AUNT BESSIE JOINS

AN ISLE OF MAN COZY MYSTERY

DIANA XARISSA

D1521165

AUTHOR'S NOTE

As this is the tenth book in the Aunt Bessie series, I feel as if there is very little I need to say here. If you haven't read any of the previous books, I always recommend that you do read them in order so that you can follow the changes and challenges in the characters' lives. Each story is designed to stand on its own, however, if you prefer to just read a single title.

If this is your first "Bessie" story, you should know that Bessie first appeared in my Isle of Man Romance, *Island Inheritance*. She provided the inheritance that brought the heroine of that story to the island. Since she was already dead when that book began, the mysteries are set about fifteen years before the romance, beginning circa 1998. There are characters that appear in both series, so if you decide to read one of the romances, you may recognise one or two people you encounter.

As the books are set in the Isle of Man, I use British spellings and terminology for the most part; some Americanisms have probably sneaked in, as I now live in the US. I also try to include a few words of Manx in every book. There are translations and explanations at the back of the book for readers in other parts of the world.

This is a work of fiction. All of the characters are a product of the author's imagination. Any resemblance to actual persons, living or dead, is entirely coincidental. Similarly, the names of the restaurants and shops and other businesses on the island are fictional. I've also taken considerable liberties with locations within the story, adding fictional shops and restaurants where they are convenient to the story rather than where any shops actually exist.

The historical sites and other landmarks on the island are all real; however, all of the events that take place within them in this story are fictional. Castle Rushen is an incredibly beautiful medieval castle in what was once the island's capital, Castletown. A photo of the castle appears on the cover of the book. "Christmas at the Castle" is an entirely made-up event that also appears in the romance *Island Christmas*.

I can't ever say enough about the hard-working and wonderful people who work for the real Manx National Heritage on the island. My characters who work for MNH are fictional, however.

The island is a unique and fascinating place, one that I hope to visit again very soon.

For all of the volunteers that help non-profit groups around the world. They work tirelessly on committees and for organizations that wouldn't be able to do all the good that they do without them.

CHAPTER 1

"No, no, this is all wrong," the man shouted, waving his arms and stomping his feet. "I said mauve. This is a sort of purple-red that simply won't do at all."

Bessie bit her tongue and counted to ten before she opened her mouth. She was quite old enough to have learned how to deal with unpleasant and demanding people. "Of course," she murmured. "We'll get it taken care of right away. It will be sorted by this afternoon."

"See that it is," the man snapped at her.

"You go and tour the rest of the castle," Bessie told him. "Mark will be waiting for you right inside the first doorway. I'll work with Laura to get this sorted."

The man made a derisory sound and then stomped across the courtyard and into the main castle building. He was short, about Bessie's height, so only a few inches over five feet tall. He wore his brown hair in a long ponytail, but it was obviously thinning on top. His clothes seemed to have been chosen at random. His trousers were a vibrant red and green plaid with a silver thread running through it. The jumper he'd paired with them was orange, and the whole effect was almost headache-inducing, at least as far as Bessie was concerned.

Bessie followed a short distance behind him, holding up her hand to stop Laura from speaking. It was only when Bessie heard the man arguing loudly with Mark Blake, Manx National Heritage's head of special projects, that she stepped back and smiled at the other woman.

"Bessie, it took three days to put up all of these decorations," Laura began. "We don't have the time or the staff to redo the whole thing before the grand opening on Friday, even if we had different decorations to put up."

"It's fine," Bessie assured her. "It's a beautiful sunny morning, but it's going to rain this afternoon. By the time Mark finishes showing Mr. Hart around the castle and they've enjoyed the lunch that Mark has arranged in the banquet room, it should be pouring. When they come back through here, the ornaments will look a totally different colour, and I'm willing to bet Mr. Hart won't hang around in the pouring rain to inspect them anyway. Get Henry to move a few of the larger pieces around and when Mr. Hart comes back through, we can say we hope he likes things better now, without actually saying what we've changed."

"It's a good idea," Laura said. "But I'm not sure it will work."

Bessie took down the nearest bauble and held it out to Laura. "Look how different this looks in sun and in shade," she said as she moved the ornament in and out of the light. "I actually noticed it the other day when I came through. The whole courtyard looks much more purple in the morning and much more red in the afternoon."

"But when does it look mauve?" Laura asked.

Bessie laughed. "Whenever Mr. Hart is here," she said firmly.

Laura laughed too, but nervously. "I'll get Henry," she said, heading towards the ticket booth.

Bessie watched her go with a smile on her face. Laura had only been on the island a short time, but Bessie had been working with her for nearly all of that time on Manx National Heritage's new fundraising event, "Christmas at the Castle." Bessie was a volunteer, talked into joining the planning committee for the event by Mark Blake, while Laura was a member of MNH's staff, but the pair worked well together and Bessie was enjoying getting to know the pretty, shy, and bright woman.

Laura was back a few minutes later with Henry in tow. "I should have known it was all going too well," Henry said, shaking his head. "We finished the decorating out here last week. I should have known we'd have to redo it."

Bessie smiled at the man. In his mid-fifties, Henry had worked for Manx National Heritage since he'd left school. His grey hair was now thinning and his brown eyes needed glasses, but he still had as much enthusiasm for the island's history as ever. Lately, he also seemed to be developing some enthusiasm for Laura, and Bessie was watching their relationship closely, not wanting to see her old friend get hurt.

"Laura said Mr. Hart wants all of the decorations out here changed," Henry said. "We don't have time for that."

"We don't have to change them all," Bessie said soothingly. "We'll move a few pieces around and make sure he doesn't come back through until it clouds over. I'm sure he'll see things differently when the light changes."

"I hope you're right," Henry said, doubt in his voice. "Mr. Hart seems, well, he's quite demanding. I found that out when I made him a cuppa."

"Don't you worry about Mr. Hart," Bessie said with confidence she didn't feel. "If he gets too demanding, the committee will handle it."

Henry and Laura exchanged glances that suggested to Bessie that they didn't put much stock in the committee's ability to deal with Christopher Hart and his demands. She didn't bother to argue, as she knew they were probably right.

A moment later, a young man with a ladder joined them. Under Bessie's direction, he moved several of the largest and most eye-catching of the decorations from one location to another. After about an hour, Bessie shrugged.

"It looks different, anyway," she said, thanking the man for his help. "I just hope it makes Mr. Hart happy."

"That's not likely," Henry said sourly. He'd just rejoined Bessie and Laura as Bessie spoke. "He was complaining constantly when I was up there," he said, gesturing towards the large medieval castle. "He doesn't like any of the rooms."

"I'm not sure I care what he thinks," Bessie replied. "The charities were permitted to decorate in any way they chose. It isn't his place to tell them what they can or can't do. He's just meant to be making sure the whole thing ties together, whatever that means."

"What does that mean?" Laura asked.

Bessie smiled at the fifty-something brunette and then shook her head. "I wish I knew," she said. "Carolyn Teare was the person who thought we needed a professional designer to, quote 'bring the whole project together under one unified festive coherence,' end of quote."

"I'm surprised she managed to talk the rest of you into hiring him," Laura said.

"Oh, she hired him," Bessie told her. "She's paying for his time as a donation towards the event. The committee couldn't find a polite way to say no, really."

"You should have tried harder," Henry muttered.

Bessie laughed. "It will all work out in the end," she said with pretend confidence. "He's only here for a few days, after all."

"He won't be here for the grand opening on Friday?" Laura asked.

"No, he's far too busy to spend more than a day or two here," Bessie replied. "I think he's meant to be flying back to London on Wednesday. I understand he's starting to film a new television series on Monday next week."

"What sort of television series?" Henry wanted to know.

"I'm hardly the one to ask," Bessie said. She'd never owned a television in her life and she didn't feel as if she'd missed anything as yet. "Carolyn said something about a new series about designing the perfect bedroom or something. I wasn't really paying attention, but apparently home makeover shows are very popular right now."

"They are," Laura confirmed. "I love watching them, although I'm not brave enough to actually try to recreate any of their designs."

"It's all a lot of fuss for nothing," Henry said grumpily. "As long as you have a roof over your head, what does it matter what colour your walls are?"

"Oh, goodness, is that the time?" Bessie exclaimed. "I need to get cleaned up for lunch."

"I'm helping to serve," Laura told her. "I'd better get ready as well."

"I'm going to find a quiet corner and have my sandwich," Henry told them both. "If you need anything, ring my mobile."

"You take a proper break," Laura said firmly. "Switch off your mobile and enjoy the peace and quiet. I'm sure the museum will be just fine for half an hour."

Henry flushed. "I won't switch off, just in case it's you who needs me," he told Laura.

She patted his arm and then, after a shy glance at Bessie, kissed his cheek. "Enjoy your break," she whispered. "We'll eat better tonight."

"We certainly will," Henry said with a bright smile.

"I'm making shepherd's pie tonight," Laura told Bessie as the two women walked across the courtyard towards the castle's staff rooms. "Henry really loves my cooking. Although I think we're both enjoying it rather too much at the moment." The woman patted her hip and gave Bessie a rueful smile. "I did promise him apple crumble as well."

"Henry seems happier than he has in years," Bessie told the other woman. "If happiness adds a few pounds, it seems worth it."

"I'm afraid it's adding more than a few, though," Laura said. "I'm going to have to start watching things after the holidays, or I'll have to start buying bigger clothes."

Bessie had always been slender, and aging hadn't changed that. She credited her daily walks on the beach outside her cottage for her continued good health and fitness, even in what she considered "late middle age." No one she knew was certain exactly how old she really was, and she wasn't about to tell.

A short time later, having changed out of her working clothes and into a skirt and jumper, Bessie washed her hands and then added a touch of powder and some lipstick to her face. "You'll do," she told her reflection. The grey-haired woman in the mirror smiled and then winked a grey eye at her.

She made her way through the castle, unable to stop herself from admiring the many beautifully decorated rooms as she went. Castle Rushen had originally been constructed in the twelfth or thirteenth century, although it had been added to and changed over the years.

The thick limestone walls always had Bessie wondering about the men who had originally been tasked with moving them into place. The castle was divided into many small rooms, some of which had served as prison cells during the eighteenth and nineteenth centuries. Now these tiny, cold and dark rooms glowed with fairy lights and colourful decorations, making the entire building feel almost magical to Bessie.

"I must remember to thank Mark for asking me to join the planning committee for this," she said to herself as she walked through one of the larger spaces that was stuffed almost full with Christmas trees. The ones nearest the entrance doorway were entirely covered in red decorations. As you walked through, you journeyed along a rainbow, so that by the time you reached the exit, the trees were all covered in beautiful violet baubles and ribbons. Bessie knew she would have visited the event even if she hadn't been involved in the planning, but she loved feeling like an insider at such a very special happening.

"I don't eat meat," Christopher Hart was saying as Bessie walked into the banquet room. "Or flour or dairy."

"I'll have to talk to the chef," Mark Blake said tightly.

Bessie could tell that he was struggling to count to ten before he lost his temper. She quickly joined the pair.

"We've just finished sorting out the courtyard," she said brightly. "I'm sure you'll like what we've done much better," she told the man who was frowning at her.

"Have we met?" he demanded.

Bessie swallowed a bubble of laughter. The man was so ridiculously rude it was quite funny, really.

"I'm Elizabeth Cubbon," she replied. "We met when you first arrived, but I know you were focussed on the site, not me."

"Are you one of the committee people?" Christopher asked. "If you are, I suppose you must call me Christopher."

"I am on the committee, yes," Bessie replied.

"Well, you lot have a great deal of work to do," he told her. "Every single room needs changes made. Some of them are absolutely appalling. Thank goodness Carolyn asked me to come over. There's so much that's wrong."

"We gave the charities free rein," Bessie said. "They were allowed to come up with their own theme and do whatever they liked in their rooms."

"Yes, it does rather show," the man said. He rolled his eyes. "Of course, they're all amateurs, which is sweet, but so unprofessional."

"I think the rooms are all lovely," Bessie said softly.

"What is it that you do for a living?" the man shot back. "Or rather, what did you do when you were younger?" he added, after giving her a once-over.

Bessie was saved from replying by a new arrival. Christopher looked past her before she'd even opened her mouth, and then he rushed away towards the door.

"Caro, darling, there you are," he shouted as he crossed the room. "It's ghastly. Thank goodness I'm here."

Carolyn Teare was a very wealthy woman in her mid-fifties. She was always impeccably dressed, and she generally wore a great deal of very expensive jewellery whatever the occasion. Today she was wearing a dark navy suit, with sapphires and diamonds sparkling at her ears and around her neck. Her blonde hair was pulled back in an intricate twist.

Carolyn had married a very wealthy and somewhat older man when she was in her early twenties, and she'd spent her time since working on keeping her body in perfect shape and volunteering all around the island. Everyone knew that she much preferred positions that would put her in the spotlight but not require her to actually do much of anything. When tasked with actual work, she usually simply threw large amounts of money at the problem, so hiring Christopher Hart to handle things at "Christmas at the Castle" was completely in character.

Bessie stayed in place as the man walked away. "This isn't going well," she murmured to Mark.

The young man flushed. "That's a huge understatement," he replied. "He wants to change every room, he has ridiculously expensive ideas for the room he's meant to be decorating, and he's incredibly rude."

"The committee will have to stand firm," Bessie said. "We're in charge, after all. He's just meant to be helping."

"Carolyn will side with him, of course," Mark answered. "I hope we can get Mary and Marjorie on our side."

"They're both far more sensible than Carolyn Teare," Bessie assured him. "I'm sure they'll both love what the different charities have done."

"I need to go and talk to the chef," Mark said. "Apparently Mr. Hart doesn't eat anything."

Bessie shook her head. Mark rushed away, leaving Bessie on her own in the centre of the banquet room. She hesitated for a moment before she walked over to join the other two.

"Oh, Bessie, how lovely," Carolyn said, giving Bessie air kisses on each cheek. "Have you been through the castle? Isn't it horrid, what they've done?"

"I think it's rather wonderful," Bessie replied.

"But there's no coherence," Carolyn said. "Luckily Christo can fix anything."

"I'm not sure anything needs fixing," Bessie said, wishing desperately that someone else would arrive before the discussion grew too heated.

"The scale of the problem is almost overwhelming," Christopher Hart said. "I suppose you can't see it because you're not looking at the big picture."

Bessie bit back the first reply that came to her lips and was saved from finding a more polite one by the arrival of her friend, Mary Quayle.

"It's just about perfect," Mary said excitedly as she joined the group.

Bessie smiled. If anyone could win a fight with Carolyn Teare, it was Mary. Mary was about ten years older than Carolyn, but equally wealthy, although far less ostentatious with it. Also beautifully and expensively dressed, Mary rarely wore more jewellery than her plain gold wedding band. The biggest difference between the two women was that Mary was a hard worker who volunteered quietly with many different organisations. She loathed the spotlight that her husband, George, embraced.

"I think it needs a few little changes," a voice said.

Bessie was surprised to see a stranger walk in behind Mary.

"Natasha Harper, I should have known you'd be here somewhere, trying to steal another commission," Christopher Hart snarled at the new arrival.

The woman laughed. "I think you'll find that's your tactic, not mine," she said. "Anyway, I'm very busy at the moment working for Mrs. Quayle. I'm not looking for any other commissions."

Christopher shrugged and rolled his eyes.

"I hope it's okay that I brought Natasha," Mary said anxiously. "She's working with me on plans for Thie yn Traie and I thought we could use her expertise." Mary and George were in the process of purchasing Thie yn Traie, a large mansion a short distance away from Bessie's beachfront cottage.

"As long as everyone understands that this is Christo's job, not hers," Carolyn said tartly.

"Oh, my goodness," Natasha said, laughing again. "This is the last sort of job I'd be interested in. I do home redecorating; I don't tart up old castles."

"I'm Elizabeth Cubbon," Bessie said to break up the awkward silence that followed Natasha's words. "Everyone calls me Bessie, though."

"Nice to meet you, Bessie," Natasha said, offering a hand. "I'm Natasha Harper."

Bessie studied the woman as she shook her hand. She looked no more than thirty, with obviously dyed blonde hair piled in a messy bun on the top of her head. She was almost shockingly thin and pale, but her expensive black dress fit her perfectly. In her black stilettos she was nearly a foot taller than Bessie.

"I'm sorry, I should have introduced everyone," Mary said, blushing.

"I'm late," Marjorie Stevens said from the doorway.

Bessie turned to greet the pretty, thirty-something blonde. "Fastyr mie," she said.

"Fastyr mie," Marjorie replied. "Kys t'ou?"

"Ta mee braew," Bessie answered. She glanced around and laughed as she realised everyone else was staring at them blankly.

"I teach a beginning Manx language class," Marjorie told the others. "Bessie is one of my favourite students."

"Even though I've taken the beginning class three times and still can't say much more than what we've just said?" Bessie asked.

"I just love that you keep trying," Marjorie told her. "We'll be starting again in Laxey in the new year."

"Maybe the fourth time around it will start to make sense," Bessie said with a sigh.

"I think I might give it a try," Mary said. "I'd like to learn a little bit of Manx now that I'm sure we're settled here."

"You'll be more than welcome," Marjorie told her.

"Charming," Christopher Hart said flatly.

"I hope everyone is hungry," Mark said from the opposite side of the room.

"Starving," Mary said.

Bessie murmured her agreement and the small group made their way to the table in one corner of the room.

"It's a special treat, having lunch in here," Bessie remarked as they all found seats. "Manx National Heritage doesn't encourage people to eat in the castle."

Mark laughed. "As we're all here working hard, it just seemed easier to have something sent in, rather than going out somewhere. Besides, the same people who are catering for the grand opening on Friday are providing today's lunch. This gives them a chance to try out the kitchen facilities we're able to provide."

"They aren't using the medieval kitchens, are they?" Bessie asked.

"Actually, they are going to be making a few things in there on Friday evening," Mark told her. "More for effect than anything else, though. They're using the kitchens that were added when the castle was a prison to prepare most of the food on Friday. That's where they prepared today's lunch."

A moment later a pair of waiters appeared, bearing trays. While they delivered bowls of steaming soup, the group was silent. Mark opened a bottle of wine and served that himself.

"I shouldn't," Marjorie told him. "I'm driving. I'm quite happy with the water that was already here."

Bessie noted that Christopher was served a bowl of plain broth, presumably the only thing the kitchen could provide that met his demands.

"This is delicious," she said as she savoured her leek and potato soup.

Warm and crusty bread rolls were passed around, and Bessie found herself spreading on the butter a bit more thickly than she normally might as she watched Christopher scowling at his broth.

The main course was lightly grilled chicken with rice and grilled vegetables, and Bessie thoroughly enjoyed it. Christopher was served his rice and vegetables with a piece of fish, but he simply nibbled on a few pieces of carrot and sent the rest back untouched. Pudding was a gorgeous Victoria sponge and Bessie was too busy enjoying it to care what Christopher thought of his bowl of red jelly. Once the plates had all been cleared away, Mark sat back and smiled at the group.

"I suppose we must get down to business," he said. " The first ever 'Christmas at the Castle' opens on Friday, and really we're just putting the final touches on things now."

"No, you aren't," Christopher objected. "Most of the rooms are simply ghastly. They're all obviously very amateur and there will need to be a lot of changes made in a hurry if you're going to open on time."

"I think the rooms are fine just the way they are," Bessie disagreed. "The charitable groups were told they could do whatever they liked with their spaces and I think they've all been very clever indeed."

Christopher sighed. "I thought you were going to be auctioning off the contents of each room," he said. "No one will want to buy them if they see them displayed as they are. The rooms are all just thrown together. With my vision, we'll be able to transform each room into a perfect little Christmas wonderland."

"Isn't he just the cleverest thing?" Carolyn said, squeezing the man's hand.

"I'm sure he's very good at what he does," Mary said. "But this isn't about perfection. This is about raising money for good causes. I think the general public will be more giving if the efforts look genuine, rather than professional."

"Good design is never the wrong choice," Christopher said sternly.

"What exactly did you want to change?" Bessie asked.

"Oh, darling, what didn't I want to change?" Christopher said, sighing deeply. "We should walk through the rooms and I'll tell you what's wrong in each of them."

"The various men and women who decorated the rooms are all going to be here soon," Mark said. "We can walk through the rooms with the representative from each charity and talk with them about any changes that might be useful."

"Excellent," Christopher said. "I'll just have some more wine while we wait."

Mark opened a second bottle of wine and topped up everyone's glasses. Bessie wasn't going to have any more, but it looked like it might be a long and difficult afternoon. Perhaps a bit more wine would help.

Half an hour later the small banquet room was full with the various volunteers and workers from the different charities.

"Let's get started, then," Mark said, his tone unenthusiastic.

"We should go down and start in the courtyard," Christopher announced. "I directed the decoration of that space myself."

Mark led the group through the castle and back down into the courtyard. It was just beginning to rain and Bessie and the others didn't waste much time admiring the space before heading back indoors.

"There, now, you see?" Christopher demanded as they all gathered in the first room. "The courtyard is done entirely in mauve, with large baubles and stars. I gave the committee very clear instructions on what I wanted to see and they've very nearly matched my vision. I realise I've set the bar rather high for the rest of you, but it's my job now to help you aspire to my level within your own tiny spaces."

A few people muttered replies, but nothing was clearly audible to Bessie. She was pretty sure she had a good idea of what was being said, however.

"For the record," Bessie said loudly now, "I think the rooms are all wonderful, and I'm looking forward to Mr. Hart's small improvements."

Christopher frowned at her. "Some of them won't be small," he muttered. He looked around the room where they were standing and then shrugged. "Who decorated this space?" he demanded.

Margaret Christian stepped forward. "I did, or rather the other ladies from Cancer Care, IOM, and I did."

"And is there a theme?" Christopher asked sneeringly.

"The theme is 'I'll be home for Christmas,'" Margaret replied. "We made the ornaments on the trees ourselves, using photographs of Manx men and women who are currently serving in the armed forces as well as pictures of men, women, and children who are fighting cancer. Our hope was that the room would remind visitors that not everyone can be home for the holidays, either because they are serving in the military or because they are too ill to leave hospital."

"Depressing," Christopher said. "This is the first room guests will enter. They'll be miserable for the rest of the tour, nay, for the rest of the month. We need to brighten things up in here. We'll add garlands in red and green on every tree and hang giant snowflakes in silver and gold on the walls. Perhaps we can distract everyone from the rather distressing photographs."

"Or maybe we could put up a table with blank Christmas cards on it and visitors could write cards for our service men and women and the people in hospital," Marjorie suggested. "I'm sure Manx National Heritage could find room in the budget for some blank cards and some postage, and it would help lift everyone's spirits to feel as if they were helping in some small way. We could even let children write letters to Father Christmas while they're here."

"That's a wonderful idea," Mary said. "If MNH can't find the money in the budget, I'll pay for the cards and postage," she added.

"I like that idea a lot better than covering the trees in garland," Margaret Christian said. "We quite like the trees exactly as they are."

"There's no accounting for taste," Christopher sniffed. "Or lack of it."

Margaret bristled, but Bessie put her hand on the woman's arm before she could speak.

"I think we're all in agreement, then," Bessie said loudly. "We'll add a card-writing table to the room, but otherwise leave it exactly as it is."

There were a few murmurs from around the room, but no one objected.

"On we go, then," Mark said.

The next room looked like the inside of a child's toy box. Giant blocks spelled out "Happy Christmas" in red and green letters, while an overstuffed, ten-foot-tall teddy bear lounged in a corner. A handful of enormous Christmas baubles were scattered around the room and oversized toys were everywhere. Bessie smiled with delight at the giant skipping rope that appeared to be tangled up with a few stray chess pieces that were larger than life-sized.

"Dare I ask who is responsible for this disaster?" Christopher asked with a dramatic sigh.

"A group of us from Manx Cloan decorated this room," Liz Martin said. She crossed her arms and stared at the man, but Bessie could see tears forming in the young woman's eyes.

Liz had been a classmate in the last Manx language class Bessie had taken, and Bessie had become friendly with the much younger woman. Liz hadn't been on the island for long. She was a stay-at-home mum to two small and energetic children, and Bessie had been impressed with the amount of time and energy Liz devoted to the small charity that worked to improve the lives of all children on the island.

"It's not very Christmassy," Christopher said sharply.

"We didn't think it would be quite right, putting a tree inside a children's toy box," Liz defended herself.

"But it's such a mess," he retorted. "It looks as if everything has just been thrown in here."

"Then we've done it all right," Liz replied. "Children don't keep their toy boxes tidy, after all."

"I did," Carolyn snapped. "Christo is quite right. This just looks like a jumbled mess. How can we fix it, Christo?"

The man sighed again and then shook his head. "If we had time, I'd suggest just starting over," he said with a sigh. "I'm going to have to think about this one. It's just, I don't know, not right."

He shook his head again and then moved on to the next room, leaving a visibly shaken Liz behind.

"I think it's perfect," Bessie whispered to her young friend. "And I'll fight him on any changes he wants to make."

"Thanks," Liz said wanly.

Bessie hated leaving the woman when she was clearly so upset, but she didn't want to miss what Christopher might be saying in the next room.

"We'll talk later," she promised Liz before hurrying after the group.

Harriet Hooper was the next to face Christopher's criticism. Unlike Liz and Margaret, she wasn't a volunteer. The Manx Animal Care Team had a paid staff of three. Margaret was their fundraiser, at least on a part-time basis, and she supported a full-time paid director for the charity. They also shared a part-time secretary. Bessie knew that more and more charitable organisations were becoming increasingly professional and were struggling to find room in their budgets to add paid staff. Harriet was a charming woman in her forties, and she'd already done a great deal of good for the small charity that employed her.

"Too many cuddly toys," Christopher grumbled. "What do they have to do with Christmas?"

"We're a charity involved entirely with animals," Harriet said in a patient voice. "We couldn't exactly fill the room with live animals, so we thought this was the next best thing."

"Live animals would be better," Christopher replied. "But really, this doesn't tie in with the overall theme of the event at all. You need a Christmas tree in every corner, not just the one, and you need proper decorations, not bones and cat toys, hanging from the branches. I'd like fairy lights on the walls and the words 'Happy Christmas' spelled out in garland across the ceiling."

"Would you?" Harriet asked. "I'll certainly take your suggestions back to the committee."

Bessie bit her lip so that she wouldn't laugh out loud. Harriet clearly knew how to deal with the difficult man, at least.

Agnes Clucas from Mannanan's Kids didn't seem the least bit bothered by Christopher's assessment of her rainbow room, either.

"You should scatter the different colours around the room," he told her.

Agnes shrugged. "I'll have to see what we can do," she mused. "I'm too old to be doing that sort of thing myself, you see. I don't know if we have anyone else who can help on such short notice."

Bessie knew the charity had a huge pool of active and enthusiastic volunteers, but luckily Christopher didn't. The Alzheimer's Research Fund had decorated the last of the rooms that had been done by an outside group. Its director and only paid employee, Michael Beach, listened with ill-concealed impatience as Christopher listed what he saw as the faults with the room. When he was done, Michael shrugged.

"Change whatever you like," he said carelessly. "I'm far too busy with my year-end fundraising campaign to get involved."

"I'm not manual labour," Christopher sniffed.

"Neither am I," Michael said haughtily.

"It really doesn't seem as if any of you appreciate what Christo is trying to do here," Carolyn said as everyone gathered in the banquet room again. "He's given up a lot of his time and energy in order to help make this event the most exciting Christmas extravaganza the island has ever seen."

"And we appreciate that very much," Mark said. "And we are enormously grateful that you're paying for his time and talents, as MNH simply hasn't the budget for such things."

"I'm sure we're all grateful for Mr. Hart's insights," Bessie said. "But as the different groups are all responsible for their own rooms, I think they'll all have to make their own choices as to how they put his advice into practice."

"Now let's talk about the room I'm going to decorate," Christopher said. "I've seen the preliminary plans, and I absolutely hate them."

Bessie swallowed hard. She's spent many hours drawing up the plans for the room being decorated by Manx National Heritage. That was before Christopher Hart had been dumped in their laps, of course.

CHAPTER 2

*M*ark glanced over at Bessie. "Manx National Heritage approved the plans," he told the man. "The theme is 'Christmas Around the World,' and we quite liked the idea of the different trees, each representing a different country and showcasing some of that country's unique Christmas customs."

"Yawn," Christopher said. "I don't like the theme, to start with, but then, if we must go with that, let's at least do something interesting and fun with it."

"Like what?" Mark asked.

"Like celebrating infamous people from each country or interesting people from each country, rather than boring old Christmas traditions," he replied.

"Infamous people?" Mark echoed.

"Sure. Every country has its share of mass murderers and the like. We could do Jack the Ripper for the UK and cover the tree in knives dipped in red paint," Christopher suggested.

" But 'Christmas at the Castle' is an event for families," Bessie said tightly. "I don't think celebrating mass murderers is what we had in mind."

"The kids would love it," Christopher said dismissively. "Look at how many flood to the wax museums. They don't go to see the pretty waxworks, they go to see the scary stuff in the basement."

"Yes, well, I think the committee will have to discuss that idea," Mark said. He looked around the room. "Perhaps everyone would like to head to their own rooms and start thinking about any changes they'd like to make? I'll walk back through with Mr. Hart for a second look and we can talk again about the best way to make each space exactly right."

"I'm a very busy man," Michael Beach said crossly. "I don't have all afternoon to waste, waiting to hear what some egotistical designer has to say about the room I decorated. As far as I'm concerned, you can do what you like with the space and simply send me a cheque for my share of the proceeds from the event."

"Why don't we start with your room," Mark suggested. "It shouldn't take long."

"I don't want to work with that man," Christopher said loudly, as Michael turned and walked out of the room. "He's very disagreeable."

"Pot," Bessie muttered to herself. Liz was standing near enough to hear her and she giggled.

"Now, darling," Carolyn said to Christopher. "You mustn't mind Michael. Not everyone can recognise genius. He doesn't have your vision or your creativity. Please, try to be patient with him."

"I'll try," Christopher said.

"Oh, you are wonderful," Carolyn cooed at him. They turned and followed Michael into the next room with Mark on their heels.

Everyone left behind began to talk amongst themselves. Only a moment later, however, conversations stopped as the sound of an argument reached them.

Michael's deep baritone carried well from the next room over. "You really are nothing but an arrogant..."

Christopher, whose high-pitched voice was raised to almost a squeal, interrupted him. "Don't you dare call me names, you horrid little man. I'll have you thrown out of here and redecorate this room myself."

"Oh, I'm scared now," Michael said mockingly. "Throw me out of here? That's the best threat you can come up with? I should have known better than to get involved in this stupid event anyway. Nearly everyone is a total amateur with no idea how to go about raising money. You can take your 'Christmas at the Castle' and shove it up your...'"

"That's enough," Mark's voice cut through the fight. "Mr. Hart, you've had your say on this room. Michael can choose to follow your advice or leave the room as it is. Let's move on and let Michael get back to his office."

"You'd better fix this room," Christopher said. "I won't be associated with this event if this room isn't redone."

Bessie could hear Carolyn saying something, but she couldn't make out the words. As nearly everyone was inching closer to the doorway in order to hear better, Bessie deliberately took a step away. She wasn't the type to snoop, at least not where other people could see her doing it.

"I can't be expected to work in these conditions," Christopher wailed.

"I'm surprised you get any work at all," Michael snarled back. "I wouldn't hire you to decorate my dog's house."

Bessie winced when she heard the slap. Now she headed straight for the door. As a committee member, she felt she should be there as things were clearly getting out of hand. She arrived in the room just in time to see Michael's fist connect with Christopher's jaw.

Christopher fell backwards, nearly knocking Carolyn over. She grabbed him almost instinctively, and then lowered him to the floor. He appeared to have been knocked out, so Bessie focussed her attention on Michael.

"Are you okay?" she asked the man, who was flexing his hand and frowning. Bessie could see a bright red mark on his cheek.

"He slapped me," Michael said. "I'm afraid I just reacted."

"I hope you're prepared for charges to be brought," Carolyn said from where she was sitting on the floor next to Christopher. "I'm going to suggest that Christo sue you as well. I doubt you're worth much, but we'll make you pay as much as we can get."

"Mr. Hart hit him first," Mark said steadily. "If anyone has to worry about charges and lawsuits, I'd suggest it's Mr. Hart and not Michael."

Carolyn flushed and shook her head. "I'm sure my advocate won't see it that way."

"I'm certain Mr. Hart won't want to press charges," Bessie said. "Think of all the negative publicity that would generate. He's about to start filming a new television show, I believe. I'm sure he'll be happy to just put the whole thing behind him."

"We'll see," Carolyn said. "In the meantime, I think he needs a doctor."

"I've rung 999," Mary said from behind Bessie. "There's an ambulance on its way."

"Maybe you should get back to Douglas," Bessie suggested to Michael. "I know how busy you are."

"I should, but I don't want the police showing up there to accuse me of leaving a crime scene or something," he replied.

"No one considers this a crime scene," Mark told him. "You go. Mr. Hart is only here until Wednesday. We can talk about your room once he's gone."

"Thanks," Michael said. "I hope he's okay," he said, gesturing towards the man on the floor. "But I can't say I'm sorry I hit him."

Bessie and Mary walked out of the castle with Michael, having suggested that they go and wait for the paramedics in the courtyard.

"They'll never find their way up here," Bessie pointed out.

Mark looked as if he didn't really want to be left alone with Christopher and Carolyn, but he agreed that they should go.

It was only a few minutes later that they were back with two paramedics. Christopher was just struggling to sit up.

"What happened?" he asked Carolyn, rubbing his jaw gently.

"That horrible man, Michael Beach, punched you," she said. "I told him you were going to press charges."

"However, you did hit him first," Mark said.

"Let's take a look at you, then," one of the paramedics suggested. He knelt down next to Christopher and shined a light in his eyes. After a short exam and several questions, he shrugged.

"Head injuries are tricky," he said. "You lost consciousness for a while. It would probably be best if you went up to Noble's for the night."

"I don't need a hospital," Christopher replied. He shook his head and then groaned. "Some headache tablets would be nice, though."

"I have some," Carolyn told him. She dug around in her handbag and then handed Christopher a small bottle. "You keep it and take what you need," she told him.

"I still think hospital is the best place for him," the paramedic said.

"I'll look after him," Carolyn replied. "He's staying at my home in Douglas tonight. If he isn't feeling well, we can take him over to Noble's at any time."

The man nodded and got to his feet. "I think my work here is done," he said with a smile. "The castle looks wonderful, by the way. I'll have to bring the kids to see it once it's open."

Mary offered to walk the men back out, but Bessie stayed behind. She wanted to make sure that nothing further was said about pressing charges against Michael.

"I think you should take the rest of the afternoon off," Mark suggested to Christopher as he slowly got to his feet. "We can look at the rest of the castle tomorrow."

"Tomorrow I shall be decorating my room," Christopher reminded him. "We still have to work out what I shall be using for that."

"We've boxes and boxes of things that we ordered when we originally chose the theme for that space," Mark told him. "I'm afraid there probably isn't time to get anything else."

"I shall have to go shopping tonight, then," Christopher replied. "I do wish I'd had more notice, but the show must go on."

He gave everyone what Bessie was certain he thought was a brave smile. It looked more like a self-satisfied grin to Bessie, but she forced herself to smile back.

"Let's talk to the woman who did that rainbow thing," Christopher said now. "I'm sure she'll be more reasonable to work with than that nasty man."

Mark found Agnes, and the group moved into the next room

together. Within minutes, Christopher had Agnes in tears and Bessie ready to scream.

"I don't think this is working very well," she said as Agnes rushed away. "Maybe we should just leave things the way they are."

"I'm paying darling Christo a lot of money," Carolyn snapped. "He's here to improve things, remember? We want this event to be a success, don't we? Christo will make everything so much more wonderful if everyone would just listen to him."

"The volunteers who've decorated the rooms have worked very hard," Bessie said levelly. "We don't want to upset them any more than we want to upset Mr. Hart. Our job, as a committee, is to make everyone happy."

Christopher laughed harshly. "Impossible," he said scornfully. "Surely you're old enough to know better than to even try."

"I'm old enough to realise that life on a small island runs much more smoothly when people make an effort to work together," Bessie told him. "You'll be gone back to London on Wednesday, but we're hoping to be working with these charity volunteers for years to come. This is meant to be the first annual 'Christmas at the Castle,' after all."

"Well, it's my last 'Christmas at the Castle,'" he replied. "By this time next year I'll be a household name, and lending my talents to dreary small town festivities like this will be nothing but a distant, albeit painful, memory. But let's move on, I don't want to be here all night."

An hour later, the man had managed to insult and upset every single person in the castle. Bessie comforted Liz and Margaret after he'd shouted at them each in turn. She also talked a furious Harriet out of leaving the castle and never coming back. When he finally decided that he'd had enough and headed back to Douglas to do some shopping for the room he'd be decorating, Bessie felt as if the castle itself let out a sigh of relief. Certainly all of its occupants did.

"I don't understand why everyone isn't embracing Christopher's wonderful ideas," Carolyn hissed to Bessie before she followed the man out of the building. "I do hope you can do something to persuade the rest of the committee to get behind him. You haven't been very supportive of him thus far."

Bessie didn't reply. She didn't want to start an argument, not when the woman was actually leaving.

"I'm going to take Christo home and then I'll be back," she told Bessie. "Mark wants the whole committee to meet just before five."

For the next hour, Bessie found herself going from room to room, working to undo the damage that Christopher had done. It was far too late to start looking for other groups to decorate rooms if anyone decided that they weren't going to take part. By the time she and the other committee members met in the banquet room, it was nearly five o'clock and time to close the castle for the night.

"People are being incredibly unreasonable," Carolyn said as she slid into a seat.

"People want to keep their rooms the way they decorated them," Bessie replied. "That seems fair enough to me. I'm sure Mr. Hart's ideas are very clever, but I'm not convinced that they're right for our event."

"You're as bad as the rest of them," Carolyn dismissed her with a wave her hand. "Mary, you have exquisite taste. Surely you agree with me."

Mary smiled tentatively. "I think Mr. Hart had some very, um, inventive thoughts, but I quite like the rooms as they are, as well."

"What about you?" Carolyn turned to Natasha. "You're a designer. You can see how amateurish the rooms look, can't you?"

"I think that's what makes them so charming," Natasha replied. "If I were in Christopher's place, I'd make a few small changes here and there, just to try to unify the themes a bit more, but I certainly wouldn't make the sweeping changes he's suggested."

"Perhaps it's time for me to resign from this committee," Carolyn said angrily. "As my contribution to it doesn't seem to be appreciated."

"We all appreciate everything you've done very much," Mark told her. "Even if we don't all agree with Mr. Hart's ideas for the rooms, that doesn't mean that we aren't enormously grateful to you for paying for his assistance. We all need to find a way to work together to make this event worthwhile. Our committee wouldn't be the same without you."

"Yes, well, I've no more time to debate things tonight. I'd better get back into Douglas and help Christo with his shopping. We'll be here bright and early tomorrow morning to start working on his room."

Carolyn sailed out of the room, her head held high. When the sound of her heels on the stone floors finally faded, Bessie sighed with relief.

"We aren't going to let him turn his room into a gallery of murderers, are we?" Bessie asked the others.

"No," Marjorie said firmly. "And I made that very clear to Carolyn earlier. She wasn't happy, but she did promise to work with Mr. Hart to find a workable theme."

"I thought the theme we had was wonderful," Mark said, glancing at Bessie. "And we've all the decorations in place as well. I'm sure he could do something quite wonderful with what we have."

"But he won't," Natasha said. "He's all about drama and conflict. I wish you all good luck. I'm ever so grateful I just have Thie yn Traie to worry about."

"At least he's leaving on Wednesday," Bessie said. "We'll have a few days to change things around once he's gone."

"I wonder why he's rushing back so quickly," Natasha said.

"Apparently he's going to be starting filming for a new television show," Bessie told her.

"Really? I'd heard rumours, but I didn't realise it was actually happening," the girl replied thoughtfully.

"Design shows are quite popular at the moment," Mary remarked. "Unfortunately, they give George somewhat unusual ideas."

"I hate to interrupt, but we're getting ready to lock up. Will you be much longer?" Henry asked from the doorway.

"No, I think we've done all we can for tonight," Mark said in a tired voice. "I'd be grateful if you could all be here tomorrow at nine. Mr. Hart and Carolyn aren't due until ten, so that gives us some time to plan a strategy to deal with the man."

Everyone made their way towards the nearest exit, with Henry following and locking doors behind them.

"Oh, Bessie, can you meet me in the car park?" Mark asked as they reached the street. "I just have to check on the catering for Friday."

Mark lived in Ramsey, so he'd kindly offered to drive Bessie back and forth to the castle when she needed to be there. As Bessie had never learned to drive, she was grateful. She'd always been very careful with her money and that meant she could indulge herself a bit now that she was older, but she'd have felt extravagant if she'd taken taxis every day that she'd needed to be in Castletown. When she'd agreed to join the committee, she hadn't given that aspect of things any thought at all.

Now she made her way across the road and into the small car park. A lone figure was sitting on the bench that overlooked the sea. As Bessie drew closer, she recognised Laura Meyers. It wasn't until she was much nearer that she realised the woman was crying. While Bessie wondered whether she should tiptoe quietly away, Laura looked up.

"Oh, Bessie, hello," she said, blinking hard and trying to smile.

"Are you okay, my dear?" Bessie asked.

"I'm fine. I'm just a little upset, that's all."

Bessie sat down on the bench beside her. She found a pack of tissues in her pocket and handed one to the other woman. Laura wiped her eyes and then blew her nose loudly. They both chuckled at the noise.

"There, all better," Laura announced. "I suppose I should find Henry."

"Are you sure you're okay?" Bessie asked.

"He's just such an unpleasant man," Laura told her.

"Henry?"

"Oh, no, not Henry," Laura exclaimed. "Henry is a dear, sweet thing. No, it's that Mr. Hart who has upset me, although it isn't really his fault."

"I'm happy to listen if you want to talk," Bessie said.

Laura shrugged. "It's nothing, really. He just, well, he reminds me of someone, that's all. His arrogance and his attitude and the way he spoke to me, they just all remind me of someone else. As I said, it isn't really Mr. Hart's fault at all."

"Can I do anything to help?" Bessie asked.

"No, it's fine," Laura insisted. "I might ask Mark to let me work somewhere else for a few days, until he's gone. I hope Mark won't mind."

"I'm sure Mark will understand. I can't imagine anyone is enjoying working with the man."

"Except for Carolyn Teare. She seems quite taken with him."

Bessie nodded. "Yes, well, I can talk to Mark if you'd like. He's driving me home."

"Could you? I'd rather Henry not know," Laura said.

"Not know what?" a voice came from behind them.

Bessie and Laura both turned around. Bessie forced herself to smile at Henry as Laura gasped.

"What's going on?" Henry demanded. "Why have you been crying?" he asked Laura.

"I was just feeling a bit overwhelmed," Laura replied slowly. "Mr. Hart reminds me of someone from my past who, well, I'd rather not think about. I was telling Bessie that I'd like to ask Mark to reassign me elsewhere until after Mr. Hart leaves."

"But I like working with you," Henry said.

"I love working with you," Laura replied. "But I'm not sure I can work with Mr. Hart again. It's only for a few days."

Henry nodded, but he looked miserable.

"Here's Mark now," Bessie said, pointing.

"Are you all waiting for me?" Mark asked.

Laura looked down at the ground. "I was just wondering if I might be assigned somewhere else for a few days," she said softly.

"Not you, too," Mark groaned. "No one wants to work with Christopher Hart. I'm awfully sorry, but I simply don't have anyone else to replace you with at this point. We're on winter staffing, which means we only have a few people to cover the entire island as it is.

The sites are mostly shut and the people who are still working are all trying to take days off to do their Christmas shopping."

Laura nodded. "It will be fine," she said in a barely audible voice.

"It better be," Henry said loudly. "If that man upsets Laura again, he'll have to answer to me."

Bessie had known Henry for many years and she'd never seen him lose his temper. If she didn't know him so well, she might have been frightened by the furious look on his face now.

"Let's go," Laura said, taking Henry's hand. "We can't let that man spoil our plans for the evening."

"I'm telling you, Mark, I won't have Laura upset," Henry called over his shoulder as Laura led him away. "If you can't keep that man under control, I will."

Bessie shook her head. "I've never seen Henry so upset," she said to Mark as they walked to his car.

"I don't like it," Mark told her. "Henry is one of our best workers, and Laura has been excellent since she's been here. We can't have people like Christopher Hart upsetting them like this. I'm going to have to talk to Carolyn. Maybe we need to send him home a little early."

Mark was silent on the drive from Castletown to Laxey. Bessie let her mind wander to more pleasant topics, like what she was going to get her friends for Christmas. She was planning a shopping trip in Douglas when they reached her small cottage by the sea.

"I'm sorry," Mark said. "I didn't say one word the entire drive, did I? I'll make it up to you in the morning, I promise."

"It's fine," Bessie assured him. "I was busy making a mental shopping list. I haven't done any Christmas shopping yet, and I certainly won't have time to do it this week. Once 'Christmas at the Castle' is up and running, I shall have to get busy."

"Hmm, Christmas shopping, that's a thought. I suppose I'll get everything I need at the museum gift shop again this year," Mark said.

"You might find a few things at our auction," Bessie suggested.

After the busy opening weekend that was rapidly approaching, the castle was going to be closed until Christmas Eve. Then, on that final night of the event there was going to be an auction. While the main event would be the auctioning off the contents of each room, several local businesses had donated items as well. Bessie had her eye on a large box of books that the bookshop in Douglas had given them. It was sealed up tightly and labeled "25 Miscellaneous Fiction Books" and Bessie could barely resist the urge to open the box and see what was inside. The only way she could open it was if she bought the box, and she was quite tempted by the idea.

"I'll be back around eight tomorrow," Mark told Bessie as she climbed out of the car. "Have a good night."

Bessie nodded and then let herself into her cottage. She took a deep breath and then sighed deeply. There truly was no place like home. The cottage was older than she was, and in some ways that showed, but she loved every single inch of the building she'd called home for all of her adult life.

She'd purchased the cottage with a small inheritance from the man she'd thought she was going to marry. After his untimely death, she'd spent many hours sobbing and feeling sorry for herself in every room. It was never her intention to stay there forever, but she'd never found a reason to leave. Her childhood had been spent in America, but the island quickly came to feel like home to her in a way that the US never had. When a second chance at marriage presented itself, Bessie declined, as it would have meant leaving the island.

Now she walked from room to room, calming her spirits after the long and emotionally fraught day. She would have rather taken a walk on the beach, but it was quite cold and dark and the rain that had started at midday was still falling. When she felt more like herself, she made a light evening meal and then found her place in the book she was reading. On a recent holiday she'd been reintroduced to Jane Austen, rereading *Emma* for the first time in a great many years. Now she was working her way through everything that Austen had written, and she was thoroughly enjoying them all. A ringing telephone interrupted Mr. Darcy as he made unkind comments about Elizabeth Bennett.

Bessie put a bookmark in the book and answered the call.

"Bessie? We have a problem," Mark's voice came down the line. "I just sent an email to all of the committee members and the volunteers who decorated rooms. It seems that Mr. Hart and Carolyn have had something of a falling out. I don't know any of the details, just that Mr. Hart has moved into a hotel in Douglas and Carolyn is suggesting that Manx National Heritage ought to foot the bill."

"But that's not right," Bessie said. "She brought him here; she should be responsible for him."

"Yes, well, there's little point in debating that at the moment. For now I'm more worried about tomorrow. I've agreed to stop in Douglas in the morning and give Mr. Hart a ride to the castle. I hope you don't mind."

"I don't see that we have much choice," Bessie muttered. "I shall give Carolyn a piece of my mind when I see her, though."

"Yes, well, she won't be at the castle tomorrow. She's staying away until Mr. Hart is finished, apparently."

Bessie sighed deeply. "What a mess," she said emphatically. "I'm sorry you have to deal with it all."

"I'm going to have to collect you a little earlier than planned," Mark said. "Probably around half seven, if that's okay with you."

"It's fine," Bessie said. "I'll be up anyway."

"I'll see you in the morning, then," Mark said. "And thank you."

Bessie found herself pacing again after she'd disconnected. When that didn't accomplish anything, she decided to have an early night. Curled up in bed, she read a bit more of her book, but found it difficult to concentrate. After a while, she gave up and tried to sleep instead. Sleep was elusive, but once she'd fallen asleep, Bessie didn't wake until her usual time of six o'clock.

The sun was trying to shine as she made her way along the beach after her shower and breakfast. She'd really enjoyed being a part of the committee that had put together "Christmas at the Castle," but there was a real danger that Christopher Hart was going to ruin her enthusiasm for the event. Determined not to let that happen, Bessie marched back to her cottage and then read until it was time for Mark to arrive. She was standing in the middle of the kitchen, waiting, when he pulled up, and she was out of her cottage and locking up before he'd parked the car.

"At least one of us is eager to get going this morning," Mark said with a sigh.

"Tomorrow is Wednesday," Bessie said with forced cheer. "Mr. Hart is going home tomorrow. We just have to survive today, and with Carolyn out of the picture, Mr. Hart should be much more easily outvoted."

Mark smiled. "I hope you're right."

"Do you have any idea what he and Carolyn argued about?" Bessie asked as they drove towards Douglas.

"None at all," Mark said. "She wouldn't tell me anything on the phone except that he'd moved into a hotel and that she wouldn't be back at the castle until he was gone."

Mark was lucky to find a parking space on the Douglas promenade right in front of Christopher's hotel. "I love the tourists, but it is quite nice when they aren't here and the parking is easier," he told Bessie.

He pulled his mobile out of his pocket and punched in some numbers. "Ah, yes, Christopher Hart's room, please."

Bessie could hear the sound of the phone ringing from her seat. After ten rings, Mark disconnected. "I rang him last night and told him we would be here by eight," he said angrily. "I don't intend to wait all morning for him to show up."

"So what are our options?" Bessie asked.

"I think we'll head down to the castle," Mark said. "I'll leave a message at the desk that he should get himself a taxi down when he finally gets up."

Mark was only inside the hotel for a few minutes. He looked happier when he came back. "Apparently Mr. Hart went out last night and brought back a large bacon pizza and a six-pack of beer. He's probably just sleeping off his excesses."

"I thought he didn't eat meat, dairy or wheat," Bessie said.

"Presumably that's only when he has an audience," Mark said dryly.

31

They were both more cheerful on their way to Castletown. Bessie found herself hoping that the man might wake up feeling too miserable to work at all that day. At the castle, Mark told all of the volunteers to leave their rooms as they were, at least until Christopher arrived. Then he and the committee, minus Carolyn, got to work on setting up the room that Christopher had been expected to decorate.

"I'm going to ring Natasha," Mary announced after a while. "She can come and help out. I'm sure she's much better at this sort of thing than I am."

"Not another designer," Marjorie groaned.

"Natasha's far more sensible than Christopher Hart," Mary assured her. "You'll see. Anyway, if she starts being difficult, I'll send her back to Thie yn Traie."

Natasha turned out to be far more helpful than Bessie had expected. They were all working steadily an hour later when Henry walked in. Bessie took one look at his face and stopped what she was doing.

"Henry, what's wrong?" she demanded.

"Thank you," the man who was behind Henry said. "I'll take it from here."

Bessie felt herself going pale as she recognised the man Henry had escorted into the room. He was forty-something, with brown hair streaked with grey, and brown eyes.

"Inspector Corkill? What's going on?" she asked.

"I'm sorry to tell you all that a body was found at the Seaside Hotel this morning. It's been preliminarily identified as that of Mr. Christopher Hart," he said.

CHAPTER 3

There were shocked exclamations from around the room. Mary Quayle turned white and Natasha quickly found her a chair. Bessie opened and closed her mouth several times as she tried to work out what she wanted to say first. Before anyone spoke, the inspector held up his hand.

"I'm going to need to speak with each of you individually," he said. "There are two uniformed officers who will sit in here while I interview you each in turn. I'd appreciate it if you didn't speak to one another until after I've talked to everyone."

"But we're trying to decorate," Natasha said.

"And I'm investigating a murder," the man snapped back. "Your decorations can wait a few hours, I'm sure."

This time no one argued. A moment later, the uniformed men walked into the room, ushering the volunteers and the site staff in with them.

"That's everyone we could find," one the men told the senior policeman. "But this place is like a maze. There could be someone hiding somewhere that we've missed."

"Who's in charge?" Inspector Corkill asked everyone.

"I suppose that would be me," Mark said after a moment.

"Is this everyone who's here today?" the inspector asked.

Mark looked around the room. "Yes, I believe it is," he said. "The volunteers sometimes bring other people with them, but they'd know if anyone from their rooms was missing."

"Is anyone missing?" Corkill demanded.

Everyone looked around, but no one spoke. After a moment, Agnes Clucas cleared her throat.

"Um, Michael isn't here," she said softly.

Mark nodded. "Michael Beach is one of the people who decorated a room," he told the inspector. "He had a bit of a disagreement with Mr. Hart yesterday and said he wouldn't be back. I haven't seen him this morning."

"And Carolyn isn't here," Bessie added.

"Carolyn Teare is on the committee for the event, but she didn't come down today to help," Mark said.

Inspector Corkill said something to one of the uniformed men, who then left the room. Now the inspector addressed them as a group.

"As I said, a body has been found in Douglas. I'm head of CID there, so I will be the primary investigator on the case. Because we believe the body to be that of Mr. Christopher Hart, and Mr. Hart was on the island to work on the event here, I shall be questioning each of you and anyone else who has any connection with the event happening at the castle. I appreciate your patience as I speak to you each in turn. Does anyone have any questions before I start?"

"Will we still be able to open on Friday?" Mark asked.

The inspector shrugged. "At the moment, I can't see any reason why not, but I'm making no promises at this point."

Mark nodded. Bessie could see that he was upset and worried.

"Miss Cubbon, I'd like to start with you," the inspector said.

Bessie swallowed hard and then put down the lights that she'd been stringing on the tree in front of her. She was conscious that all eyes were on her as she followed the policeman from the room. They walked down the corridor and through a door marked "staff only" before the man stopped. He pushed the door shut behind them and then turned to Bessie. His formidable frown was replaced by something like a smile as he gave her a quick hug.

"Looks as if you're tangled up in another murder," he told her. "I'm really sorry."

"Not half as sorry as I am," Bessie said with a sigh. "I don't suppose there's any chance it was an accident?"

"No, no chance," the inspector replied.

"That's awful. I mean, he wasn't a very nice man, but no one deserves to be murdered."

"He wasn't nice? Can you expand on that?"

"Maybe we should sit down," Bessie suggested. "This might take a while."

"Oh, sorry," the man flushed. "Do sit down."

Inspector Corkill sat down behind the small desk and Bessie took the chair across from him. She glanced around the room.

"I've been in this castle hundreds of times and I didn't realise this little office was here," she remarked.

"Apparently, they aren't using it at the moment, so they offered it to me as a space for interviews. Henry told me that it used to be a guard station when the castle was a prison. I've no idea what it was used for before that."

"It's quite small. It was probably used for storage," Bessie guessed.

"As much as I'd love to talk about the history of Castle Rushen all day, we really need to focus on my investigation," the man said. "I'd appreciate it, well, I mean, when there are other people around, I think it might be best if you didn't call me Pete. I don't want anyone thinking you're getting special treatment because we're friends."

Bessie smiled at his bright red face. "I'm happy to call you Inspector Corkill all the time," she said. "I was brought up to believe in showing respect for authority figures, even if you are friends with them."

"Oh, no, I do want you to call me Pete, maybe just not in front of Carolyn Teare."

Now Bessie laughed. "Yes, she'd be the first to complain about special treatment, unless she was the one getting it," she said. "I'll do my best to remember."

"Right, let's start with what you can tell me about our victim, then. I understand he arrived on the island on Sunday. Can you tell me why he was here?"

"There are five of us on the planning committee for 'Christmas at the Castle,'" Bessie began. "Myself, Marjorie Stevens and Mark Blake from Manx National Heritage, Mary Quayle and Carolyn Teare. We've been working for a month or so with volunteers from various charitable groups around the island to get the castle decorated for Christmas. We're meant to open on Friday for the weekend, and then on the final night, Christmas Eve, we will be auctioning off all the contents of the rooms as well as a number of other prizes that have been donated. All of the proceeds from the event will be shared between the groups that took part and Manx National Heritage."

"I have tickets for Christmas Eve. I'm bringing Helen."

Bessie was pleased to hear that the couple was still together. She knew Helen Baxter, a nurse at Noble's, because the woman was interested in the medical history of the island. The pair occasionally met at lectures and conferences at the museum and elsewhere on the island.

"I think she'll love it," Bessie said. "At least, I hope you both do. We've worked really hard getting everything ready and it's just about done."

"So where does our dead man fit into it?"

"Last week, when we met here to look at the various rooms as they were being decorated, Carolyn said that she thought the rooms needed to work together better. She proposed having a designer work with the groups to, well, unify things in some way."

"And the committee agreed?" Pete asked.

"Not really. There isn't any money in the budget for a designer, so Mark told her that we'd just have to work with what we had. The next day, Carolyn told us that she'd hired Christopher Hart to come across and, well, fix everything, I think was how she put it. As she was paying for it and it was expected to bring us some extra publicity, we couldn't really say no."

"So he arrived on Sunday?"

"You'd have to check with Carolyn on that," Bessie replied. "I met him yesterday morning around nine when he first arrived at the castle."

"I'm going to have you walk me through your entire day, but let me ask you this first. What was your first impression of the man?"

"I hate to speak ill of the dead," Bessie said with a sigh, "but, as I said, he wasn't very nice. He shouted at Laura because he didn't like the colour of the decorations we'd used in the courtyard, even though he'd specified he wanted mauve there and that's exactly what we'd used. He seemed to feel that he was a very important person and expected all of us to treat him as such."

"Okay, walk me through yesterday," Pete said. "I want every little detail you can remember."

Bessie took a deep breath and then began. She told him about changing the placement of the ornaments in the courtyard, the tensions at lunch and the disagreements that had followed. When she mentioned Michael Beach's well-aimed fist, Pete shook his head.

"I'll have to get a copy of the report from the ambulance personnel on the incident here yesterday," he told Bessie as he made a note.

Some time later, Bessie finished up by telling Pete about the phone call from Mark and their trip into Douglas that morning to collect the man.

"So everyone on the committee knew that Mr. Hart had moved into a hotel?" Pete checked.

Bessie thought for a moment. "I think Mark said that he'd emailed the committee and all of the volunteers, but you'll have to check with him. I don't know if he mentioned which hotel in his email, although there aren't that many options this time of year."

"No, I think there are only a handful of places open to guests at the moment," Pete agreed. "Everyone else is remodeling, renovating, or wintering somewhere warm and dry."

"I don't know what else I can tell you," Bessie said.

"Who do you think killed him?" Pete asked.

"Oh, goodness," Bessie exclaimed. "I've no idea. No one liked him, but it's a huge step from there to murder. He upset a lot of people here yesterday, but he was only going to be here for another day and a half. I can't see any reason for anyone to kill him."

"What did he and Carolyn fight about?"

"I haven't the foggiest idea," Bessie replied. "I know she said she'd used him before to decorate several rooms in her home. They seemed to be getting along just fine when they were here yesterday."

"What about Richard Teare?"

"Her husband? I think I've only met him once or twice."

"He wasn't involved in the planning for the event here?"

"Oh, no, he's far too busy making money in the city. Carolyn makes sure that she's on all the right committees and appears at the important social events, while he makes piles of money for her to spend. I don't even know if he's on the island at the moment. He rarely is, as I understand it."

"He's here," Pete told her. "He drove Mr. Hart to the hotel last night."

"How interesting," Bessie murmured.

Pete walked Bessie back to the partially decorated room, where everyone else was sitting around looking miserable. The inspector took Mark away for questioning. The silence in the room was stifling, and after a moment, Bessie felt as if she couldn't stand it any longer.

"I'm sorry, but can I put the radio on?" she asked one of the uniformed officers.

"Sorry, but we can't risk anyone hearing the news just now," the man replied.

"What if we play a tape?" Bessie asked. "We have several tapes of Christmas music."

The two men exchanged glances, and then one nodded. "I suppose that can't hurt," he said. "Inspector Corkill might not agree when he comes back, though, so you may have to switch it off."

"That's fine," Bessie replied. She walked over and put in the first cassette tape she picked up. A few minutes later a traditional Christmas carol filled the air. Bessie adjusted the volume down so that it was unobtrusive, but it helped to fill up the tense silence, at least.

She sat back down for a few moments, but felt too restless to stay seated.

"Is it okay if I get back to work on my tree?" Bessie asked the uniformed man now.

He looked at his colleague and then shrugged. "We were told you weren't to speak to one another," he said. "If you can decorate without speaking, I suppose it should be okay."

"I'll be good," Bessie promised. She quickly returned to stringing up lights, and after a few minutes, most of the others went back to work as well. Bessie found herself smiling as the music played and the room began to take shape. If she ignored the two men in the doorway, she could almost forget about Christopher Hart's untimely death.

When Inspector Corkill returned a short time later, he stopped in the doorway and stared. "Music? And decorating? Shall I guess that Miss Cubbon is behind it all?" he asked.

Bessie turned and smiled at him. "We aren't speaking to one another," she told him. "We're just getting on with our work."

"I suppose I can't complain, then, can I?" He shook his head and then asked Mary Quayle to join him.

The morning dragged on as everyone was interviewed in turn. Bessie's tummy was growling by the time the police had finished interviewing the last volunteer. She was also nearly desperate to speak, even though she had nothing in particular to say.

"Thank you all for your cooperation," Pete said from the doorway after he escorted Liz back into the room. "As our investigation progresses, I expect I'll need to speak to all of you again, but I won't take up any more of your time today. I've given you all my card. Please get in touch immediately if you think of anything that could be relevant, no matter how insignificant it might seem."

He spoke to the two uniformed men and then looked over at Bessie. "I'd appreciate another quick word, Miss Cubbon."

Bessie crossed to him and followed him and the uniformed men out into the corridor.

"I'd be grateful if you could ring me later and tell me about your afternoon," he told her. "Let me know if anyone is behaving at all oddly or says anything interesting or out of character."

"I'll ring you," Bessie promised. "But as everyone is quite upset, I suspect we'll all be acting out of character."

"Thank you," was the man's only reply.

Bessie watched as the trio made their way towards the exit. She didn't like feeling as if she were spying on her friends, but the idea that one of them might be a murderer was even more upsetting. Sighing deeply, she turned and walked back into the room that was still unfinished. If they were going to open on time, that had to be their priority, she thought. Maybe after lunch, her tummy added.

Mark suggested ordering pizza so that they could keep working through lunch, and no one objected. As Bessie returned to work on yet another tree, Liz approached her.

"Bessie, I don't quite know how to put this, but what are we meant to do now? I mean with Mr. Hart gone, do you still want us to make the changes he suggested or should we leave our rooms alone?"

"That's a great question," Bessie told her. "Let's see what Mark thinks."

"Let's wait to make any decisions until after lunch," Mark suggested when the pair approached him. "I rang Carolyn and Michael and they're both going to be here within the hour. We can all sit down and work out exactly what we want to do at that time."

"Can I help in here until the pizza arrives?" Liz asked.

Bessie gladly handed the girl a box of decorations and pointed her towards the nearest bare tree. The other volunteers quickly joined in and by the time the food was delivered, the room was starting to look like Bessie's plan.

"This is going to be my favourite room," Mark told Bessie as they helped themselves to lunch.

"It is looking rather nice," Bessie said. "And I think it's interesting to learn about Christmas customs in other parts of the world."

"Absolutely," Mark agreed. "I love that our event is fun and educational, all while supporting great not-for-profit groups. 'Christmas at the Castle' was one of my better ideas, I do think."

By the time everyone was stuffed full of pizza, garlic bread and fizzy drinks, Michael and Carolyn had arrived. Mark spoke to each of them in turn and then called the group to order. Before he began, Mary spoke up.

"I've been talking with Natasha," she told the group. "She has some ideas for little things that can be done to improve each room. I'm happy to pay for her time here, if you're all willing to listen to her ideas."

Bessie thought all of the volunteers looked uneasy with the idea.

"As long as everyone is free to leave their rooms the way they are if they choose," Mark articulated what Bessie was sure the rest were thinking.

"Of course they can," Mary assured him. "And I promise they're only small changes, as well."

"I think we ought to fix everything exactly as dear Christo wanted it," Carolyn said loudly. "The whole event should be a tribute to the dear man and all that he tried to do here."

"Perhaps we should donate some portion of the proceeds to his favourite charity in his name," Bessie suggested. "Surely that would be a more fitting tribute than trying to rearrange things based on our memories of what he said."

"I can remember exactly what he said about every room," Carolyn said.

"I think Bessie's idea is a good one," Mark interjected. "And I think letting Natasha have a turn at improving the rooms is also wise. Mr. Hart's ideas were, well, divisive might be the best word. I think it's important that we all work as a team to make this event the best it can be."

"Perhaps it's time for me to resign from the committee," Carolyn said crossly.

"What did you and Mr. Hart fight about last night?" Bessie blurted out.

Carolyn flushed. "That's certainly not any of your concern," she snapped. "And it certainly has no bearing on my determination to honour the memory of my dear friend."

"Maybe you could decorate a room in his honour," Marjorie said. "We haven't used every room in the castle, by any means. Perhaps MNH could find a small space that you could decorate in Mr. Hart's style."

Carolyn looked as if she wanted to argue, but after a moment she simply sighed dramatically. "If that's the best I can get, I suppose that will have to do," she said with an injured sniff. "I have all of the decorations that Christo purchased last evening. I'll have my staff get to work right away."

Mark and Marjorie had a quick conversation before Mark led them all down one of the corridors. "We didn't want to try to do too much, as this is our first year," he explained. "So we have an entire wing of rooms that we aren't using. This is the largest of the unused spaces. You're welcome to decorate it in honour of Mr. Hart."

Carolyn looked around the large and empty room. "It's cold and dark," she said. "But I suppose, if it's all I can have..." she trailed off and looked at Mark expectantly.

"There are smaller rooms on either side if you'd like one of those instead," Mark told her.

"This will do," she said sourly. She pulled out her mobile and within minutes she was shouting orders into it. Bessie felt sorry for the woman's employees, now tasked with bringing several boxes of decorations to the castle, where they would be expected to decorate the large drafty space Carolyn had been given.

"What should we expect?" Mark asked when Carolyn finally disconnected her call. "What theme was he planning to use?"

"I'm not sure exactly what he was planning," she replied. "I suppose you could call it 'Deadly Christmas,' but that seems, well, inappropriate, especially under the circumstances."

Mark nodded. "We'll decide what to call it after you're done decorating," he said. "Now, the rest of the committee probably needs to get back to our room. Mary, how about if you and Natasha start working with the volunteers to see what you can do?"

It was nearly five o'clock when Bessie stood back from a tree and smiled. "I think we're about done," she said happily. She looked around the room at all of the bright and cheery trees and smiled more deeply. The finished room was every bit as beautiful as she'd hoped it would be.

"I'm so going home to soak in a bath," Marjorie said, climbing down from a ladder. "I've been reaching over my head all afternoon. My arms and my back are really stiff."

"But the garland looks wonderful," Bessie said. A long garland of pine branches, with fairy lights woven through it, now stretched all around the room. Marjorie had spent all day measuring and hanging it so it was perfect.

"It wasn't easy on these old stone walls," Marjorie admitted. "But I think it was worth the effort."

"I had it easy," Mark said. "I was just doing trees."

"Wow," a voice from the doorway said. "You've been working really hard in here."

Bessie turned and nodded at Mary and Natasha, who were standing in the doorway. "We have, but we think we're done."

"And I wouldn't change a thing," Natasha told her.

"But come and see what she's done elsewhere," Mary urged them. "I think she's amazing."

They all followed Mary back down to the courtyard where Natasha had had a few ornaments rearranged. For some reason, those few changes made the space feel brighter and Bessie was immediately impressed with the woman.

An hour later, she was wishing she had the money in her own budget to have Natasha redesign her entire cottage. None of the changes the designer had made were huge, but they'd all made a significant difference to the feel of each room.

"I can't believe how different it all feels, even though nothing much has changed," Bessie said as they ended the tour in the banquet room.

"I love what she's done in our room," Liz told Bessie. "I never thought that moving the giant teddy to the opposite wall would make any difference at all, but it seems to make the space feel warmer and more enclosed, like a real toy box should."

It seemed that everyone, even Michael Beach, was happy with Natasha's input.

"Let me buy you dinner," he suggested to the young blonde as the group made their way out of the castle a short time later. "We can go anywhere you'd like."

"I wish I could," she replied. "But I've been here playing with Christmas decorations all day. I have to get back to my plans for Thie yn Traie. I'm on a tight deadline there."

Bessie expected Mary to insist that the woman take the evening off, but Mary didn't say a word. In the car park, everyone went their separate ways, with Bessie dropping onto the bench to wait for Mark to finish locking doors in the castle. She was surprised when Michael sat down beside her.

"So, I understand you're friends with half the police force on the island," he said. Bessie could tell that he was trying to sound offhand, but she could hear tension in his tone.

"I wouldn't say that," she replied. "I do know a few members of the police, but nowhere near half the force."

"You know Inspector Corkill, though, right?"

"I do," Bessie agreed.

"Does he think I killed Christopher Hart?"

Bessie stared at him for a moment. "Why would he think that?" she asked eventually.

"Because I punched him yesterday," Michael said. "Our little altercation seems likely to have made me the number-one suspect."

"I don't know what the inspector thinks," Bessie told him. "But I don't think your disagreement about Christmas decorations is much of a motive for murder."

Michael nodded. "There was a lot of name calling and ugly remarks," he said. "I suppose people have been killed for less."

"Unfortunately, you're probably right," Bessie said. "But there's a big difference between punching someone in the heat of anger and seeking them out many hours later to kill them."

"I didn't have to seek him out," Michael said. "He rang me from his hotel room."

"He did?"

"Yeah, he wanted to tell me that he was seriously considering taking the whole story to the press. He said he was certain I'd want to avoid negative publicity, especially on behalf of the Alzheimer's Research Fund, and he suggested that I might like to buy him a few drinks and discuss how we might smooth things over before he went back to London and started doing press interviews for his new series."

"That sounds a lot like blackmail to me," Bessie said.

"It sounded like blackmail to me, too," Michael agreed. "But he was right, I can't afford for the story to hit the papers. I'd probably lose my job over it."

"What did you do?"

"I agreed to meet him. I didn't feel as if I had much choice."

"And what happened over drinks?"

"I didn't go," Michael told her. "I drove down to Douglas and parked by the pub, but I didn't go in. I sat outside, watching the sea and thinking. I finally decided that I'd have to take my chances that Mr. Hart would rather not have everyone know that I knocked him out with one punch and I drove away."

"You're probably right," Bessie said after a moment's thought. "I can't see him telling people that he slapped you, either, and you have enough witnesses on your side that he would have had to tell the whole story if he started spreading it around."

"The problem is, I don't have any alibi and it seems like I have a motive," Michael told her. "I was hoping you might have some ideas as to how I can persuade Inspector Corkill that I didn't do it."

"The best thing you can do is tell him the whole story, if you haven't already," Bessie replied. "The more quickly the inspector can solve the case, the sooner you're in the clear."

"But who else had a motive?" Michael asked.

"I don't know, but maybe you weren't the only person Mr. Hart was trying to blackmail," Bessie suggested.

Michael sat back, a smile slowly spreading over his face. "I didn't think about that," he said. "You've made me feel much better."

"I'm glad," Bessie said.

She was going to remind him that he should tell the police everything he'd told her, but before she could speak, he jumped up.

"Must go, lots to do," he muttered, dashing away.

Bessie settled back on the bench, but Mark was there a moment later. "Ready for home?" he asked.

"Oh, definitely," Bessie replied.

At her cottage, she made herself a light meal and then rang Pete Corkill at home. She told him about everything that had happened that afternoon, including her conversation with Michael Beach.

"That's interesting," Pete remarked when she'd finished. "I think I need to have a word with Mr. Beach tomorrow morning."

Bessie asked a few questions, all of which the inspector politely refused to answer. When she disconnected, Bessie was feeling quite dissatisfied. When there was a case in Laxey and Inspector John Rockwell was investigating, she could sometimes get answers to her questions. She thought about ringing John and asking him for an update on the case, but she knew that doing so was inappropriate. With nothing better to do and her books lacking appeal, Bessie took herself to bed early.

CHAPTER 4

*H*aving had an early night, Bessie found herself awake early the next morning. After a shower and breakfast, she took a long walk on the beach, stopping frequently to simply listen to the waves. The walk had its usual calming effect on her and Bessie returned to her cottage feeling refreshed. She was surprised to see a car parked outside the cottage as she approached.

"Good morning," John Rockwell called to Bessie as he emerged from the car.

Bessie rushed over to give him a hug. Doona climbed out of the passenger side and came around for a hug of her own.

"This is an unexpected pleasure," she told the pair as she led them into the cottage.

"I brought some pastries," Doona said, holding up a bakery box.

"Tea or coffee?" Bessie asked.

"Coffee, if you don't mind," John replied. "I had a late night."

"Coffee sounds good to me, too," Doona said.

Bessie set the coffee maker going and then switched on the kettle as well. She preferred tea, at least when she wasn't overtired. Doona unpacked the box of goodies onto a plate and the trio sat down with their hot drinks to enjoy breakfast together.

"So, what's brought you here this morning?" Bessie asked after she'd finished a croissant.

"We wanted to make sure you were okay," Doona said. "John rang me last night to tell me that you were stuck in the middle of another murder investigation. I hope it hasn't upset you too much."

"I'm fine," Bessie told her. "I barely knew the man, after all."

"You may know the killer somewhat better," John said softly.

Bessie nodded. "I've been thinking about that," she admitted. "But maybe Mr. Hart's death has nothing to do with 'Christmas at the Castle.'"

"That's always possible," John replied. "And I'm sure Pete will be considering every possibility."

"Can't you take a few days off from working at the castle until the murder is solved?" Doona asked.

"We open in a few days," Bessie answered. "I have to be there to help finish everything. We're nearly done with the decorating; today we're meant to start setting up for the big auction on Christmas Eve. All of the items up for bid will be on display this weekend. We're hoping that encourages people to come back on Christmas Eve for the actual auction, although we're allowing sealed bids to be submitted if people prefer."

"You aren't auctioning off anything of great value, are you?" John asked.

"Not really," Bessie said. "A few of the local hotels are giving away weekend packages which are worth something, but I can't tell you exactly how much. We have some jewellery and gift certificates to various shops around the island. I don't think any one item is worth more than five hundred pounds or so, though."

"So nothing worth killing someone over," Doona said.

"Mr. Hart didn't have anything to do with the auction, anyway," Bessie said. "I can't see how his death could possibly be connected with that."

"I was more concerned about security," John told her. "How are the items being displayed and what security is in place for them?"

"You'd really have to talk to Mark about that," Bessie replied. "I'm sure he said something about only displaying pictures of the items that are available, at least until the actual auction evening. Mark and Marjorie are in charge of the auction, though, so I didn't pay that much attention to the plans they made."

"I'm sure the police in Castletown know all about it," John said. "It's their problem, after all, not mine. I'm just concerned about you."

"I'm fine, and 'Christmas at the Castle' is going to be wonderful," Bessie said firmly. "Perhaps Mr. Hart just met with an unfortunate accident."

"His death wasn't an accident," John told her.

"Oh, dear," Bessie sighed. "In that case, we just have to hope that Pete can work out who killed him as quickly as possible."

"I don't suppose you have any thoughts on the matter," John said.

"I don't, really," Bessie replied. "I did think about it, quite a lot actually, but I haven't come up with any answers."

"What was he like?" John asked.

"He was very demanding," Bessie began. "And he was somewhat difficult as well. I think he upset every single one of the volunteers who had decorated rooms at the castle."

"Upset them enough to make them want to kill him?" Doona asked.

"Over a few Christmas decorations?" Bessie shook her head. "People had hurt feelings, but that isn't a very strong motive for murder."

"I understand he'd had a disagreement with the woman who brought him over to help with the event," John said.

"Yes, apparently he and Carolyn Teare had some sort of falling out Monday evening," Bessie told him. "That's why he moved to the Seaside Hotel. He was meant to be staying with her while he was here."

The pastries were all gone and the coffee pot was empty. Doona got up and started to tidy the kitchen.

"We need to get to work," John said after glancing at his watch. "I'd love to stay and hear more about the case, but that will have to wait for another time."

"Come over any time," Bessie told him. "Although I'd much rather find other things to talk about."

John nodded and then gave her a hug. "I'm hoping Pete will have the whole matter resolved in a day or two."

"Me, too," Bessie said.

She let the pair out, smiling as she watched John hold Doona's door for her. The pair seemed to be back on friendly terms after their awkward patch. Back in the cottage, she quickly finished the tidying and then checked her appearance. She'd only just finished combing her hair when Mark arrived to take her to the castle.

"I was wondering," Mark said as they made their way south. "That is, I thought maybe you might be able to find time to talk to everyone today."

"Of course I can. What do you want me to talk to them about?"

Mark chuckled. "I'm explaining myself badly," he said apologetically. "I was just thinking that you've been through murder investigations before, and I thought maybe you could take time to reassure everyone, that's all. I'm certain some of our volunteers are quite upset about the whole thing."

"Has anyone said they won't be coming back to the castle?" Bessie asked.

"Oh, no, at least no one has rung me. Never mind, I'm rather upset about it all myself, you see."

"I do see," Bessie told him. "And it's understandable that you're upset. But it's quite possible that whoever killed Christopher Hart had nothing whatsoever to do with our little event. He certainly seemed like the type of person to have more than one enemy, didn't he?"

Mark nodded. "You're making me feel better, which is exactly why I want you to try to chat with everyone else. I'm sure you'll make all of our volunteers feel better as well."

"What about the others on the committee? Do they need reassurance as well?"

"I spoke with Marjorie last night. She was caught up in the murder investigation at the museum in May, so this isn't exactly new to her. I think she's holding up just fine. I don't know how Carolyn and Mary are feeling. I haven't had a chance to speak to either of them except in passing."

"I'll make a point of talking to everyone today," Bessie told him. She smiled to herself. She'd been planning to try to do that anyway, but with a rather different motive. Bessie was determined to help Pete solve the murder as quickly as possible, ideally before "Christmas at the Castle" opened.

Before they'd even walked into the castle, Bessie had her first opportunity to speak to one of the volunteers. Agnes Clucas pulled her car into the space next to Mark's as Bessie climbed out.

"I'll just wait for Agnes," Bessie told Mark. "You go on ahead."

"How are you, Bessie dear?" Agnes asked as she stepped out of her car. "I just need to get some things out of the boot."

"I'm fine," Bessie told her. She watched as Agnes unlocked her boot and pulled out a large box. "But how are you?"

Agnes shrugged. "I'm doing just fine," she said. "I was thinking about what Mr. Hart said about the rainbow trees, though. I found a few ornaments at home that I thought might help fix the room."

She opened the box and showed Bessie several boxes of multi-coloured ornaments. "Mr. Hart said the trees were all too alike and the end result was boring," she told Bessie as Bessie admired the beautiful glass baubles. "I thought if I scattered these throughout the room, it might make the room more interesting, without upsetting the rainbow theme."

"They're wonderful," Bessie said. "And I think they'll be perfect."

"That's what Ms. Harper said, too," Agnes said. "I told her I had these baubles and she thought they'd be exactly what the room needed. I hope she still thinks so when she sees them."

"I'm sure she will," Bessie said. "But I'm worried about everyone," she told Agnes in a confiding tone. "It isn't very pleasant, being mixed up in a murder investigation."

"Oh, I'm sure someone from across came over and killed Mr.

Hart," Agnes said. She picked up the box and stepped back from the car. "If you could just shut the boot?" she asked Bessie.

Bessie complied and then fell into step with her. "So you don't think Mr. Hart's murder has anything to do with 'Christmas at the Castle?'" she asked.

"Oh, I can't see how it could," Agnes replied. "No one would get that upset about a few Christmas decorations, would they? But having met Mr. Hart, it wouldn't surprise me to learn that he upset people just about everywhere he went. I suppose some of those upsets must have been over things rather more serious than our holiday happening."

"And you think they followed him over here and killed him?"

"I should imagine they'd want to do it as far away from their own home as possible," Agnes said.

Bessie couldn't argue with the logic of that. She held doors open for the other woman, stopping with her in the room Agnes had decorated.

Agnes put the box down and quickly added a few baubles to one of the trees. "It does work rather well, doesn't it?" she asked, looking at Bessie.

"It really does," Bessie agreed.

She crossed Agnes off her mental list of people to see and then made her way to the banquet room. Mark had called a committee meeting for first thing this morning. Bessie could only hope she'd have time to chat with some of the members before the meeting got started.

Mary was standing in the centre of the banquet room when Bessie arrived.

"Ah, I was starting to think I was in the wrong place," she greeted Bessie. "It's quite spooky in here when you're all alone."

"As far as I know, there's only one ghost in Castle Rushen and she haunts the throne room," Bessie told her.

Mary shivered. "I can't help but feel as if poor Christopher Hart is haunting the castle now," she said. "I think I would, if I were him."

"I think, if I were able to come back as a ghost, I'd haunt somewhere lovely and warm, like the French Riviera," Bessie said. "I'd much rather watch people enjoying themselves than skulk around an old castle that's cold and damp."

Mary laughed. "I wonder if ghosts get a choice," she said thoughtfully.

"If I get a chance, I'll let you know," Bessie said, laughing.

"Oh, I do hope we get a choice and we can haunt people together," Mary said. "I think I'd like to haunt a few houses and scare one or two people who have been quite terrible to George and myself after all the unpleasantness."

George's former business partner had recently disappeared, taking a large amount of stolen money with him. While George had been cleared of any wrongdoing in the matter, there was a small segment of the island's population who were now avoiding the couple. As George was a lively and gregarious man who thrived on social interaction, he was struggling to accept a quieter lifestyle. Mary was very shy, and Bessie had no doubt that she didn't miss their formerly active social life even the tiniest bit. But Mary loved her husband enormously and Bessie wasn't surprised that the woman resented the way he was being treated.

"Let's go to the French Riviera instead," Bessie said. "Or maybe somewhere exciting, like New York City or Paris."

"I've never been to New York," Mary said thoughtfully. "I suppose that could be fun."

"But how are you?" Bessie changed the subject. "Not too upset by Mr. Hart's untimely death, I hope."

"Oh, I'm okay," Mary replied. "I barely knew the man and I didn't much like him, although that's a terrible thing to say."

"I didn't like him, either," Bessie told her. "He didn't try to be likeable."

"No, I suppose not," Mary agreed. "Anyway, aside from talking to the police, which always makes me nervous even though I've not done anything wrong, I'm just fine."

"Good. I know some of the volunteers are a little upset," Bessie said. "I'm going to try to speak to them all today."

"That's good of you. I'm sure none of them could be involved in Mr. Hart's death, though. What possible reason could anyone on the island have for wanting him dead?"

Bessie shrugged. "That's for the police to work out," she said firmly.

"Of course it is," Mary agreed.

"I do hope I'm not late," Marjorie said from the doorway.

"Not at all," Bessie assured her. "Mark still hasn't made his way up here yet and I've no idea where Carolyn is."

"She'll be running late," Marjorie said with a laugh. "She always is."

Bessie nodded. Carolyn was nearly always the last to arrive for their committee meetings.

"I'm just going to ring George," Mary said. "He's meant to be bringing Natasha down in a little while. I don't want him to forget."

She walked to the far end of the room to make her call, leaving Bessie with Marjorie.

"So, how are you?" Bessie asked her friend.

"I'm fine. How are you? Is it awful being caught up in another murder investigation?"

"It isn't pleasant," Bessie admitted. "But it is starting to feel rather routine."

"I was up half the night, thinking about Christopher Hart," Marjorie said. "I tried to sleep, but I couldn't. I just can't help but wonder who could have killed him. I can't seem to work out a motive."

"He wasn't a very nice man," Bessie remarked.

"No, but lots of people aren't very nice and no one kills them," Marjorie said.

"Maybe someone followed him from across," Bessie suggested. "I'd like to think that his death has nothing to do with anyone I know, anyway."

"Oh, I hope you're right. I'm looking forward to Friday and the big grand opening. I really think this event is exactly what the island needs at Christmas. It should be perfect for families, young couples, grandparents, everyone, really."

Bessie laughed. "I hope it lives up to your expectations," she said.

Before Marjorie could reply, Mark walked into the room. Mary ended her call and joined the others before Mark spoke.

"Carolyn just rang," he said, frowning. "Something has come up and she's asked us to postpone the committee meeting until one o'clock this afternoon. Is that okay with everyone?"

"It doesn't matter to me. I was planning to be here all day, anyway," Bessie replied.

"So was I," Mary said. "Natasha is coming down soon and we were going to work with everyone on the last finishing touches."

"I have to run back up to Douglas for a meeting," Marjorie said. "But I can be back for one, or a little after."

"Great, thanks, everyone," Mark said. "I'll be in the office downstairs going over ticket sales and other paperwork if anyone needs me."

Marjorie disappeared behind Mark, and Mary was quickly back on her phone. That left Bessie free to start trying to find everyone so that she could speak to them. She headed towards the nearest decorated room. Michael was standing in the centre of it with his back to Bessie, talking on his mobile.

"I'd love to come for an interview after the holidays," Bessie heard. "I have family in Cumbria, so it's probably my first choice for relocating."

Bessie took a few steps backwards and then stomped heavily into the room. Michael spun around and flushed when he saw her there.

"I'll check my calendar and ring you back in an hour or so," he said into the phone. "Thank you again."

"I hope I'm not interrupting anything," Bessie said brightly.

"No, not really," Michael muttered. He glanced down at the phone and then shook his head. "You heard that, didn't you?"

"I'm sorry, yes."

"I hope you won't think too badly of me, wanting to leave the island," he said. "I just feel as if I've done all I can here."

"You've only been here three months," Bessie pointed out.

"Yes, but it's such a small island. There simply isn't any real opportunity for career advancement. I didn't do enough research into the island before I moved over. It's a nice enough place to live, but it's a little bit, well, boring, if you're young and single."

"Does the board of directors at the Alzheimer's Research Fund know you're job-hunting?" Bessie asked.

Michael flushed. "Not yet," he said. "I've only really just started looking in the last few days and I'll only leave if the perfect job turns up, so I didn't mention it yet."

"I hope none of this has anything to do with Mr. Hart's death," Bessie said.

"No, of course not," Michael replied very quickly.

Bessie raised an eyebrow. "Really?"

"Oh, I can't say it isn't upsetting," Michael said. "I've never been tangled up in a murder investigation before, after all, but I'm really just concerned with my career, nothing else."

"And you've no idea who might have killed Mr. Hart?" Bessie asked.

"The more I think about it, the more I'm sure you were right," he told Bessie. "He must have been blackmailing someone and they must have finally had enough. In a way, whoever killed him did me a favour, actually, as I might have trouble finding another position if word did get out that I'd punched him."

"Well, I wish you luck," Bessie said. "But we'll be sorry to lose you. I know you've raised a lot of money in the short time you've been here."

"That's my job," Michael replied.

Bessie nodded and then made her way through his room and into the corridor beyond. She felt uneasy about Michael's sudden desire to leave the island, but his explanation made sense. The board at the Alzheimer's Research Fund wouldn't be happy. Bessie knew it had taken them nearly six months to find Michael. They wouldn't be eager to start looking for a replacement so soon.

Bessie was pleased to find Liz hard at work in her room. "I do hope you're not changing much," she told the girl as she walked in. "I loved this room just the way it was."

"Just moving a few things around like Natasha suggested," Liz told her. "She's going to be bringing a few things with her today to make the room look more festive, as well. Mr. Hart was right about that; it doesn't feel very Christmas-like in here."

"I'll look forward to seeing what Natasha has come up with," Bessie said. She had a quick chat with the woman, who insisted that she wasn't upset about the murder.

"Someone from London or somewhere like that must have come over and killed him," Liz insisted. "I'm sure he had a great many enemies. He seemed like the type." Bessie left Liz happily rearranging the oversized toy box.

The castle felt very quiet this morning and Bessie found herself wandering into the courtyard. While she would never have chosen mauve Christmas decorations for the space, she had to admit they looked good against the stone walls. Noticing movement in the ticket booth, Bessie headed there.

"Good morning, Laura," she said to the woman who was sitting behind the desk, which was covered in tickets and envelopes.

"Good morning," she replied, smiling at Bessie. "I don't suppose you've come to help?"

"What are you doing?"

"Posting out tickets. It seems, with everything else going on, that that little job has been rather neglected. We're okay for Friday and Saturday this week, but I don't think any of the tickets for Sunday have been posted yet, and we've sold quite a lot. I'm afraid to look at the list for Christmas Eve."

"I'll come back and help later," Bessie promised. "After I've checked in on everyone."

"Is everything okay?" Laura asked.

"As far as I know, everything's fine," Bessie assured her. "But Mark was worried that some people might be upset about Mr. Hart's death, that's all."

"I think we're all upset about that. I thought about taking a few days off, you know, just to avoid the whole thing."

"We just have to hope the police sort it out quickly," Bessie said, patting the woman's hand. "Inspector Corkill is very good at his job. I'm sure he'll work out what happened soon."

"I hope so. I hate feeling as if I'm a suspect."

"We're all suspects," Bessie told her. "I'm sure you and I are quite low on the list, though. I wonder who is highest on that list."

"I'm sure it must be someone we don't know," Laura said. "I'm sure Mr. Hart had lots of enemies. Someone must have sneaked over from across just to kill him, don't you think?"

"That's certainly one possibility. I'm sure the inspector is doing everything he can to investigate just that."

"If you can get back to help out later, I'd be ever so grateful," Laura changed the subject. "I'm meant to be helping Henry with setting up the auction as well."

"I thought the committee was supposed to be helping with that," Bessie said.

"Henry's moving furniture and rearranging the room," Laura told her. "Then you and the committee can come in and set things up."

"Perhaps I should go and see how he's getting on. I hope he isn't rushing. The committee meeting has been rescheduled for this afternoon, and we won't be ready to do anything in there until after that."

Bessie took a shortcut up to the large room where Henry was hard at work. She was pleased to see that two young men were doing all of the heavy lifting under Henry's direction, rather than Henry trying to move furniture by himself.

"Ah, Bessie, just in time for a tea break," he greeted her. "Joe, pop the kettle on, will you?"

One of the men filled the kettle and switched it on before pulling out his mobile. The other man was already talking to someone on his.

"How are you?" Bessie asked Henry as the man found mugs and dumped biscuits onto a plate.

"I'm good," he replied. "I was worried about Laura, because that Mr. Hart upset her, but she's okay now."

"I think we'll all feel better when the police arrest someone," Bessie said.

"I bet whoever did it is long gone," Henry told her. "They will have come over and killed him and then headed back where they came from. Inspector Corkill will never find them."

"I hope they do find him, or her, but I'd be happy if the killer turned out to be someone from across. I'd hate to think that anyone from 'Christmas at the Castle' could be involved."

She enjoyed tea and biscuits, chatting with Henry and the two young workers. Bessie found that spending time with young people was energising and she always felt as if she'd learned something from them as well. Today they told her all about a new movie that was just out. As she headed back down to look for the others on her unwritten list, Bessie was mentally shaking her head at what Hollywood seemed to think was entertaining these days.

Harriet was in her room, rearranging cuddly toys. "Natasha suggested that I try sorting them in some way," she told Bessie. "I'm trying to arrange them by size, but only very approximately."

"I like what you've done so far," Bessie told her. "I hope you're happy with Natasha's changes?"

"Oh, yes, she's so much nicer and easier to work with than Mr. Hart was," Harriet replied.

"And you aren't too upset about his untimely death?"

Harriet shrugged. "I barely knew the man, and what I knew about him, I didn't much like," she said. "I'm sorry he was killed, but if he'd simply decided to leave, I would have been happy to see him go."

"Do you have any idea who killed him?"

"If it wasn't someone from across, then the only suggestion I have is Michael," Harriet replied. "He might have been in a lot of trouble if Mr. Hart had followed through on his threat and pressed charges after that punch."

"We were all witnesses that Mr. Hart struck Michael first."

"But when you're looking for a new job, having police charges brought against you won't help."

"Michael is looking for a new job?"

"Unlike the rest of us, working for non-profits is Michael's career. The best and fastest way to get ahead in that business is to switch jobs regularly. I've no doubt Michael started looking for his next job as

59

soon as he accepted the one here. And I wouldn't be surprised if he's disappointed in the position here, as well. I'm sure he thought he'd be able to bring in more staff once he got started, but even with his success so far, the charity simply isn't big enough to warrant hiring on more people. He seems like the type that would resent having to type his own letters, though."

"It's a long way from that to murder," Bessie said.

"I don't know anything about how Mr. Hart died, but I think we all know that Michael has a temper. If he met up with Mr. Hart later that day and they argued, well, I can see Michael hitting him again."

Bessie frowned. "You could be right," she said reluctantly. She didn't exactly like Michael Beach, but he'd worked hard on his part of "Christmas at the Castle." She'd much prefer it if the killer was a total stranger.

With Harriet's words replaying in the mind, Bessie headed towards the front of the building. She still hadn't found Margaret Christian. This time, when Bessie walked into her room, Margaret was there.

"Just getting the Christmas card table sorted," she told Bessie.

"It's just the thing this room needed," Bessie replied.

"I'm so glad that Marjorie suggested it and MNH offered to fund it. I think it's just the right touch."

"But how are you?" Bessie asked.

"I'm keeping busy so I don't think about that poor young man, if that's what you mean."

"We don't have to talk about it," Bessie assured her. "I just wanted to check on everyone, that's all."

"I know the nice policeman said it wasn't, but I still think he must have simply met with an unfortunate accident," Margaret said. "Such a dangerous world we live in, really. I feel sorry for his family, losing him this close to Christmas."

"I haven't heard anything about his family," Bessie said. "Of course he must have had someone who'll miss him."

"I wouldn't count on it," Natasha drawled from the doorway. "He lost both of his parents when he was quite young and he and his older

60

brother had a falling out about twenty years ago and never spoke again. He was currently between women, as well, and believe me, none of his exes will miss him."

"You knew him better than I realised," Bessie said, studying the young woman who was framed in the doorway.

"He was a competitor," she said with a shrug. "I keep track of all of my competitors."

"He said something about you stealing customers," Bessie recalled.

Natasha flushed. "He liked to throw that accusation around whenever he had a chance," she replied. "I think, over the years, he managed to accuse just about every other designer out there of stealing clients from him. The simple fact was that a lot of his customers chose to switch designers, often in the middle of projects with him, because they simply didn't like what he was doing. Ironically, he was the one who stole clients now and then. He even sent some design ideas to Mary, suggesting that he might be a better choice for Thie yn Traie."

"Do you have any idea who might have killed him?" Bessie asked.

"So many possibilities," the woman replied. "An ex-girlfriend whom he treated badly, another designer who had clients stolen from him, a former customer who felt that he ruined his or her home. The list is endless."

"It appears the police have a big job to do, then," Bessie said.

"I'm much happier with my job," Natasha replied. "I'm thrilled with how everything is coming together here, and Mary seems to like my ideas for Thie yn Traie, as well."

Before Bessie could reply, Carolyn Teare rushed into the room. "Ah, Bessie, there you are. You're just the person I wanted to see."

Bessie looked at the woman in surprise. Carolyn's hair was a tangled mess, her skirt didn't match her jumper and she looked as if she'd been crying.

"What's wrong?" Bessie asked.

Carolyn looked around the room and shook her head. She took Bessie's arm and pulled her through the castle, ignoring everyone they passed. When the pair finally reached an empty room, Carolyn stopped. She pressed her hand to her head.

61

"Carolyn, what's wrong?" Bessie asked, staring into the other woman's eyes.

"You've been involved in murder investigations before," Carolyn said. "You'll know what to do."

"What to do about what?"

"I think my husband killed Christo," Carolyn hissed.

CHAPTER 5

*F*or a moment, Bessie could only stare at the woman. "Pardon?" she said eventually, certain that she must have misheard.

"I think Richard killed Christo," Carolyn wailed. "What can I do? I can't tell the police. I don't want Richard to go to prison. I need him."

Bessie shook her head. "Why do you think Richard killed Mr. Hart?" Bessie asked.

"He took him to the hotel," Carolyn replied. "But it was hours before he came home. When I asked him what he was doing for all that time, he wouldn't answer me."

"But what possible motive did he have? I didn't think he even knew Mr. Hart."

"He was, well, he thought, that is, he didn't like my friendship with Christo," Carolyn said, flushing. She turned and walked a step away from Bessie. "Richard thought I might be having an affair with Christo," she said quietly.

"But you weren't," Bessie said, trying to make it sound more like a statement than a question.

Carolyn glanced over at her and turned a darker shade of red.

"Christo liked his women young," she said. "He wasn't interested in me."

From the bitterness in the woman's tone, Bessie had to assume that Carolyn had made an offer that Christopher Hart had turned down. Perhaps that was what the fight that got him kicked out of Carolyn's home was about.

"I've only met Richard once or twice," Bessie said. "He doesn't seem like the violent type." Besides the fact that he's in his late sixties, Bessie thought, but didn't add.

"He has a terrible temper," Carolyn replied.

"You should talk to Inspector Corkill," Bessie told her.

"Oh, I couldn't possibly. What if Richard did kill Christo?"

"You don't want him to go to prison?"

"Of course not," Carolyn said. "All the money is his, after all. Knowing him, he'd spend a fortune on his defense and then go off to prison and leave me with nothing."

Bessie found herself staring at the woman again. "You think he killed someone, but you don't want the police to know," she said slowly.

"Exactly; you've been involved in lots of murder investigations. How can I divert suspicion onto other people? Who else had a motive? You must know."

"I haven't the slightest idea who might be a suspect. I can assure you, though, that Inspector Corkill will be taking a good look at you and your husband, whether you tell him about your suspicions or not."

"Richard will have to go away," Carolyn said. "Perhaps he should go and visit his brother in California for a while. The police can't question him if he's in America."

"They might not let him go," Bessie told her. "I don't think they'll want anyone involved in the case travelling right now."

"They can't stop him," Carolyn said tartly. "He's been thinking about going to visit his brother for months."

"I think you'll find that they can stop him," Bessie told her.

"You aren't any help at all," Carolyn complained.

"What did you and Mr. Hart fight about the night he died?" Bessie asked.

"Christo and I didn't fight," Carolyn replied. "We never fought. We were the very closest of friends."

"So why did he suddenly move to a hotel?"

"Christo and Richard had a difference of opinion on something," Carolyn muttered.

"Has he told the police that?"

"I don't know what Richard has told the police," Carolyn said with a sigh. "We aren't, that is, I haven't really seen him since, well, since that argument. Richard left to take Christo to the hotel. He didn't get home until quite late. I was already in bed. Of course, he had to go to work the next morning, and we've both been quite busy. We simply haven't had time to talk."

"But you told the police about the argument."

"Of course not. That would only give them the idea that Richard had some sort of motive for killing Christo."

Bessie sighed. "If you don't want the police to know things, you shouldn't be telling me," she told the woman. "I expect I'll be questioned again and I'll have to tell Inspector Corkill what you've told me."

Carolyn shrugged. "I thought you'd be like that," she said. "But I can just deny everything. I have an advocate on speed dial. He'll sort it all out."

"If I were you, I'd tell the police everything," Bessie said.

"Too much risk. I can't have Richard locked up. He needs to be out here, earning money."

"And you're prepared to live with a murderer, for the sake of the money?" Bessie asked.

"You make it sound so dramatic when you put it that way," Carolyn complained.

"You're the one who said you think he did it," Bessie pointed out.

"Well, maybe he didn't," Carolyn snapped. "Maybe it was Michael. He'd already punched Christo. Maybe he found Christo in Douglas and finished the job."

"Several people here seem to think that someone followed Mr. Hart from across," Bessie said. "Maybe Mr. Hart's death had nothing to do with anyone on the island at all."

"That's probably it," Carolyn said. "I did my best to let people know he was coming. It was all meant to be good publicity for our event. I do hope I didn't accidently let his killer know where to find him. Oh, goodness, his death could have been my fault."

Bessie had had enough of the other woman's drama. "Why don't we leave the investigation up to the police, and we can focus on getting the castle ready for Friday?" she suggested. "We have the auction to set up and I'm sure we need to do some finishing touches around the place."

"And I still have to set up my tribute room," Carolyn said. "Although I think my staff has that well in hand. Anyway, it's time for the committee meeting. We really must get going."

She headed off towards the banquet room, leaving Bessie shaking her head behind her. I've been here all day, Bessie thought as she followed Carolyn. We've been waiting for you.

The committee meeting didn't take long. They went over everything that still needed to be finished and then split into groups to get to work. No one mentioned Christopher Hart or the murder investigation. Bessie spent an hour helping Laura with tickets and by five o'clock everything was just about finished. The only thing left to do was add some fresh flowers in some of the rooms. Those were due to be delivered on Friday morning.

"I dare say we can take tomorrow off," Mark told Bessie as he drove her home. "All of the last-minute jobs can't be done until Friday, so there's no reason for anyone to even be at the castle tomorrow."

"I can't believe, after all the hard work, that we're done a day early," Bessie replied. "There were times when I didn't think we'd ever finish."

"I was worried, when Mr. Hart first arrived and wanted to change everything, that we were in trouble," Mark confided. "Natasha's changes have been much more manageable."

"And she's done wonderful things," Bessie said. "I thought it all looked beautiful anyway, but it looks even better now."

Mark dropped Bessie at home. They agreed that he'd collect her on Friday morning. She planned to spend the day at the castle, bringing her formal wear for the evening grand opening with her.

"I'll ring you if anything comes up between now and then, otherwise I'll see you on Friday," Mark told her.

With an unexpectedly free day to fill, Bessie made herself a light evening meal while she tried to decide what to do with her Thursday. She missed spending time with her friends in Laxey, but they would all be at work during the day. She was just about to ring to book a taxi to take her to Ramsey the next day when the phone rang.

"Hello?"

"Ah, Bessie, it's Pete Corkill. I was hoping I might be able to come to see you tomorrow morning before you head down to Castletown."

"I'm not going to Castletown tomorrow. We're all ready for Friday, and Mark has given us all the day off."

"In that case, can I buy you breakfast somewhere?"

"Why don't you come here?" Bessie asked. "I can do a full English breakfast. I haven't done that in ages."

After the inspector agreed, Bessie checked her refrigerator. She hadn't done a proper grocery shop in weeks, because she'd been so busy going back and forth to Castletown. Without a trip to the shops, she'd never be able to make breakfast the next day.

Bessie quickly made a list of what she needed and then headed out the door. She walked up the hill to the small shop at the top. Fully expecting the disagreeable young woman whose father owned the shop to be behind the till, she forced a smile on her face before she walked in.

"Anne? Are you working here again?" she asked, surprised to find her old friend, Anne Caine, stocking shelves.

"Would you believe the owner's daughter has run off to Scunthorpe with some lad she met at TT? Apparently, they met in the beer tent and stayed in touch after he went home. I gather she and her dad had a disagreement about something and off she went," Anne told her.

Bessie shook her head. "Good luck to her," she said. "I hope she's happy there. She always seemed miserable here."

"Oh, aye," Anne laughed. "She never made a secret of that, did she? Her father is furious, of course, but she's over eighteen and can make her own mistakes."

"Are you back for good, then?" Bessie asked.

"Oh, I don't know," Anne said, waving a hand. "I don't have to work, which is the ultimate luxury. But I really miss working, as well. I told the owner that I'll cover until the new year and then we'll have to talk. The shop is closed from Christmas Eve until the second of January, anyway, so it isn't much of a commitment."

Bessie found what she needed for the breakfast she'd promised Pete. "Is Andy coming home for Christmas?" she asked as Anne rang up her items.

"Only for a few days," Anne replied. "He's going to be here for Christmas Eve and then he's going back on Boxing Day. He's been invited to be the resident chef at some fancy country house from Boxing Day until the new year."

"That should be good experience for him," Bessie said.

"Yes, and his friend, Sue, is going as well. She's going to be his assistant chef for the week. I think that's the main reason he took the job."

Bessie chuckled. "They seemed well-suited when I met her at my Thanksgiving dinner."

"They're perfect for each other," Anne agreed. "I really liked her and I know Andy thinks she's wonderful. He just has to persuade her to see him as more than just a friend."

"Did you get tickets for 'Christmas at the Castle?'" Bessie asked.

"I did. I'm bringing Andy and Sue with me, as well. We're coming on Christmas Eve for the auction. Now that we have a little bit of money, I think we should be supporting local charities."

Bessie smiled at the woman. Anne had worked hard, often holding down two jobs at once, to support herself and her son over the years. A recent inheritance had given her access to more money than she'd ever imagined having. Bessie had wondered if Anne and Andy might spend at least some of it on extravagances, but thus far she'd seen no sign of them doing anything but behaving very cautiously and sensibly with their new wealth. That Anne was looking to give back to the community only reinforced Bessie's delight in Anne's good fortune.

"If I don't see you between now and then, I'm sure I'll see you at the castle on Christmas Eve, then," Bessie told Anne before she headed back down the hill.

At home, she put away her shopping and then got ready for bed. Feeling like a change, she found a book she'd hidden away for a rainy day. It was the newest title by one of her favourite authors. When it had arrived from the bookshop in Ramsey in one of their regular shipments, she'd hidden it from herself, determined to wait to read it when she knew she needed a real treat. Tonight felt like the right night for her indulgence.

With a box of chocolate truffles on the bedside table, Bessie climbed into bed and got lost in one of her favourite fictional worlds. Hours later, the chocolates were gone and Bessie was blinking hard and trying to pull herself back to reality.

"Reality is overrated," she told her mirror image before she brushed her teeth and went to bed.

She kept her walk short the next morning, and had breakfast ready to go when Pete Corkill arrived.

"I didn't actually start cooking yet," she told him as she let him in. "Everything cooks so quickly, it seemed better to wait."

He sat at the kitchen table while Bessie began to cook. "You can talk while I work, if you want," she told her guest. "I've made breakfast often enough that I don't really need to concentrate."

"Why don't we talk about 'Christmas at the Castle', rather than the case," the inspector suggested. "I'd like more background, if possible."

"I think I told you everything I know," Bessie said. "Was there something specific you were wondering about?"

"You said that Carolyn Teare brought Christopher Hart across. Do you know how she happened to choose him, rather than some other designer?"

"I'm sorry, but I haven't the slightest idea," Bessie replied. "I didn't know we needed a designer until she announced that she was providing one. I'd also never heard of the man before she mentioned him."

"Who selected the members of the committee?" Pete changed the subject.

"I suppose that was Mark Blake. He asked me to join. I'm sure when he asked me, he told me that Mary Quayle and Marjorie Stevens had already agreed to help. He also asked me if I had any suggestions for other members, but I couldn't think of anyone to add."

"So who suggested Carolyn Teare?"

"You'd have to ask Mark," Bessie said. "I'd say, but no, I shouldn't."

"Yes, you should," Pete told her. "Whatever you were thinking, I'd like to hear it, even if it's just speculation."

Bessie shook her head. "I was just going to say that it's likely she suggested herself, but that doesn't sound very nice."

"But she might have?"

"She often volunteered for committee positions, especially where there was expected to be a lot of publicity," Bessie said.

"So she likes to do volunteer work?"

"I wouldn't say that exactly," Bessie said ruefully. "She likes to serve on various committees, but I don't think she particularly likes to work."

Pete chuckled. "I take it you aren't fond of her," he said.

"I just feel that, if you're going to volunteer for something, you should be prepared to work hard," Bessie explained. "Carolyn prefers to throw money at the first sign of any work that needs doing." She sighed. "There's always a place for that, of course, especially with non-profit organisations."

"Who selected which non-profits would be involved?" Pete changed the subject again.

"At our first meeting, Mark asked for suggestions," Bessie said. "We ended up inviting about ten different groups to take part, but only five of them were interested or able to put something together in time."

"I don't suppose you remember who suggested which groups?"

Bessie thought while she turned over bacon and sausages. It was no good. "It was too long ago and it didn't seem important at the time," she told the man. "We were all throwing out ideas and discussing different groups. I don't recall anyone being strongly in favour of any one group over any other, if that helps."

"Was anyone particularly opposed to any group?"

Bessie shook her head. "I don't remember anyone opposing any of them," she said. She pulled down plates and piled food onto them. After delivering the plates to the table, she poured coffee for them both and then sat down opposite the man.

"There was a short debate about whether we should allow groups that use professional fundraisers rather than groups that just use volunteers," she said after she'd taken a few bites. "Marjorie really wanted to only use volunteer groups, but Carolyn felt that the Alzheimer's Research Fund was worth including, no matter how they raise their money."

"How did you feel?"

"I wanted the event to be as inclusive as possible. I thought we should ask every non-profit on the island to take part."

"Why didn't you?"

"It was a question of scale," Bessie explained. "This is the first year MNH is trying this and Mark didn't want things getting too big too fast. We'd have had enough problems if all ten groups we did ask agreed to take part, as we only wanted to use a handful of rooms. I think, for the first year, the size is just about right."

"If Marjorie had won the argument, who wouldn't have been included?"

"Michael Beach and the Alzheimer's Research Fund, and Harriet Hooper and the Manx Animal Care Team," Bessie replied.

"That would have made it a much smaller event," Pete remarked.

"That was one of the points that was raised in the discussion," Bessie recalled. "We hadn't actually asked anyone yet, but both of those groups were on our short list and we didn't want to cut the list down too far. It turned into a fairly long discussion, actually."

"Did it become heated?"

71

Bessie shook her head. "Everyone kept calm and presented their point of view politely. It was our first meeting, after all. We were still trying to work together."

"But that changed? When?"

"I wouldn't say it changed," Bessie prevaricated. "As we got to know one another better, there were, of course, some disagreements, but mostly we stayed focussed on creating the best possible event."

"Tell me about the disagreements," Pete invited her. "Breakfast is excellent, by the way."

"Thank you. I should make myself a proper breakfast more often," Bessie said. "As for our disagreements, most of them were just over silly little things. We couldn't agree on how to decorate the courtyard, for example."

"And who won that argument?"

"We were still debating the issue when Carolyn brought in Christopher Hart and told us all that he would be deciding what would be going in that space. He sent his instructions to MNH and they ordered and hung the decorations."

"And you all went along with that?"

Bessie sighed. "Sometimes it's better not to argue," she said. "Carolyn offered to pay for all of the decorations if we went with Mr. Hart's plan. The less MNH has to spend for the event, the better, of course."

"So Carolyn won that argument. Tell me more."

"Carolyn wasn't happy about the plans for the MNH room, either," Bessie recalled. "She wasn't at the meeting where it was discussed and voted on, and when she found out we'd decided in her absence, she put up a bit of a fuss."

"Let me guess, Mr. Hart was going to change that room," Pete said dryly.

Bessie chuckled. "He was, now that you mention it. And no, I really hadn't realised that Carolyn was using Mr. Hart to get everything the way she wanted it at 'Christmas at the Castle.' I suppose, because I'm not the scheming type, that I simply never thought about it."

"I'm not sure that it has anything to do with Mr. Hart's murder, but it's interesting," Pete said.

Bessie cleared away the breakfast dishes and poured more coffee. "Surely, Carolyn wouldn't have killed him if he was helping her get her way."

"Unless that's what the argument was about," Pete suggested. "But what can you tell me about Richard Teare, Carolyn's husband?"

"Carolyn told me yesterday that she thinks he killed Mr. Hart," Bessie said.

"But you don't agree," Pete said. "Or you would have brought it up before now."

"I don't know," Bessie said. "You would think a wife would know her husband better than anyone. I've only met Richard Teare a few times, but he really doesn't seem like a murderer to me."

"Experience has taught me that most murderers don't seem like the type," Pete said.

"Carolyn said that she thought Richard killed Christopher because he thought she was having an affair with the man," Bessie said. "Maybe I simply don't think he cares enough about Carolyn to kill over an affair."

"You don't think he loves his wife?"

"She was a trophy wife when she was young," Bessie explained. "Richard is quite a bit older than she is and I suspect her charm has faded somewhat over the years."

"But maybe she'd never cheated on him before?"

"I don't think she cheated this time," Bessie said. "I didn't get the impression that Mr. Hart was interested in anything other than Carolyn's money."

"Whether they had an affair or not, what matters is what Richard Teare thought was happening," Pete pointed out. "Does he seem like the jealous type?"

"I've probably only spoken to him ten times in my life," Bessie said. "I remember, vaguely, when he and Carolyn were first married. He was very possessive of her then, but in the last few years they seem to have drifted apart."

"No children?"

"No, Richard has some from his first marriage. I'm sure Carolyn said something once about him not wanting to go through all of that again."

"So if he wasn't jealous over Mr. Hart's relationship with Carolyn, what other possible motive could Richard have had for killing him?"

"I have no idea," Bessie said. "I don't know anything about Richard's business interests, so I couldn't tell you if they were tied to Mr. Hart in any way. If Richard was going to kill someone, I'd be inclined to think it would be over money matters, rather than his wife, though."

Pete made a note in his notebook and then nodded at Bessie. "Okay, so that's a possible motive for Richard Teare to investigate. Who else had a motive?"

"You know he and Michael had a fight earlier in the day. I don't think that gives Michael a motive for murder, but it might be worth looking at."

"We're looking very closely at Michael, actually," Pete told her. "He has a temper and he's admitted to being in Douglas that evening. If he's telling the truth about Mr. Hart's attempt to blackmail him, he seems to have given himself a fairly strong motive."

"Why would he lie?"

"Maybe he's trying to distract us from something else we'd find if we dig," Pete said. "Or maybe he's trying to justify the murder, to himself, if not to us."

"Blackmail is a nasty business."

"It is, but murder is worse."

Bessie nodded. "I don't know anything about Natasha Harper, except that she's much better to work with than Christopher Hart was. Mr. Hart accused her of trying to steal his clients when she first arrived at the castle, but she explained that away when I asked her about it later."

"What have I told you about questioning suspects?" Pete asked.

"Yes, well, we were talking and it came up," Bessie muttered, flushing.

74

"I'd really rather you stayed well away from the castle and all of the suspects until the case is wrapped up," Pete told her. He held up a hand as she opened her mouth to argue. "I know you can't or won't do that, but I want you to understand how I feel about the whole matter. Whoever killed Christopher Hart knew what he or she was doing. If the murder had happened anywhere near Castle Rushen, I'd cancel 'Christmas at the Castle' to try to keep everyone safe."

"Nearly everyone I spoke to thinks the killer came from across, just to kill Mr. Hart," Bessie said. "Have you considered that possibility?"

"Of course; I'm considering every possibility," he replied. "Getting to the island isn't the easiest of tasks, though. If someone did come over, they'd have left a trail behind them. The airlines and the ferry service keep records of who travels and when. You need a credit card to check into a hotel, et cetera. If that is what happened, whoever did it probably would have been better off attempting to kill the man in London."

"But going through all those records takes a lot of time," Bessie said. "Whoever it was is probably long gone, back where they came from."

"We have a small number of staff going through flight, ferry, and hotel records as we speak," he told her. "We're just lucky it's December. There's far less to check through than there would have been in June or July."

The inspector drained his coffee cup. "I really must get into the office," he told Bessie. "I really appreciate your taking the time to share your perspective with me, though. And breakfast was wonderful. Thank you."

"I'm here any time you want to talk," she assured him. "I just wish it could be all sorted before the grand opening tomorrow night. It's going to keep us from truly enjoying the evening."

"I'm doing my best," he replied. "And I'll just remind you to leave it all to me. A murder investigation is no place for an amateur."

Bessie nodded and bit her lip. She'd helped the police with more than one investigation in the past, including one that had been Pete's case. She wasn't going to just sit around while the police did their slow and methodical job, not if there was something she could do to speed up the investigation.

"I hope you have a wonderful grand opening, in spite of everything," Pete said now.

Bessie walked him to the door. "I'm really looking forward to it, in spite of everything," she told him.

"Helen and I are looking forward to Christmas Eve, assuming I don't have to work, of course."

Bessie nodded and then watched him walk to his car. She wondered about the women who fell in love with policemen, or the men who fell for policewomen, at that. It had to be difficult. Police work was demanding and never-ending. Bessie hoped that Helen and Pete would find a way to make their relationship work. She liked them both and thought they were well-suited.

Bessie tidied up the kitchen and then waited for her taxi. She was going to do some grocery shopping with her unexpectedly free day. Her favourite driver, Dave, dropped her off in front of the bookshop.

"It looks really busy today," he said, frowning. "If you decide you want collecting early or you get held up, ring me directly. That's easier than ringing through the office."

Bessie spent a few minutes in the bookshop, but she soon found herself agreeing with Dave. It was far too crowded with Christmas shoppers for her to enjoy a leisurely browse. She headed towards ShopFast, thinking she might stop in a few shops along the way, but the street was full of people rushing about, which made it difficult to look in windows. ShopFast was also busier than normal for a Thursday morning. She pushed her shopping trolley through crowded aisles.

"Bessie? How are you?" a friend asked in the bakery.

"I'm feeling a bit overwhelmed," Bessie answered honestly. "I just came in for a few things, but the craziness of the crowd seems to be contagious. I can't seem to stop myself adding more and more to my trolley."

The woman laughed. "I know what you mean. Christmas is still over a week away but I'm buying up food like the shops are going to be shut from tomorrow."

Bessie looked down at her trolley and sighed. "I just hope I manage to eat it all," she said.

There were long queues at the tills, but because she hadn't bothered with any other shopping, she walked out of the shop more or less on time to meet Dave.

At home, with the shopping all put away, Bessie had a light lunch and then decided to take a long walk. When she reached Thie yn Traie, she spotted Mary coming down the steep steps.

"I've been watching your cottage from my windows all day," Mary told her when she joined her on the sand. "I was sure you'd be out for a walk before too long. The weather is too perfect to miss."

Mary was right; it was a surprisingly mild day for December. "Let's hope the good weather continues through Christmas," Bessie said. "There will be a lot of disappointed people if the ferries can't sail."

"Including me," Mary told her. "I've ordered a whole feast from across."

"Will you be celebrating Christmas at Thie yn Traie?"

"I wish," Mary told her. "We haven't quite completed the purchase yet, although Daniel Pierce has told us we can move in anyway, if we want to. He and George were business associates for a few years and we all know how badly they want rid of the house."

"You are definitely buying it, then?"

"Oh yes, and we've already started redoing it all. I'm hoping we can have enough of it finished in time to have a small New Year's Eve party. You will come, won't you?"

"Of course," Bessie told her. "Although New Year's Eve parties can be difficult. You always feel rather stuck until midnight, even if you aren't having a nice time."

Mary laughed. "I promise you'll enjoy yourself. If nothing else, you can stay in the library until quarter to twelve."

"I didn't know Thie yn Traie had a library."

"It does. I don't know that anyone ever read any of the books in it, but it's very well stocked with both fiction and non-fiction. I'm going to have to hire someone to catalogue it and then we'll have to check that against the catalogue from our library in Douglas. I imagine we'll have a lot of books to get rid of, once we've done that. You'll have to help me find good homes for them."

Bessie smiled. "That sounds like a wonderful job," she said. "But you said you were watching for me," Bessie recalled. "I hope nothing is wrong."

"Oh, no, I was just bored," Mary admitted. "Natasha is hard at work on various plans, so I need to be here to consult with her, but mostly she's working on her own and I'm just sitting around."

The pair chatted for a few minutes longer and then Bessie headed back to her cottage. She enjoyed the quiet day after all of the hard work she'd put into "Christmas at the Castle," but after dinner she found she was quite restless. After all of the time and effort, she was ready for the grand opening.

CHAPTER 6

*B*essie woke up early the next day, feeling like a small child on Christmas morning. "This is silly," she told herself as she tried to get back to sleep. "It's only a charity fundraiser."

But she'd been involved in "Christmas at the Castle" from the very beginning and she was very proud of what they'd accomplished at Castle Rushen. She'd never held down a paying job, but she was sure she felt much like someone would when a huge project finally came to fruition. Giving up on getting back to sleep, she showered and then patted on the rose-scented dusting powder that reminded her of the man she'd loved and lost when she had been much younger. If she'd married Matthew, she would have left the island and her life would have been completely different.

"You've ended up exactly where you ought to be," she told her mirror image. "Now quit talking to yourself and get moving."

Laughing at herself, Bessie made breakfast and then packed a few sandwiches into a bag. She wasn't sure she would have time for a proper lunch later. The grand opening reception was going to be catered, but she didn't want to be starving by the time that was ready.

Mark was a few minutes early. "I'm sorry," he said. "I couldn't sleep last night and I ran out of things to do to kill time this morning."

Bessie just laughed. "I know what you mean," she replied.

"This is the biggest project I've done for MNH, and having a murder happen right in the middle of it hasn't done much for my confidence," he confided. "I sure hope everything goes right today."

"It's going to be wonderful," Bessie said. "We've worked too hard to see it all fall apart now."

At the castle doors, the pair parted. "I have a lot of last-minute paperwork to sort through," Mark told Bessie. "Make sure you're in the banquet room at midday, though, and bring everyone who's around with you."

Bessie spent her morning wandering around the beautifully decorated castle, checking on everyone else. It seemed to her as if everyone was in high spirits, anticipating a very successful opening night. The only person who wasn't happy was Carolyn Teare.

"Oh, Bessie, thank goodness you're here," she exclaimed as Bessie peeked into the room Carolyn was decorating. "I've had ever so much trouble getting staff down here to help with this. You'll give me a hand, won't you?"

"For a short while," Bessie replied, looking around at a room that was still mostly empty, aside from a stack of boxes in the very centre. "It's nearly half eleven and we all have to be in the banquet room for midday, but I can work with you until then."

"Excellent," Carolyn said. "If you could just decorate that tree, I'd appreciate it." She pointed to a large white artificial tree that was standing alone in one corner. It was completely bare. "There's a box of decorations next to it," she said in a helpful voice.

Bessie opened the box and shook her head at the stark black baubles that were inside. She began to hang them on the tree, but was soon interrupted.

"Oh, I do think the tinsel should go first," Carolyn called from the corner of the room.

Bessie looked over and saw the woman sitting on a chair. She had her mobile out and was frowning at the display. As Bessie took the ornaments back off the tree, Carolyn punched numbers on her phone.

"Ah, hello, darling. I just wanted to see how you were this morning," the woman cooed into her phone.

Bessie didn't like to eavesdrop, but Carolyn made no attempt to lower her voice as she chatted. Half an hour later, Bessie knew far more than she wanted to know about Carolyn's marriage. It had quickly become apparent that Carolyn was talking to her husband, Richard, and from what Bessie could hear, Carolyn sounded madly in love and deeply devoted to the man. Bessie was surprised at what she heard, given the other woman's suggestion that her husband had murdered Christopher Hart, but she kept her thoughts to herself as she wound black tinsel around the tree and then added ornament after ornament in the same colour.

"You've done quite well," Carolyn said when she finally put her phone away. "Only another ten to go and we'll be ready."

Bessie stared at her for a moment. "I don't see how we'll get another ten done before we have to start getting ready for tonight," she said after a moment.

"We'll have to get the whole committee in here to help, that's all," Carolyn said with a shrug.

"I think most of them have other things to do this afternoon," Bessie pointed out.

"You'll help, won't you?" Carolyn pleaded. "Only Richard is quite cross with me and he won't let me bring my staff down to help out. I was trying to make up to him, but he won't change his mind. I simply can't do it all on my own."

Since I haven't seen you do anything, that's hardly surprising, Bessie thought to herself. "Let's see what happens after the meeting," Bessie said noncommittally. "We'd better get over to the banquet room now, though."

Bessie left the room before Carolyn could object. She wasn't sure what Mark had planned for their meeting, but she didn't want to be late. As she got closer to the room, her mouth began to water. Something smelled like tomatoes and garlic. She quickened her pace.

In the banquet room, two large tables had been set up. One was nearly full with serving platters of food. The second was covered in a linen tablecloth with wine bottles in the centre.

"I think just about everyone is here," Mark said as Bessie and Carolyn walked into the room. "I just wanted to take the time to thank each and every one of you for all of your hard work over the last month. We should have allowed a lot more time for planning, and we will in the future, but this time we managed to get the job done and I'm grateful to you all."

"We had a great leader," Bessie said loudly.

"Thank you," Mark said, blushing. "Anyway, lunch today is my thank-you gift to you all. There's plenty of wine to go around as well, but do keep in mind that we still have a lot to get through tonight. Anyway, help yourselves and enjoy."

Everyone applauded lightly. The charity volunteers insisted that the committee members make their plates first, and Bessie quickly found herself pushed to the front of the queue. For a moment she wasn't sure where to start. There was grilled chicken, pasta with tomato or Alfredo sauce, grilled vegetables, salad, garlic bread, and a huge tray of pastries and cakes for pudding.

With a very full plate, Bessie took a seat at the empty table and let Mark pour her a small amount of wine. Mary Quayle and Marjorie Stevens soon joined her.

"I was late," Marjorie said after a sip of wine. "So I came straight up here the back way. Are all of the rooms ready to go?"

"We put the finishing touches on everything this morning," Natasha said as she slid into a chair opposite Mary. "I'm really pleased with how it has all turned out."

"My room isn't done," Carolyn said loudly as she moved to the head of the table. She put her plate down and then grabbed the nearest wine bottle. She poured herself a full glass of wine and then took a large drink. "I need everyone's help this afternoon," she added, nearly shouting. "I've barely started in my room. I've only managed to get one tree decorated."

That would be the tree I decorated, Bessie thought but didn't say.

"I'm afraid a lot of us have other things to do this afternoon," Mark told Carolyn. "Marjorie and I will be doing press preview tours most of the afternoon and all of the charity representatives are meant to be at the press conference later."

"You can't do press previews," Carolyn wailed. "My room isn't ready."

"We can't reschedule them," Marjorie said firmly. "We're relying on getting a lot of publicity for this to sell out Christmas Eve. We need the press to come through today."

"But what about my room? What about my tribute to Christo? I want it to be perfect before it's seen."

"We'll have to shut the door while the press is here," Mark said. "At least then they won't see it before it's finished."

Carolyn frowned and drained her wine glass. "But that doesn't solve the problem," she said. "I suppose I don't mind if the press can't see it, but it needs to be ready for the grand opening."

"I'll help," Michael Beach shouted from the other end of the table. "My room is done and ready to go. My car is in the shop, so I took a taxi this morning. I've no interest in paying their exorbitant rates to get back home and then back again for tonight. I was just going to wander around Castletown, but I can help you instead."

"Thank you," Carolyn said happily. "Now, who else can help?"

In the end, just about everyone agreed to spend their afternoon working on Carolyn's room. Henry offered to send one or two of the younger members of the paid staff up with a ladder to help with hanging things. Bessie was tempted to make up an excuse, but with everyone else helping, it sounded like it might be quite fun, really. With very full tummies, the group eventually made their way back to Carolyn's room.

"Now, before we start, let me share my vision," Carolyn said from the doorway. "Christo wanted to celebrate some of the things we usually shy away from, like death and murder. I don't want to take things quite that far with my tribute, because he was actually murdered. There will be eleven white Christmas trees with black decorations in a circle in the centre of the room. The walls will be draped in black crepe. Instead of a nativity scene, on the table in the centre of the room, we'll have the four horsemen of the apocalypse."

Carolyn opened a box and held up a small ceramic figure. "He's meant to be a wise man, but I thought, if we put horses with him, people will understand the symbolism."

Bessie turned her head and bit her lip. The four wise men of the apocalypse, more like, she thought. She was just grateful that the press weren't going to see this room. Maybe they could forget to open the door tonight as well.

No one said anything; they all just exchanged glances and then began to assemble white Christmas trees. As Bessie began to decorate one, she heard raised voices.

"It's close enough," Michael was saying. Bessie looked over to see him standing next to a very lopsided tree. "Once everyone sees the apocalypse in the centre, they aren't going to care about a few crooked trees."

"I'd like it done correctly," Carolyn said tightly.

"Have some more wine," Michael suggested. "Then you won't be so bothered."

He picked up the backpack he'd carried in with him and pulled out a bottle of wine and some of the paper cups that had been provided at lunch for water and fizzy drinks. He poured wine into a cup and held it out to Carolyn. "Go on, you know you want to."

Carolyn took the cup and took a small sip. "I still want the tree fixed," she said.

"You're really pretty," Michael told her. "I hope your husband knows how lucky he is." He poured himself a cup of wine and took a large drink.

Carolyn blushed. "Thank you. I'm sure he does."

"I doubt it," Michael replied. "You don't seem happy. I don't think your husband appreciates you at all. I'd appreciate you, lots."

Bessie watched, appalled, as the man leered at Carolyn. "I don't think this is the time or the place for this conversation," she said, walking over to join the pair. She glanced around the room, fully aware that everyone was watching the scene with keen interest.

"Maybe we should take a short break," Michael suggested to Carolyn. "Care for a walk?"

Before Carolyn answered, her mobile rang. She glanced at the display and then shook her head. "I have to answer this," she said, walking quickly from the room.

"You don't think the tree is too bad, do you?" Michael asked Bessie.

Bessie sighed. "Maybe you should go and get a cup of coffee," she suggested to the man.

"Nah, I'm having way too much fun," he told her. He grabbed a string of tinsel and rolled it into a ball. Taking a step back from the crooked tree, he squinted at it and then threw the ball at the top of it. He laughed as the tinsel rolled down the tree, catching on a low branch and then hanging half on and half off the tree.

"It's how Picasso would have done it," he told Bessie.

"I think we need to straighten things up," Natasha said. She quickly pulled the tree apart and snapped it together again, this time correctly.

"You should have wine," Michael told Natasha. He found another paper cup, splashed wine into it, and then handed it to the woman.

"Gee, thanks," Natasha said. She put the cup to her lips, but Bessie could see that she didn't actually drink anything. "Maybe we should have a quick stroll," she suggested to Michael.

"Yes, let's," Michael agreed. He picked up his backpack, but Natasha shook her head.

"Leave that here. We won't be gone long," she told him.

Michael hesitated and then dropped the pack. Bessie heard several bottles clink together as the pack hit the ground.

"I'll try to get him to have some coffee and sober up a bit before I bring him back," Natasha whispered to Bessie. "I'm sorry I won't be here to help, though."

"Getting rid of him for a little while is a big help," Bessie said quietly.

A couple of hours later the little group had the trees just about done.

"All of the charity volunteers are supposed to be at the press conference in ten minutes," Henry reminded everyone from the door-way. Agnes, Harriet, Margaret and Liz quickly finished what they were doing and headed out.

Bessie exchanged glances with Mary, who was now the only other person in the room, the men from MNH having hung the crepe and departed.

"Well, I suppose it's just us to finish everything," Bessie said with a sigh.

"I don't mind," Mary told her. "I love feeling useful, really."

"I like being useful," Bessie agreed. "But I'd much rather Carolyn was doing the bulk of the work, seeing as it's her room."

"Well, yes, you make a good point," Mary said.

"Once you've finished that one, we've done the trees," Bessie said as she hung the last ornament on the tree she was decorating. "I suppose I should start on the horsemen."

Bessie began to unpack the box that Carolyn had left on the table in the centre of the room. The four men were clearly meant to be wise men, although it appeared that they had each come from a different nativity set. Bessie unpacked the first horse and began to laugh.

"Is that a plastic toy horse?" Mary asked as she walked over to join Bessie.

"It is," Bessie told her.

The four horses were also all different, and different sizes. "This one is smaller than the wise men," Mary said as she unwrapped the last horse.

"How are we meant to make this look like anything other than a mess?" Bessie demanded.

"We need Natasha," Mary replied. She pulled out her mobile and had a short conversation. "She's on her way," she told Bessie after the call ended.

Natasha walked in a moment later. "This is meant to be the four horsemen of the apocalypse?" she demanded as she looked at the figurines. "I'm not sure even I can fix this mess."

Bessie turned back to the trees, giving them all a careful inspection and rearranging a few ornaments here and there. By the time she got back to the centre of the room, Natasha was finished.

"There. I've done my best," the woman muttered.

"It's better than I imagined," Bessie told her, surprised at what Natasha had accomplished.

Natasha had used several small boxes to create a multi-dimensional display. After covering the entire table in black cloth, she'd staggered the wise men and horses and arranged them in such a way that their height differences were less noticeable. By swirling the black cloth around them, she managed to give the whole scene a somewhat menacing look that felt more apocalyptic than Bessie had expected.

"It's really very good," Bessie said.

"It is," Mary agreed. "It's creepy and I don't like it at all."

"The whole room is creepy," Natasha said. "I think Christopher Hart would have loved it."

"And that's the whole idea," Carolyn said grandly from the doorway. "Oh, it's just about perfect," she exclaimed, turning slowly to take it all in.

"We weren't sure how you wanted the figures on the centre table," Bessie said.

Carolyn looked over the display. "That's very good," she said. "I was worried because I couldn't get the exact pieces I wanted, but in the end they work really well."

"Because Natasha spent a lot of time and effort on them," Bessie said.

"Oh, did she?" Carolyn said idly.

"We all put a lot of time and effort in," Bessie added. "While you were talking to your husband."

"He's very demanding just now," Carolyn replied. "I think we both need a little holiday. Maybe we'll go away for Christmas."

Bessie didn't bother to reply. If they did go and that got them into trouble with Pete Corkill, it wasn't her problem.

"Where's Michael?" Bessie asked Natasha.

"He said something about a press conference," she replied. "He wasn't in any fit state to talk to the press, but he wouldn't listen when I told him that."

"Where's Michael?" Henry asked from the doorway.

"Wasn't he at the press conference?" Bessie asked.

"No, he never turned up," Henry replied.

Bessie looked at Natasha, who shrugged. "He told me he had to get back for the press conference and left me watching the sea. I wasn't in any hurry to get back here." She glanced around and then frowned. "That didn't come out right. I love helping out here, but I was enjoying the fresh sea air and the break, that's all. Michael and I talked for a while and then he said he needed to get back and I told him I'd see him later."

"Well, he never made it to the press conference," Henry said. "Which means he missed out on some publicity."

"The board at the Alzheimer's Research Fund isn't going to be happy about that," Mary said.

"I'm on the board," Carolyn said airily. "I'll make certain they don't fire the poor man."

"Maybe we should go and look for him," Bessie said, a worried feeling growing inside her. "It isn't like him to forget about work responsibilities."

Henry stared at her for a moment and then sighed. "Here we go again," he muttered as he turned and left the room.

Bessie pulled out her mobile and rang Mark. "I'm sorry to interrupt. I know you're really busy, but Michael seems to have wandered off and we're all a bit worried about him."

"How's Carolyn's room coming?" Mark asked.

"It's finished," Bessie told him.

"Excellent. Why don't you all come down to the courtyard and we'll work out what we need to do next."

In the courtyard, the press were still milling around with glasses of wine and canapés. Bessie said hello to a few people she knew as she crossed the space. Mark was talking to Henry.

"I don't think we need to involve the police," Mark was saying as Bessie joined them.

"I wouldn't normally, but after the murder and all," Henry argued.

"What do you think, Bessie?" Mark asked.

"I think we should look for him, at least a little bit, before we bother the police," Bessie said. "He might have just sat down on a bench and forgotten all about the press conference. I dare say he might have even fallen asleep."

"Was he that drunk?" Mark asked.

"He was still drinking while he was helping with the decorating," Bessie replied.

Mark sighed. "Where did Natasha see him last?"

Mark quickly organised the castle staff into a search party. Natasha and Henry headed back towards where she had last seen the man and the others spread out to cover the small centre of the town. Half an hour later, everyone was back.

"How could he have just disappeared?" Mark demanded.

"Maybe he decided to head home for a short while before the party tonight," Mary suggested.

"He didn't have his car," Bessie reminded her. "Not that he should have been driving if he had, but he did say he wasn't going to take a taxi again."

Mark tried ringing both Michael's home and mobile phones, but no one answered.

"Now I'm starting to worry," Bessie admitted as the search party headed out to do a second turn through town.

"Maybe we should ring the police," Mary said.

"That seems extreme," Carolyn said. "He's only been missing for what, an hour or two? I'm sure he'll turn up."

When the search party returned again, having had no more success, Mark rang the Castletown police. After a short conversation, he put the phone down and turned to the group.

"The police aren't really interested," he told them. "Michael is a grown man and he's only been missing for a very short time. They've said I should ring again in the morning if he hasn't turned up."

"And look at the time," Mary gasped. "I have to get changed."

Bessie glanced at her watch and sighed. She needed to change and get herself ready for the grand opening party. With Michael missing, she wasn't in the mood for a party, even this one that she'd been anticipating for weeks.

"I've taken a room at the Castletown Hotel," Carolyn said. "That way I have plenty of space to get ready." She was quickly on her way out of the castle, leaving Bessie shaking her head.

"You're welcome," she muttered. "We all really enjoyed doing all of the work getting your room ready for you."

Mary chuckled. "She's so used to having staff that she simply doesn't think to thank people."

"Do you thank your staff?" Bessie asked.

Mary frowned. "Well, yes, I do, really. But Carolyn isn't the type."

"No, she isn't," Bessie agreed.

Mark had set aside several large rooms that weren't part of "Christmas at the Castle" for everyone to use. Bessie and Mary changed, and then Bessie combed her hair and added a bit of lipstick to her lips. That was more makeup than she usually wore, and it was quite enough for her. Mary spent a good deal longer fussing over her hair and face, but she was ready with time to spare anyway.

"Let's go down and see if Mark needs any help," Bessie suggested after she'd admired Mary's dress.

"I'm not even certain what we're meant to be doing tonight," Mary whispered as they walked through the castle.

"Hopefully we're meant to be eating lots of lovely canapés," Bessie replied. "I know I ate a huge amount of lunch, but I'm starving again."

"Lunch does seem to have been a rather long time ago," Mary said.

In the courtyard, Mark looked extra handsome in his tuxedo, and Bessie was surprised to see Henry in one as well.

"Don't you look dashing," she said to the man, who coloured brightly.

"It's not very comfortable," he hissed at her. "But Laura seems to like it."

Bessie smiled. "Where is Laura?" she asked.

"She's taking tickets at the entrance," Henry told her. "Or she will be in a few minutes, when we open. Wait until you see how gorgeous she looks."

"I'm sure she looks wonderful," Bessie replied. She frowned as her mobile rang. She'd only just managed to cram it into the small evening bag that went with her black dress. At least that made it easy to find, she thought as she pulled it out of the bag.

"Hello?"

"Bessie? It's Pete Corkill. What's this I hear about someone disappearing from down there?"

"It's Michael Beach," Bessie explained. "He had a few too many glasses of wine with lunch and then went for a walk with Natasha. He was meant to be back for a press conference, but he missed it."

"What does Natasha say?"

"That he told her he was coming back to the castle and left her sitting by the sea."

"You should have rung me," he told her.

"Mark rang the local station," Bessie replied.

"But I'm investigating Christopher Hart's murder."

"Surely this doesn't have anything to do with that," Bessie argued.

"I certainly hope not. We'll know more once we find the missing man."

"I'm sorry I didn't ring you."

"Please ring if he suddenly turns up," Pete said. "I'm going to start doing some checking around."

After Bessie put her phone away, she rejoined the party. Everyone was busy complimenting one another.

"I feel as if I'm playing dress-up," Liz confessed to Bessie. "I never wear long gowns."

"Well, you look lovely and very comfortable in it," Bessie told her.

"It certainly isn't that," Liz laughed. "It's quite tight and I can barely walk in it." She leaned in close to Bessie and whispered. "I was really worried about fitting into it, actually. We just found out we're having another baby and I feel as if I've grown two sizes already."

"Congratulations," Bessie exclaimed, delighted for her young friend.

Liz flushed. "We aren't really telling anyone yet," she told Bessie. "But some days I feel as if I'll burst if I don't tell someone."

Bessie laughed. "Well, I'm honoured and delighted that you told me, and I won't say a word to anyone else about it."

"Thanks," Liz said. "I've only a few weeks to go before we'll feel more comfortable telling people, but I feel as if I'm gaining so much weight that people are going to start to notice anyway."

"I don't think you look as if you've gained weight," Bessie told her. "And anyway, this time of year you can always blame mince pies and Christmas pudding."

Liz laughed. "I hadn't thought of that. What a great idea."

"What's a great idea?" Mary asked as she joined them.

"Having another mince pie before it gets busy," Liz told her. She turned and walked away, leaving Bessie with Mary.

"Only a few minutes before the doors open," Mary said. "Are you nervous?"

"Not really," Bessie said after a moment's thought. "I know the rooms look good. The only worry is that people won't know what to expect and might be disappointed, but I think Mark did a great job in describing the event in all of the publicity, so we should be fine."

"I wish Michael were here," Mary said.

Bessie glanced around the space and sighed. "I'm trying not to worry about him," she said. "Carolyn's not here, either."

"She'll be waiting to make an entrance," Mary predicted.

A moment later, Mark cleared his throat loudly. "I know I thanked you all at lunch today, but I just wanted to say it one more time. You should all be really proud of what we've accomplished here. Now let's just hope we raise lots of money for all of our respective groups."

While everyone was clapping, Carolyn made her entrance. She swept into the courtyard with a long red cape flapping in the wind behind her. Stopping a few paces into the courtyard, she paused and smiled before unhooking the cape and dropping it to the ground behind her. Bessie nearly gasped when she saw the tight-fitting and very short black dress Carolyn was wearing. It didn't seem at all appropriate for the grand opening of an event that was being promoted as being family-friendly. Before anyone in the courtyard spoke, a voice came from behind Carolyn.

"Wow-wow-wow! That is some dress," Michael said. He took a step forward and then stumbled, but caught himself before he fell to the ground. "We need some wine, darling Carolyn," he said, slurring his words.

Carolyn laughed. "Come along, then," she said.

Michael slid an arm around her waist and the pair headed straight towards the bar that was set up in one corner of the space. Mark was quick to follow them, and Bessie was sure he was planning to have a serious conversation with Michael. Now Bessie needed to ring Pete.

CHAPTER 7

*I*t was a short conversation, as all Bessie could tell him was that Michael was at the castle.

"See if you can find out where he's been," Pete said before Bessie disconnected.

An hour later, the castle was full of people and Bessie was overwhelmed by how much everyone seemed to be enjoying the event.

"It's going well," Mark whispered to her as they passed one another in one of the rooms.

"The door to Carolyn's room isn't open," Bessie told him. "I'd almost rather it stayed shut, but Carolyn will be upset when she finds out."

"One of the staff locked all the rooms while we were getting ready, at least the rooms that can be locked. When Henry unlocked everything just before we opened, he didn't realise that room was finished. I'll have someone get it opened as soon as I can, but it isn't really a high priority for me right now."

Bessie hid a smile. If she were in Mark's place, it wouldn't be a priority for her, either. "Maybe Carolyn won't notice," she suggested.

Mark shrugged. "She seems to be spending her evening with Michael. Last time I saw them, they hadn't left the courtyard."

With that in mind, Bessie headed towards the courtyard. It took her a while to get there, as she knew many people and they all wanted to stop her and congratulate her on the event. When she finally reached the large outdoor space, it was nearly empty. Henry was hard at work, clearing up rubbish and collecting glasses. Laura was standing near the entrance, watching for late arrivals. A man was behind the corner bar, idly polishing glasses and watching his only two customers. Carolyn and Michael were standing very close together and talking quietly.

"'Christmas at the Castle' seems to be a success," Bessie said as she reached the couple. "I've heard nothing but compliments from the guests."

"Have a glass of wine," Michael suggested. "Surely you've earned one."

Bessie smiled and nodded at the man behind the bar.

"Red or white?" he asked.

Bessie couldn't have cared less. "White," she said, as that was what Michael and Carolyn were drinking.

"We were worried about you," she said to Michael as she took the glass from the bartender.

"Carolyn was telling me," Michael replied. "I didn't realise I had to account for all of my movements to your committee."

Bessie flushed. "We probably overreacted," she admitted. "But Mr. Hart's murder is still on everyone's mind. Since we've no idea who killed him or why, I think we're all worried about everyone who is involved with 'Christmas at the Castle.'"

"And yet here we are at the grand opening," Michael said, waving his drink. "If the police were worried about it, they wouldn't have let us carry on, surely."

Bessie shrugged. "I'm just glad you turned up safe and sound."

"If a little bit drunk," the man said, laughing.

"Maybe you should have a walk around the castle," Bessie suggested. "The lights on the trees are much more effective now that it's dark outside. We were always working in daylight. I've never seen it quite like this."

Michael shrugged. "I'm enjoying the courtyard," he told Bessie. "And the company." He waved his glass again, this time towards Carolyn. She giggled.

"It is nice and quiet out here," she agreed. "Or it was." She gave Bessie a pointed look.

"We were sorry you missed the press conference," Bessie said to Michael, ignoring Carolyn.

"Couldn't be helped," Michael told her. "I tripped on the castle steps on my way in, you see. Tore the knee in my trousers. I had to go home and change. I couldn't possibly have stayed like that for tonight."

"Mark has more press events coming up, in the lead-up to the auction on Christmas Eve. I'm sure you'll be able to get lots of publicity for your charity anyway," Bessie told him.

"What time does all of this finish?" Carolyn demanded. "I'm getting quite bored."

"You should go around the castle and talk to the guests," Bessie suggested. As a committee member, it was what she should have been doing all night.

"Or we could get out of here," Michael said in a low voice. "We could go back to my flat and relax."

"Is that a proposition?" Carolyn asked, giggling.

"It's whatever you want it to be," Michael told her with a wink.

"I need to get back to our guests," Bessie said stiffly. She put her almost untouched glass of wine on the bar and turned to walk away.

"Oh, Bessie, don't mind us," Carolyn called after her. "We're just playing."

Bessie didn't bother to reply. She was nearly back to the castle entrance when she heard Carolyn yell.

"Richard? What are you doing here?"

Bessie turned and walked back to the bar, where Richard Teare was smiling humourlessly at his wife.

"I was invited," he told her. "It's the grand opening and I thought it would be interesting to see exactly what you've been doing for the last month or so." He turned and looked at Bessie. "Bessie Cubbon, you look beautiful tonight."

Bessie smiled and offered her hand. As the man shook it, she studied him. He was tall, with broad shoulders. His expensive suit had clearly been made for him. His hair was silver grey and his brown eyes, when they met Bessie's, looked both tired and angry.

"Richard, it's lovely to see you again. Let me take you on a tour," Bessie suggested.

"I think that's a job for my devoted wife," he growled. "Come on, darling, show me around."

"I'm too tired," Carolyn said. "Let Bessie do it. She knows far more about it all than I do, anyway."

"I don't believe that. After all the hours and hours that you devoted to the site, you must know every inch of it," Richard said mockingly.

"I'm going back to my hotel," Carolyn said. "Bessie can show you around or you can just go home and stop being silly."

"Silly? What's silly about wanting to see what my wife has been doing for the month?" Richard asked. "I thought you liked it when I showed an interest in your little projects."

"I'll walk you to your hotel," Michael offered. "I've had enough 'Christmas at the Castle' for today."

Richard turned and looked the man up and down. "I do hope you aren't serious," he said sharply. "I know my wife has had a few drinks, but she isn't about to fall into bed with someone like you because of it."

Michael flushed. "I was just offering to escort her to her hotel, nothing more."

Richard chuckled. "Yes, of course," he said. "Just remember that I control the purse strings in our house. My darling wife isn't in a position to buy expensive presents for her little diversions and she isn't going to convince me to make a huge donation to your charity, either."

"I was just trying to be helpful," Michael said through gritted teeth.

"Don't argue over little old me," Carolyn simpered. "I'm sure

Michael's intentions were honourable," she told her husband. "He's kind and sweet, really."

"And far too young for you, dear," Richard said.

Carolyn's face reddened. "You know I'm devoted to you," she said.

Richard laughed. "I know you're devoted to my money," he said. "I don't think you care about me in the slightest."

"There you all are," Mary's voice floated across the courtyard. "You're missing all of the fun."

She and Natasha crossed over to the bar and Mary smiled brightly at everyone. "Ah, Richard, how wonderful that you were able to make it. Come and see what we've done. I'm sure you'll be impressed," she said, taking Richard's arm.

"I thought I would have Carolyn show me around," he said.

"Oh, leave her here to relax," Mary replied. "She worked hard all day to get the last room finished. She's earned a break and a glass of wine."

Bessie sighed with relief as Mary pulled Richard away into the castle.

"He's very handsome," Natasha remarked with a sly smile.

"And he's very married," Carolyn snapped at her.

"Maybe I should walk you to your hotel before he gets back," Michael suggested to Carolyn.

"I don't know," she replied. "I think maybe I should stay and see what he thinks of it all."

"Mary and I can look after him," Natasha said. "He'll be in very good hands."

Carolyn narrowed her eyes at the younger woman. "You need to keep your hands off my husband," she hissed.

"I hope you aren't implying that I would chase after a married man," Natasha said angrily. "There are plenty of men out there; I don't have to chase after yours."

Carolyn didn't reply, she just stared hard at Natasha. After a moment, Natasha laughed and turned her attention on Michael.

"Maybe you could buy a girl a drink?" she said, winking at him.

"I'd be happy to," he said. "There's a great little pub just across the road."

Natasha laughed again. "I think I'll settle for a glass of wine here for now," she said. "But the night is still young."

The bartender poured wine for Natasha and she moved to stand close to Michael. Carolyn sipped her drink while glaring at the pair of them. Bessie wanted to head back into the castle, but she worried about leaving the unhappy little group behind. The last thing they needed during the grand opening was a huge altercation, and with tensions as high as they were, it seemed like that could happen at any moment.

"Do you think we should close the bar?" Henry whispered to Bessie as he passed used glasses to the bartender.

"Mark wanted drinks available until the end of the night," Bessie said. "He thought people might like to stop for another glass of wine before they leave. It's meant to be a party, after all."

"Doesn't feel too festive with that lot bickering," Henry grumbled.

Bessie patted his arm. "You're doing a wonderful job. Don't you worry about anything."

"I can't help but worry," he replied. "I keep thinking someone's going to find a body somewhere."

Bessie shook her head, even though she'd had the same feeling. "It's going to be fine," she insisted. "Even better once we get Carolyn and Richard out of here."

"Preferably not together," Henry muttered.

People were beginning to leave now and Bessie wasn't surprised to find that Mark had been correct. A number of guests stopped at the bar on their way out to have a quick drink before heading home.

"It was wonderful," one of Bessie's friends told her. "I'd have loved to see the whole castle decorated, not just a few rooms."

"Maybe next year," Bessie replied. "We started planning far too late to do any more than what we did."

She was so busy chatting with guests that she didn't notice Richard's return until he spoke to her.

"You're to be congratulated," he said. "It's much nicer than I imagined it would be."

Bessie smiled at the oddly worded praise. "Thank you. Carolyn worked very hard, you know."

"Carolyn flitted around and got in the way and whenever there was real work to be done, brought in hired help," he corrected her. "I know my wife and her, um, limitations, shall we say."

"We couldn't have done it without her," Bessie replied truthfully. Carolyn's paid staff had done a great deal of the work over the last month.

"Is Carolyn involved with that young man, then?" he asked.

"You mean Michael Beach? I hardly think so."

"He's only after her money and position in Manx society," Richard said. "Although Carolyn doesn't seem to mind being used if she also gets what she wants."

Bessie bit back a dozen retorts. "Maybe you two should have a holiday somewhere," she suggested after a moment.

"I'm too busy with work at the moment to even consider that. I was thinking maybe we should simply go our separate ways."

Bessie tried not to look as shocked as she felt. "I'm sure that would devastate Carolyn."

"Maybe I'm just tired of being used myself."

"Bessie, what are you and my darling husband chatting about?" Carolyn asked in an artificially light tone.

"Just telling her how much I enjoyed the display," Richard said.

Carolyn wound her arm through her husband's. "You should be telling me that," she pouted. "I worked hard, too."

"I'm sure you did, dear," he said, patting her hand.

"I have a hotel room all booked and paid for," she said to the man in a loud whisper. "Why don't we both go back there and celebrate a successful grand opening together."

"I'd rather sleep in my own bed, thank you," he replied stiffly.

"Did you enjoy the display?" Natasha asked Richard as she joined them.

"I did, very much," he replied. "I understand you were instrumental in fine-tuning every room. You did an excellent job. Perhaps we could talk about you doing some work for me."

"I'm in charge of the decorating in our house," Carolyn said angrily.

"I'm thinking of redecorating my offices in Douglas," Richard told her.

"We just did those last year," Carolyn snapped back. "Christo did them for you. They're perfect."

"They're totally lacking in functionality," Richard replied. "One conference room looks like a prostitute's bedroom, full of soft couches with pillows and curtains and drapes everywhere, and the other one looks like a doctor's surgery, all stark white and stainless steel surfaces and hard plastic chairs. I feel as if every time I have a meeting I have to chose between seducing my clients or trying to stick a knife in them."

"But that's exactly what you do," Carolyn told him.

"Perhaps, but one must be subtle about such things," Richard replied.

Bessie hid a smile by taking a sip of wine.

"I really must see those rooms," Natasha said. "They sound awful, and exactly like Christopher Hart."

"He did amazing and interesting things," Carolyn said loudly. "Anyone can put a table and chairs in a room and call it a conference room. Christo gave everything he designed its own unique personality."

"Are you staying in Douglas?" Richard asked Natasha.

"I am, yes," she replied. "Actually, at the Seaside Hotel."

"Why don't I give you a ride back to your hotel," Richard suggested. "We can stop in my office on the way there and I can show you the rooms I want redoing."

"I'll come, too," Carolyn announced.

"Don't be silly, darling. You have a hotel room here for tonight," Richard said.

"I can cancel that," Carolyn replied. "I didn't know you were coming down, that's all. Of course I'll come home with you."

"You know I hate to waste money," Richard told her. "I've paid for that hotel room. I want you to use it."

Carolyn stared at him for a moment and then tossed her head. "Of course, if that's what you want. I'll just have Michael walk me over there."

"Whatever you like," Richard said, waving his hand as if he wasn't interested.

"Ladies and gentlemen, the castle will be closing in thirty minutes. If anyone wants a last look around, now is your chance," Mark announced from the centre of the courtyard.

A few people headed back towards the castle entrance. Bessie decided to join them.

"I know I've seen it a hundred times," she said to no one in particular. "But I really want to see it again."

"I'd love to show you around again," Natasha said to Richard. "I can point out some of the little changes I made."

"That sounds interesting," Richard said. He offered the woman his arm and she took it with a satisfied smile.

"Shall we?" Michael asked Carolyn as he rejoined the group. Carolyn nodded grimly and took Michael's arm. The pair followed Natasha and Richard towards the castle entrance.

Bessie followed more slowly.

"May I join you?" Mary Quayle asked as Bessie crossed the courtyard.

"Of course," Bessie replied. "I feel as if we need to keep an eye on those four," she muttered as they entered the first room.

"I know what you mean," Mary whispered. "My children were less work when they were toddlers."

Bessie chuckled. Across the room, Natasha was whispering to Richard while Carolyn glared at her. Michael was talking to her, but she didn't seem to be listening.

The same pattern continued around the castle. By the time they reached the banquet room, Bessie had had enough.

"I'm going home," she announced to everyone.

"There's only my room left," Carolyn said. "I do wonder what people have had to say about it."

"Unfortunately, the door has been locked all evening," Mark said.

Bessie hadn't seen him come up behind them all, but she felt relieved when she saw him. Surely he could calm the volatile situation.

"Locked? How did that happen?" Carolyn demanded.

"We were concerned that some of the items you used for decorating might be valuable, so we locked the door while everyone was getting ready for this evening," he explained. "Unfortunately, no one remembered to unlock it once everything got underway."

"Someone should lose their job over this," Carolyn said darkly.

"That would be me," Mark replied. "You are, of course, free to share your thoughts with my supervisor at MNH."

"I didn't mean you," Carolyn replied. "Who was responsible for unlocking the door, exactly?"

"As site supervisor, the ultimate responsibility was mine," Mark said smoothly. "I was tied up at the front gate, but I should have come through and checked that everything was done before we opened. As I said, you can complain to my supervisor."

Carolyn flushed, but didn't speak.

"No one will be complaining about you," Richard called from where he was whispering with Natasha. "You've done a good job with this whole thing. But if the room can be open now, let's take a look."

Mark nodded. "I've brought up the key," he told them.

Mark crossed the room and walked down the short corridor to the room that everyone had worked so hard on decorating that day. He turned the key in the lock and then pulled the door open.

"Don't switch on the lights," Carolyn shouted. She pushed past him. "I'll plug in the trees. They should be the only light in the room. Oh, ouch."

"What's wrong?" Mark called from the doorway.

"I fell over something," Carolyn shouted back. "And I can't find the main plug for the trees, either. I was sure it was right at the doorway."

Mark switched on the overhead lights and gasped. Bessie crossed to him quickly, ready to help preserve what she was sure was going to be a crime scene. She looked into the room. Trees had been toppled to the ground, and smashed ornaments were everywhere. In the centre of the room, the four wise men and their horses were in pieces on the table. Black crepe hung in tatters where it had been torn from the walls. Carolyn was sitting on the floor just inside the door and as she looked around, she began to scream.

"We need to ring the police," Bessie told Mark.

"My beautiful room," Carolyn sobbed. "All my hard work, gone."

"Come on," Mark said. He offered Carolyn his hand and pulled her to her feet. "We shouldn't touch anything. The police need to investigate."

"Oh, sure," Carolyn said sarcastically. "Maybe they can learn something from fingerprints. Oh, that's right, there were a dozen people in there today, decorating."

"We still need to ring them before we touch anything," Bessie told her, even though she agreed with the woman's words. She couldn't imagine that the police would be able to do much.

"Who had access to the keys?" Richard asked Mark as they all stood around awkwardly waiting for the police to arrive.

"The main site custodian keeps a set with him and there is a second set kept in the desk in the ticket booth," Mark explained.

"Who is the site custodian?" Richard asked.

"That would be me," Henry said from the doorway. "Please don't tell me you've found another body," he added.

"No, nothing like that," Mark assured him. "But someone has destroyed the decorations in this room."

Henry stuck his head in the room and then shook his head. "I didn't even look when I locked everything up," he said. "I just shut the door and locked it."

"What time was that?" Carolyn asked.

"About four, I think," Henry said, frowning. "The charity volunteers had all gone down to the press conference and everyone else went off to get changed. Mark didn't want any doors that could be shut and locked left open when the site was deserted."

"Why didn't you reopen it before the guests began to arrive?" Carolyn demanded.

"I wasn't aware that it was ready to be seen," Henry said. "I opened up the rest of the site and then I went to find Mark to ask him about this room, but he was busy with a group of people and I never got a chance. I thought it was better to leave it locked up than open it if it wasn't ready."

"And you were right," Mark said firmly over whatever Carolyn began to say. "Why don't we all move back into the banquet room? It's far more comfortable than standing around in the corridor."

The group walked back to the large room. Everyone stood alone, and Bessie thought she saw more than one suspicious look on various faces. A few moments later a uniformed constable arrived. He took a look at the room and then shrugged. "It's a mess," he said. He pulled out his mobile and made a call. While he was doing that, Bessie quietly made a call of her own.

"No one was hurt?" Pete Corkill asked when Bessie finished telling him about the room.

"No, but the room has been pretty well destroyed. At least, the decorations have been."

"I can't see how this connects with Mr. Hart's murder, but I'm going to come down and have a look anyway," he told Bessie. "I'll ring the local constabulary and let them know I'm on my way."

"My wife and I are tired," Richard announced a moment later. "We'll just be going."

"I'm sorry, sir, but I've been told to ask everyone to remain here for the time being," the uniformed constable said. "One of our inspectors will be coming over to ask you all a few questions."

"Someone didn't like the colour theme and tore the room up a bit," Richard said. "That's hardly a police matter."

"Criminal damage," the man replied. "MNH could press charges."

"But they won't," Richard said. "I'll pay for any damage to the castle itself, although there doesn't actually appear to be any. The decorations were all my wife's property and she won't want to press charges, I'm certain."

"Some of those figurines were valuable," Carolyn protested.

"But we won't be pressing charges," Richard repeated loudly.

"MNH would like a thorough investigation," Mark said quietly. "A lot of hard work has gone into this event and we can't afford to worry about vandalism."

The man that walked into the room now was a stranger to Bessie. He was in his thirties and he was wearing a dark suit that matched his dark hair and eyes. He looked around the banquet room and then focussed on the uniformed constable.

"What?" he demanded.

"It's down here, sir," the man said, walking down the corridor.

Bessie watched as the uniformed man gestured towards the still open door. The man in the suit glanced inside and then shrugged.

"I take it that wasn't a design choice?" the man asked the room at large.

"Of course not," Carolyn snapped. "The room was beautifully decorated as a tribute to Christopher Hart, the wonderful designer who helped so much with getting the rooms throughout the castle decorated."

"I see," the man said. "Seems like your little tribute made someone angry."

Carolyn gasped. "Whoever murdered poor darling Christo must have done this," she exclaimed. "They hated Christo and couldn't stand to see such a beautiful tribute to his memory."

She glanced over at her husband, and snapped her mouth shut.

"Last I knew, the murderer was still at large," the policeman replied. "I suppose it's just possible he or she was responsible for this mess."

Bessie had been thinking along the same lines, but really, she thought, anyone who didn't like Carolyn might have destroyed the room just to get at her, and that included an awful lot of people.

"I'm Inspector Armstrong," the man told them all. "Let's see if we can work out when this happened."

It was quickly established that the room had been locked at around four, and as far as anyone knew, not opened again until

Mark had done so and discovered the damage more than five hours later.

"Now I suppose we should talk about alibis," Inspector Armstrong suggested. "I know the castle was open to many hundreds of guests tonight, but as you are all still here, I'd like to be able to clear as many of you as possible."

That may have been his intention, but it quickly proved impossible. With everything that had been going on around the site, no one was able to prove where they were at any given time, let alone for the entire period that the room had been locked up.

"Who knew where the keys were kept?" the inspector asked after several frustrating minutes of trying to work out people's movements.

"All of the MNH staff, everyone on the committee, and probably all of the volunteers," Bessie supplied.

The inspector groaned. "It's too late at night to get involved in this mess," he said. "Especially as it seems nothing is missing and no one was hurt. For tonight we'll just lock the door and I'll come back in the morning and start investigating."

"I'd like to ask a few questions before everyone leaves," a new voice said from the doorway.

"Inspector Corkill, no one told me you were coming down," Inspector Armstrong said, his cheeks reddening.

"I informed your office," Pete said easily. "I gather they never passed the message along."

"No, they didn't," Armstrong said coldly.

Bessie felt sorry for whoever had failed to inform Inspector Armstrong of Pete's interest in the case. She was sure they were going to be in a good deal of trouble when the inspector next saw them.

"I'll just take a look, if I may?" he asked.

Inspector Armstrong waved a hand. "It's fairly hopeless," he said. "The room is a mess, but everyone here and about two hundred other people had access to it during the relevant time. It's not on the path through the museum for the Christmas thing, so sneaking back here would have been easy."

Pete stuck his head in the door to the room and then came back to the banquet room. "It looks as if several of the nativity figurines are missing," he said. "I couldn't quite make out what the smashed figures were, but there doesn't seem to be enough of them for a full nativity scene."

"It wasn't a nativity scene," Carolyn told him. "It was the four horsemen of the apocalypse."

"Happy Christmas," Pete muttered under his breath as he turned and looked around the crowd. "Ah, Miss Cubbon, there you are," he said as his eyes met hers. "Can I have a quick word?"

Bessie nodded and followed him out of the room, down the corridor towards the damaged room.

"Any thoughts?" Pete asked her as soon as they were out of earshot of the others.

"Anyone could have done it," Bessie told him. "At least anyone associated with the event. We all knew where the keys were kept and we all knew how to access this room through the back corridors, as well."

"Motive?"

"Anger at Christopher Hart? Anger at Carolyn? Just tired of the whole 'Christmas at the Castle' event?" Bessie rattled off the first three things that crossed her mind. "I don't think anyone liked what Carolyn did with that room. It was dark and depressing, and it actually could have generated some negative publicity for us. I wasn't the least bit disappointed when Mark told me it had been left locked up, I will say that."

"But you weren't tempted to destroy it all."

"No, of course not, but clearly someone was."

"Did you find out what happened to Michael?" Pete asked.

"He said he fell and tore his trousers and had to go home and change."

"And did he?"

"How should I know?"

"I mean, did he return wearing different clothes?"

Bessie shrugged. "I didn't pay any attention to what he was

wearing this morning," she said. "I'm not even sure I could tell you what he's wearing now."

Pete nodded. "How was the grand opening?"

"The guests seemed to have a good time, but Carolyn, Michael, Richard, and Natasha seemed to be having some sort of elaborate battle amongst themselves."

She gave the inspector a brief run-through of the evening, which left him shaking his head.

"Maybe I should take a few of them in for questioning," he suggested. "Although I can't touch Richard or Carolyn. They have friends in high places."

"That isn't fair," Bessie complained.

"I doubt anyone would tell me anything at this point," he said. "Most of them probably don't know anything and the person who does is too well covered. I think we'll have to leave it for tonight and see if we can pick up any fingerprints tomorrow."

"Everyone here had a hand in decorating that room," Bessie told him. "You're going to have fingerprints on top of fingerprints."

"Ah, but I'm hoping we might find a few on the insides of the broken pieces of those figurines," Pete said. "Only one person could have touched the insides, I reckon."

"That's why you're the police inspector and I'm just a nosey middle-aged woman," Bessie said with a laugh. "That never crossed my mind."

Pete walked Bessie back to the banquet room. Everyone looked at them expectantly.

"As Inspector Armstrong pointed out, it's getting late. As nothing seems to have been stolen and no one has been hurt, as far as I'm concerned, we can leave the investigating until tomorrow," Pete announced.

"Thank goodness for that," Carolyn muttered.

"Everyone is free to go," Inspector Armstrong announced. "I'll expect to see all of you here in the morning."

"I have nothing to do with this mess," Richard objected. "If you want to talk to me, you'll have to do so at my offices in Douglas."

"I'm sure we can arrange something that will be convenient for everyone," Pete murmured, looking at Armstrong for confirmation.

"Of course," the man said, nodding curtly at Richard.

"Excellent," Richard replied, smiling smugly.

Bessie stood back and watched as everyone slowly filtered out. Carolyn and Richard left together, whispering back and forth. Michael said something to Natasha, who shook her head and then swept out alone. Mary hurried after her, leaving Michael to walk out behind them.

"That was not how I wanted the evening to end," Mark complained to Bessie as they made their way out, locking every door they could behind them.

"No, but at least it was just us when the mess was found," Bessie pointed out. "No one else need know about it."

CHAPTER 8

They were both too tired to talk on the journey home. Bessie wasn't sure what she could say to the man who'd put so much time and effort into "Christmas at the Castle," only for this to happen. Aside from confirming what time he would collect her in the morning, Mark didn't speak at all.

It was only half ten, but it felt like midnight when Bessie finally got to bed. She pulled the covers up over her head and tried to forget about everything that had happened at Castle Rushen. Her brain refused to cooperate, instead insisting on replaying the various conversations she'd overheard or been a part of.

"What were Carolyn and Richard playing at?" she demanded as she sat up in bed. "And why did Natasha and Michael get in the middle of it all?"

She slid back under the covers and sighed. Even with all of her years of experience, she still didn't really understand how people could treat other people so badly. She could only hope that everyone went home and calmed down, and that they would all behave better on Saturday. The more she thought about Michael, the more puzzled she became. He'd acted as if he was really drunk some of the time, but he hadn't sounded all that intoxicated later in the evening. Neither had Carolyn, really.

"This isn't helping," she said loudly. Giving up on sleep, she grabbed the first book she came to on the closest shelf and found herself rereading an old favourite. Nero Wolfe never suffered from sleepless nights, she thought, as the overweight detective played with his orchids and sent Archie out into the big bad world to detect things. By chapter four she was yawning. She'd read the book too many times to lose sleep over it, so she set it down on her nightstand and slid under the covers. She was asleep as soon as her head hit the pillow.

Her internal alarm gave her an extra twenty minutes of sleep the next morning, which meant Bessie had to hurry to be ready when Mark arrived to collect her.

"Good morning," he said as Bessie buckled her seatbelt.

"Good morning," Bessie replied. "Let's hope the police can work out what happened in Carolyn's room quickly so we can just get on with having 'Christmas at the Castle.'"

"Don't tell anyone," Mark said, "but I'm not the least bit sorry this happened, assuming the damage remains confined to Carolyn's room. I hate what she did with it and I don't think it adds anything to our event."

"I'd have to agree with that," Bessie told him. "I didn't like the room either, and I've no idea what the four wise men of the apocalypse were doing there."

Mark laughed. "You do make me feel better," he told Bessie. "I couldn't sleep last night for worrying about our vandal."

"I'm sure whoever it was deliberately targeted that room," Bessie assured him. "I'd be tempted to suggest that Mr. Hart's murderer was behind it, but I'd rather think that whoever killed him is long gone back across."

"I was thinking something similar," Mark said. "Whoever destroyed the room had to know where the keys were kept, which makes it seem likely that it was someone connected to the event."

"So maybe it has nothing to do with the murder," Bessie said cheerfully. "Maybe someone just got tired of doing Carolyn's work for her and threw a fit."

"A pretty dramatic fit," Mark said. "I only glanced into the room, but it looked as if just about everything was broken or damaged."

"That had to take some time," Bessie mused.

"I don't know," Mark replied. "Smashing things doesn't take all that long. Someone could have pulled down the wall fabric in seconds, pushed over all the trees and then spent less than five minutes with a hammer on the figurines."

Bessie sighed. "After all of our hard work, it's sad that it could all be destroyed that quickly, but I think you're probably right."

"I'll have Henry check today to see if any hammers are missing."

"But if someone took it, they could have simply returned it when they were finished," Bessie said with a sigh. "I noticed you have a few small hand tools in the ticket booth. It would have been easy enough for someone to take the hammer when they took the keys and then return both when they were finished."

"Maybe the hammer will have fingerprints on it," Mark said.

"Haven't we all borrowed that hammer in the last few weeks?" Bessie asked. "I know I used it at least a couple of times."

Mark sighed. "Maybe someone will simply confess," he said tiredly.

"Anything's possible," Bessie said, patting his arm.

Mark parked near the castle and the pair walked up the stone steps together. Mark unlocked the first door and Bessie followed him inside.

"We'll just wait here for Henry," Mark said. "He can send up the committee and the volunteers as they arrive and keep everyone else out."

"What time do we open today?" Bessie asked. She flushed. "I know I ought to remember, but I don't."

"We're open from one to five today, and then again tonight from seven to nine," he reminded her. "That is assuming we have police permission to carry on."

"Oh, I do hope they don't make us cancel," Bessie said. "We're raising a lot of money for all of the good causes with every ticket we sell."

"I just hope people don't stay away when they hear what happened," Mark said.

"Maybe we can keep it quiet," Bessie suggested. She and Mark exchanged glances and Bessie laughed.

"Okay, there's no way we can keep it quiet, not on this island, but why would it keep people away? A little light vandalism in a room that wasn't even open to the public shouldn't bother anyone."

"I hope you're right," Mark replied.

Bessie patted his arm again. She hoped she was right as well. They'd put too much time and effort into the event to see it fail now.

Once Henry was in place at the door, Bessie and Mark headed up to the banquet room. Mark unlocked doors as they went, and both he and Bessie inspected each room along the way.

"Everything looks perfect," Bessie said.

"I don't suppose we ought to open up Carolyn's room," Mark said.

"You can, as I'm here," Pete Corkill said from the doorway behind them.

"I was rather expecting Inspector Armstrong," Bessie told the man.

"He's agreed to leave it with me," Pete told her. "He's very busy with other things and there might be a connection between this and my murder, so he was happy to turn the whole thing over to me."

Bessie doubted that happy was the right word, but she didn't question the man.

Mark unlocked the door. "The switch for the overhead light is on the left," he told Pete.

Pete turned on the light and sighed deeply. "I suppose it looked a lot better before everything was smashed," he said, looking at Bessie.

"I thought it was rather awful," Bessie admitted. "It certainly didn't look festive or merry."

"I have a crime scene team coming to start processing the mess," Pete told them. "In the meantime, I'm going to start working on trying to work out some other things."

Bessie and Mark walked back to the banquet room and took seats at the long table. "What do we need to do today?" Bessie asked.

"Nothing much," Mark replied. "I originally asked everyone to come in this morning so that we could tidy everything up. I thought the rooms would be more disturbed than they are. I was surprised at how good everything looks this morning."

"I suspect we'll have more work to do after the afternoon hours," Bessie predicted. "We should get lots of families through this afternoon and small children are far more likely to want to touch things than the adults were last night."

Over the next half hour the charity volunteers and the rest of the committee slowly trickled in. By the time Pete's crime scene team arrived, everyone was there except for Michael.

"Is everyone here, then?" Pete asked from the doorway.

"Michael isn't," someone answered.

"I wasn't sure if you wanted Natasha," Mary said hesitantly. "She was planning to fly back across this morning to spend the weekend at home, but I suggested she probably shouldn't. She didn't feel up to coming back down here again, though. She's at her hotel in Douglas, working on the plans for Thie yn Triae, if you want her."

"I'll have someone talk to her there," Pete said, sounding unconcerned. "I'm already accommodating Richard Teare in that way."

"I'm not sure why I had to come back," Carolyn grumbled loudly.

"You'd be here anyway to help us get ready for the afternoon opening," Mark reminded her.

She frowned and looked down at the table in front of her. Bessie thought she looked older today, and far less attractive, even though her outfit probably cost more than Bessie spent on clothes in several years.

"I'm sure those of you who weren't here last night have been informed as to what was discovered when we opened the door to the room that Mrs. Teare decorated," Pete said. "For now we're assuming that everyone associated with the event knew where to find the keys and how to get into the room unseen. What I'd like to do is take everyone's fingerprints so that we can compare them with the prints that we know we'll find on the ornaments and other decorations."

"Finding our prints in there won't prove anything," Harriet argued. "We all did at least some of the decorating in there."

"Exactly, and I'm hoping, once we can eliminate all of you, that we have a set of prints we can't identify," Pete told her.

Harriet didn't look as if she believed his explanation, but she didn't argue further.

"If we could just set up on a table somewhere?" Pete asked Mark.

Mark rang Henry at the gate and asked him to send up a spare table and some chairs with one of the staff on duty. Everyone watched silently as the table was set up on one side of the room with two chairs behind it and one in front.

"Who'd like to go first?" Pete asked.

"I'm happy to," Mark said, stepping forward.

Bessie watched as everyone took their turn to have their fingerprints taken. Pete asked each person a few questions before sending them away to wash their hands in the nearest sink.

"Miss Cubbon, I think you're next," Pete said eventually.

Bessie walked over and sat down. "I'm sure you have mine on file," she said as she offered her hands to the man on the opposite side of the table.

"It's easier for us if we take a fresh set today, if you don't mind," Pete told her. "That way we can do comparisons on the spot."

"I don't mind at all," Bessie said.

"Do you know who took Michael home last night?" Pete asked as the man pressed each of Bessie's fingers into the ink and then on to the cards.

"No," Bessie replied. "He left after Carolyn and Richard, walking out with Natasha, but I don't know what happened once they all got outside. Mark and I were quite a bit behind them because Mark was locking up. Everyone was gone by the time we got to the street."

"The man seems to have disappeared again," Pete said grumpily. "He isn't answering his home phone or his mobile."

"I hope he's okay," Bessie said, feeling slightly worried for the man, but only cautiously so after his disappearing act the previous day.

"You don't know if he has a girlfriend or anything like that?" Pete asked.

Bessie shook her head. "I really rarely spoke to him," she explained. "He came and decorated his room the first day we were open for decorating, and then he didn't come back until the day Mr. Hart arrived to assess everything."

"When did his relationship with Carolyn begin?"

"I don't know that they have a relationship," Bessie replied. "There seemed to be something going on between them last night, though."

"Did they meet when Michael came to decorate his room?"

Bessie thought back. "I don't think so," she said after a moment. "I don't think Carolyn was spending much time down here then. She came to committee meetings but otherwise, she wasn't here. Mark and I are the only two committee people who've been on site pretty much nonstop since early December."

"I'm going to let you go because I don't want people to think I'm spending more time with you than I am with everyone else," Pete told her. "But I'd really like to talk to you again later today."

"I'm here all day," Bessie told him. "Although I'll probably be quite busy when the castle is open."

"Maybe I can buy you dinner between sessions," Pete suggested.

Bessie nodded. "I can pay my own way," she told him.

"But you'll let me buy anyway," Pete added.

Bessie stood up. Before she could walk away, Pete had one final question.

"Do you have any idea where we might find some of Michael's fingerprints?" he asked.

Bessie laughed. "I think I might, actually," she said, sounding as surprised as she felt. "In the room he decorated, there might be at least one really good set of prints, now that I think about it."

Pete frowned. "I'll have you show me after we're done here," he said.

Bessie nodded and walked away.

"Mrs. Teare, I believe you're the only one we've missed," Pete said.

"I was just speaking with my advocate," Carolyn replied. "He says I don't have to give you my prints."

"Of course you don't," Pete agreed easily. "But we would greatly appreciate your cooperation."

Carolyn frowned and stared at her mobile. Bessie could see indecision etched across the other woman's face. When the mobile buzzed, everyone in the room seemed to jump.

"Yes, yes, I see, okay, thank you," Carolyn said on her end.

"Richard would prefer it if I decline," she said stiffly. "He won't be providing his either."

Pete nodded, clearly unsurprised by the news. "Miss Cubbon, if you could show me what we were discussing, then?" he asked.

Bessie stood up and the pair left the room. She could feel the curious stares that followed her out of the space. When they reached it, Michael's room felt weirdly empty to Bessie. She scolded herself for her overactive imagination and led Pete to the large tree in the back of the room.

"All of the ornaments on this tree were donated by the families of men and women who were diagnosed with Alzheimer's disease," Bessie told Pete. "Michael was here when we opened that first morning, and just after lunch I came up to see how he was doing. He'd finished the entire room, except for this tree. As you can see, many of the ornaments are old and some of them were quite dusty. Michael was polishing them, one at a time, before hanging them on the tree."

"Was he now?" Pete asked.

"See that shiny silver one at the top?" Bessie asked. "I teased him about getting fingerprints on it, because it's so shiny."

"So he was extra careful not to," Pete guessed.

"No, he grabbed it with both hands, pushing his fingertips against it," Bessie said. "We were both laughing about how if he robbed a bank, we had all the evidence we needed."

Pete nodded. "I do hope he didn't give the ornament another polish after you left," he muttered. He took gloves and a plastic bag from his pocket and carefully put the ornament into the bag.

Bessie followed him back to the banquet room, where Mark was anxiously looking at his watch.

"It's just about midday," he said as Bessie walked in. "We open in about an hour. I didn't have lunch catered today, because I didn't realise we were going to be tied up all morning."

"The pub across the street has excellent food," Bessie suggested.

"And I'll treat because we've all been working so hard," Mary added.

A few people cheered and then everyone headed for the exit. Bessie waited while Mary had a quick word with Pete and then they followed the others out of the castle and across the road.

Lunch was delicious but rushed. It was a small pub that wasn't used to unexpected and large groups at that time of day, but they managed to get everyone happily fed with five minutes to spare. Mark thanked Mary repeatedly, until he had to hurry back to the castle to make certain everything was ready. Mary had insisted on including Henry and Laura as well as the three young MNH staff members who were helping at the castle that day in the invitation to lunch, and they were all quick to follow Mark back across the road. The charity volunteers and the committee members were a bit slower.

"I should hurry," Marjorie said as she swallowed her last bite of sticky toffee pudding. "I'm MNH staff, after all."

"But today you're 'Christmas at the Castle' committee, really," Bessie said. "Knowing MNH, you aren't getting paid for all the extra time and effort you've put into this little event."

"I'm not," Marjorie agreed. "But I love it anyway."

"If I had to work for a living, I certainly wouldn't give up my free time," Carolyn sniffed.

"When you work for a non-profit, you often find that your desire to help them succeed overrides your self-interest," Marjorie replied.

"If you say so," Carolyn said doubtfully.

"You do a lot of volunteer work," Bessie said. "Surely you get a great deal of satisfaction from that."

Carolyn raised her eyebrows at Bessie. "Satisfaction? Hmm, yes, I suppose so," she replied. "But really, I do what I have to as a result of my husband's position in Manx society, that's all. Mary understands, don't you, my dear?"

Mary smiled thinly. "I only volunteer for projects I'm interested in and where I think I can actually make a difference," she told the other woman. "I'd like to think I was a real help with 'Christmas at the Castle.'"

"You were," Bessie said emphatically.

Carolyn looked at Bessie expectantly, but Bessie couldn't bring herself to say what she knew Carolyn wanted to hear. Fortunately, the waitress interrupted before she could reply.

"I have everything you ordered ready to go," the girl told Mary as she handed her the bill.

Mary glanced at it and then gave the girl a stack of notes. "Thank you," she said.

The girl brought three large and very full carrier bags over to them. "Here you are," she said brightly. "Was there anything else today?"

Bessie assumed, from the girl's suddenly increased enthusiasm, that she'd counted the money she'd been given and just realised that Mary had added a very generous tip. Mary always did.

Marjorie insisted on carrying two of the bags, leaving just one for Bessie and Mary to fight over.

"I paid for it," Mary argued.

"All the more reason for me to carry it," Bessie replied. "But what is it all for?"

"Inspector Corkill and his men," Mary told her. "He wouldn't let any of them take a break to join us, so I told him we'd bring lunch to them."

Bessie smiled at her friend. Unlike many wealthy women, Mary was always thinking of others. She'd also allowed Pete to take her fingerprints without a murmur.

A long queue had built up in front of the castle, so Bessie and the others headed around to the side door. They slipped inside quickly and took the back stairs to the banquet room.

"We're just about to open for business, so you really can't eat in here," Mark said apologetically when he walked through as Mary was handing the feast over to Pete. "We can open another room for you, though, and move the table you were using in there."

"That would be great," Pete said. "And we all truly appreciate your kindness," he told Mary. "I could get into a lot of trouble for accepting gifts from a suspect," he added.

"It's only lunch," Mary told him. "And I promise not to expect special treatment because of it."

"You won't get it," Pete told her seriously.

Mary laughed. "I wouldn't have it any other way," she assured him.

Two policemen quickly moved the table into the small room that Mark unlocked for them.

"I'll have a member of staff stationed in here," Mark told Pete. "They'll keep our guests from taking a wrong turn into this corridor."

"I appreciate that," Pete told him. "The crime scene is enough of a mess without adding to it."

The sound of a bell ringing alerted everyone that the castle was now open for business. Bessie rushed down to the courtyard to help greet the afternoon's guests. For the next four hours, she had little time to do anything but answer questions and thank people for coming. When five o'clock finally arrived, she was grateful to see the last of their afternoon guests leaving.

"That was exhausting," she said to Laura as they made their way back to the banquet room. Mark had requested that everyone attend a very short meeting to discuss how things had gone before they all took a much deserved break before the evening session.

"I think it went brilliantly," Agnes said. "Our little donation box was stuffed so full that we had to empty it twice. And it wasn't all one-pound notes and coins, either. There were fives and tens in there as well."

"We must have three or four hundred cards for sick children and our military personnel," Margaret said. "And at least that many letters to Father Christmas. The children were all very excited about that."

"I was wondering if we ought to have Father Christmas visit the site," Mark said thoughtfully.

"Not this year," Bessie said emphatically. "We have quite enough going on for this year."

"I'm with Bessie on that one," Marjorie said. "We can add it to the list of things to do differently next year, but let's not complicate things now."

After a quick check that no one had any concerns or problems, Mark sent them all away to rest and relax until half six. "All of the rooms will probably need a bit of straightening up," he said. "But go and have something to eat and relax for a while first. The committee members will come around starting at half six to help anyone who needs it as you fix up your rooms."

The group slowly began to disperse. Bessie waited to see if Pete still wanted to have dinner with her.

"Ah, Bessie, I'm a bit too busy with, um, something, to leave right now," he said when she stuck her head in the room where he was working. "Maybe I could drive you home later and we can talk then."

"I'm happy with whatever works for you," Bessie assured him.

As everyone else seemed to have disappeared, Bessie took herself off to a small café she liked that was only a short distance away. She'd been something of a regular for lunch during the last month while she'd been working at the castle, and she couldn't help but think that she'd miss their warming comfort food after the next week when she would be back to rarely visiting the south of the island.

She ate cottage pie with jam roly poly for pudding and drank several cups of tea. Having lived alone for all of her adult life, she was quite content to eat on her own, but it hardly felt like she was alone, as all of the different waitresses who'd looked after her during the month made a point of stopping to chat. She returned to the castle feeling content and surprisingly well rested, all things considered.

For half an hour, she went from room to room, chatting with everyone and helping tidy up odd sweets wrappers and the like. Margaret's room was in the worst shape and Bessie spent several minutes hunting down pens and pencils that seemed to have wandered all over the room, under Christmas trees and behind decorations. With Mary's help, they managed to get everything tidied up with a fresh pile of blank letters to Santa and cards ready to go.

"There should be fewer children here tonight than there were this afternoon," Bessie remarked.

"I certainly hope so," Margaret said with a rueful laugh. "It was exhausting trying to keep up with them all this afternoon."

Bessie made a mental note to try to spend more time with Margaret when the castle was open, especially during afternoon hours. It sounded very much like a second pair of hands would be welcome.

The other rooms needed little more than a bit of straightening and Mark and Marjorie had already helped the others get that done by the time Bessie arrived in them. They all ended up in Michael's room with only a few minutes left to spare.

"It doesn't look too bad," Mark said as he looked around.

"No, I expect the children were getting tired by the time they got to here," Bessie said with a laugh.

"I did the MNH room first, and it needed even less work," Marjorie told her. "As it's the very last stop in the castle, I think there might be something to your theory."

"Sorry I wasn't here this morning," Natasha said as she walked into the room.

"You don't have to be here now," Mary told her.

"I know," Natasha said with a laugh. "But I really missed being a part of it. I know that's weird, but it's such a wonderful thing you're all doing here. I hope I'm not in the way."

"Not at all," Mark said. "We can use all the help we can get. Now, I need ideas. With Michael not here, I stationed one of the MNH staff in here this afternoon, but the poor man didn't know anything about the Alzheimer's Research Fund and apparently he got a lot of questions."

"I'm happy to hear that people were asking questions about the charities," Bessie said.

"I was, too," Mark agreed. "I don't suppose any of you know enough about Michael's work to be able to cover for him tonight?"

Everyone exchanged glances. After an awkward silence, Bessie finally spoke up.

"I don't know a lot, but I'll stay in here and do my best," she offered.

"Thank you, Bessie," Mark said. Bessie could hear how tired he was in his voice.

"I hope you have a nice long holiday booked for the new year," she said to him as everyone else scattered back to their rooms or to the courtyard to greet guests.

"I do, actually," Mark said. "But if they don't get Mr. Hart's murder solved, I might not be allowed to go."

"I'm sure Pete will have it all sorted by then," Bessie said confidently.

"Let's hope so," Mark muttered as he headed out.

The two hours that Bessie spent in Michael's room felt long and tedious. She smiled and chatted with all of the visitors and told them everything she could remember about the Alzheimer's Research Fund. She did her best, but she couldn't help but feel as if someone else could have done a much better job.

It was nearly nine when Mark came in. "Inspector Corkill wants to see all of us in the banquet room once the last of the guests have left," he told Bessie.

"That sounds ominous," Bessie said.

Mark shrugged. "He wouldn't say anything more than that," he replied.

Time seemed to slow down even further now as Bessie wondered what the inspector wanted. The possibilities raced each other around Bessie's mind as she absentmindedly greeted the last few guests who straggled through. A few minutes after what she'd hoped were the last of the guests, Bessie heard voices in the corridor.

"Come on," Mary called to her from the doorway. "Henry is chasing everyone out and Mark wants us all in the banquet room."

Bessie followed the others who were all chatting amongst themselves.

"You're very quiet," Mary said as they reached their destination.

AUNT BESSIE JOINS

"It was a long day," Bessie replied.

"I'll come and help you tomorrow, if you get stuck in Michael's room again. I'll bring Natasha and we'll have fun," Mary offered. "Really, Carolyn should have done it anyway; she's on the board."

"I forgot about that," Bessie exclaimed. "She really should have."

In the centre of the room, Pete cleared his throat. "I have a few things I want to discuss with you all," he said. "I know it's late and you're all tired, but I need to ask each of you a few questions, one at a time. I'd like to start with Bessie Cubbon, please."

"What's going on?" Agnes demanded.

"I want to go home," Carolyn snapped. "You can question us in the morning."

"I'll try not to keep you here for too long," Pete said. "But I really must talk to you all before you leave."

"Something has happened to Michael," someone guessed.

Pete held up a hand. "I'd like to speak to each of you in turn," he repeated. "Miss Cubbon?"

Bessie stood up and followed him out of the room. He stopped at the door to the room they'd used for lunch and gave Bessie a grim smile. "I didn't mention that we have company," he said as he pushed the door open.

Bessie frowned as she walked into the room and spotted the man behind the table. John Rockwell got to his feet and frowned back at her.

125

CHAPTER 9

"Your being here can't be good," Bessie said as she crossed the room.

"No, it isn't," John replied. He stepped around the table and gave Bessie a quick hug.

"You shouldn't hug suspects," Pete said from the doorway.

"And I'll deny I did it if Bessie ends up being the murderer," John said with a tight smile.

Bessie forced a smile onto her own lips and then, at John's invitation, sat down opposite him.

"What's happened?" she asked.

"Two things," Pete said as he joined them at the table. "First of all, we've made a tentative identification of some of the fingerprints that were found on the inside of one of the smashed ornaments."

"And they were Michael's," Bessie guessed.

"Why do you think that?" Pete asked.

"Because he has a temper, because it seems like something he might have done after a few too many drinks, and because you haven't arrested anyone else," Bessie replied.

John and Pete both smiled. "She's very good," John said to Pete.

"I know," Pete replied.

"We aren't going to be telling the others about that," John told her. "For now we're officially leaving the vandalism as unsolved."

"What happened to Michael?" Bessie asked.

"A body was found in Lonan this morning in a house that was empty and on the market. A neighbour saw lights on in the property late last night and rang the office, but when a constable went to check, the property was dark and everything looked secure. He wrote up a report and the information was passed on to the real estate company handling the sale. They sent someone around to check everything this afternoon and found the body."

"And it's Michael," Bessie said sadly.

"We haven't had a formal identification yet," John said. "But Pete's provided a preliminary one."

Bessie nodded. "Another murder connected to 'Christmas at the Castle,'" she said sadly.

"No one has said anything about murder," John told her.

Bessie looked up at him in surprise. "He killed himself?" she asked, feeling confused.

The two policemen exchanged glances. "It will be some days before we have a proper cause of death determined," Pete said.

"But it could have been suicide?" Bessie asked. "Or an accident?"

"It could have been one of those," John agreed. "It's definitely not as clear-cut as Mr. Hart's death was, at least."

"Can you think of any reason why he might have killed himself?" Pete asked Bessie.

She took a deep breath and then sat back, feeling shocked. "He wasn't happy on the island," she said eventually. "But he was exploring other job opportunities, not talking about killing himself."

"His altercation with Christopher Hart was public knowledge," Pete pointed out. "That might have limited his job options."

"Even so, Carolyn was standing behind him, at least for the moment. His job here was safe."

"But he didn't want to be here," John reminded her.

"No, but suicide is quite a long way away from being somewhat dissatisfied with your current job," Bessie replied.

"What if he'd killed Mr. Hart?" Pete asked. "Was he the sort who might have let guilt eat away at him until he took his own life?"

"I barely knew the man," Bessie said. "But I would have said no; at least before yesterday I would have."

"What happened yesterday?" John asked.

"He was behaving strangely yesterday," Bessie told him. "He drank a lot, and I'd never seen him have more than a single glass of wine before. Of course, I'd only seen him at one or two social gatherings early in the planning stages for our event. Maybe he was out drinking every other night and I never knew about it."

"And he disappeared for a while," Pete said thoughtfully.

"It wasn't like him to miss the press conference," Bessie said. "He was very ambitious, and a lot of his success at work was dependent on his raising both money and awareness. I was shocked that he'd miss an opportunity to gain publicity for the charity."

"Who knew him best?" John asked.

"I don't know anything about his private life," Bessie said. "Carolyn was on the board at the charity he worked for, but I don't know how well they knew one another. Harriet said something about having worked with him previously, I think." Bessie shook her head. "I'm feeling all muddled up," she said. "It's such a shock."

"He went for a walk with Natasha yesterday afternoon," Pete said. "Do you think they were some sort of a couple?"

"I thought at the time that Natasha was being nice and getting a rather drunk man out of our hair while we finished decorating," Bessie recalled. "But after everything that happened last night, I'm not sure what they were doing."

Pete and John took Bessie back through the entire previous day before having her walk them through her Saturday. When she was finished, John sat back with a sigh.

"I have a number of questions for you, but I think I'd rather talk to the others before I ask them," he said.

"No doubt Carolyn Teare is kicking up a major fuss," Pete added. "We'd better get her sent home before her advocate arrives and we have to deal with him, too."

"Bessie, would you mind waiting until I've spoken to everyone else so we can talk again?" John asked. "I can give you a ride home, if that makes it any more tempting."

Bessie chuckled. "You don't have to tempt me," she told him. "I'll do whatever you think will be most helpful."

"Why can't all witnesses be like Bessie?" Pete muttered as he ushered Bessie out of the room.

"Please don't talk to anyone," he told Bessie loudly as he walked her back into the banquet room.

Bessie shrugged and crossed to a chair in an empty corner of the space.

"I demand to be allowed to leave," Carolyn said angrily. "I've been saying that for over half an hour and these men wouldn't let me go."

"I'm sorry for the inconvenience," Pete said without conviction. "Come on back and I'll get your statement and then you'll be free to go."

"Why isn't Bessie free to go?" Carolyn demanded as she stood up. "Don't tell me you suspect Bessie of anything criminal."

"No comment," Pete replied. He gave Bessie an amused grin before he led Carolyn down the corridor.

As soon as they were gone, several people started to speak. Mark held up a hand.

"We all heard the inspector tell you not to talk to anyone," he said, glancing around the room. "But I do hope you're okay."

"I'm fine," Bessie assured him. "But I can't say anything more."

Mark nodded and the room fell into an awkward silence. To Bessie, time seemed to stand still. When she checked her watch, she worked out that she'd spent about half an hour with the two inspectors. She was surprised to see Pete back only twenty minutes after he'd left with Carolyn.

"Mark, I'd like to talk to you next," he said.

Mark got up and followed him out of the room, leaving everyone to shift in their seats and wonder what had happened to Carolyn.

Mark was back only fifteen minutes later. "Just to set your minds at rest," he said in the doorway, "Carolyn has been sent home. Once you've had your turn with the inspector, you'll be allowed to leave as well. I need to wait and lock up, but if anyone has a particular reason for being questioned sooner rather than later, let me know."

A few people muttered under their breath, but no one spoke. After a minute, Mark continued.

"Liz, I know you have small children to get home to. Why don't you go next?"

"Thanks," Liz replied, getting slowly to her feet.

Bessie hated how exhausted the poor girl looked. It had been a very long day for a pregnant woman. This time it was only ten minutes before Pete reappeared.

"If I could have Agnes next, please," he said.

Bessie amused herself with trying to guess whom the two inspectors would send for next. She decided that they were working through the charity volunteers, and was strangely pleased when, less than ten minutes later, Pete asked Margaret to come through. After Harriet, the questioning seemed to go even more quickly as Henry, Laura and the three young MNH staff members were questioned in very short order. When Marjorie went back with Pete, Mary exchanged glances with Natasha.

"It looks as if they're leaving us for last," she said. "I hope that doesn't mean they think we did something wrong."

Natasha yawned. "I'm going to fall asleep in this incredibly uncomfortable chair in a few minutes," she replied. "I don't even like the hotel bed, but it's definitely calling to me at the moment."

When Pete came back in a short time later, he looked exhausted. "Thank you both for your patience," he said to Mary and Natasha. "Mrs. Quayle, your husband insisted that we wait to question you until your advocate could be with you. He's arrived now, so if you'd like to come with me, please."

"Oh, goodness, George is such an idiot sometimes," Mary said affectionately. She left the room with Pete. They were both back about twenty minutes later.

"I'll just wait here for you, dear," Mary told Natasha. "Then I can give you a ride back into Douglas."

"Thank you," the girl told her. "I hope I won't be long. Do you think I need to borrow your advocate?"

"Oh, he was nothing but an inconvenience," Mary told her. "I sent him home after the third question."

Bessie laughed and Mary turned and winked at her.

"You run along and see if you can help the police work things out," Mary told Natasha. "You can bring fresh perspective. We all know each other too well, I think."

Natasha nodded and then followed Pete down the corridor. Mary took a seat next to Bessie and patted her hand.

"I know you aren't allowed to talk about anything, so let me bore you with tales of my grandchildren, please. I think I'll go mad if I have to sit here in silence again."

Bessie smiled. "I'd love to hear about your grandchildren," she told Mary.

When Natasha walked back into the room half an hour later, Bessie was laughing over the antics of the newest addition to the Quayle family.

"He's too smart for his own good, that child," Mary said. "But I love them all so very much."

"We can go now," Natasha told Mary. "I do hope you aren't expecting me to help out again tomorrow," she added, looking from Mary to Mark and back again.

"I said you weren't expected today," Mary reminded her. "Of course you may take tomorrow off and just rest. Take Monday as well and then you can start back on Thie ny Traie and forget all about Castle Rushen."

"I'm not sure I'll manage two days off," Natasha replied. "But I will take tomorrow to rest, at least."

"We're meant to be open from one to five tomorrow," Mark said. "I'm hoping the police aren't going to make us close."

"No need, at least at this point," Pete said. "We'll have a crew here tomorrow working on processing the vandalised room further, but as long as we can keep out of the way of your event, you can go ahead."

"Excellent," Mark said with a sigh.

Bessie couldn't help but think that it would be easier for everyone if the police had cancelled their Sunday hours. She didn't feel as if she'd be at all ready to be cheery and bright again the next day.

"Bessie, I can take you home now," John Rockwell said from the doorway.

"I'll just lock up behind us all," Mark said.

Natasha and Mary left with a uniformed constable as an escort. John, Pete, Mark and Bessie walked out together, checking and locking up as they went.

"We're going to have to do some tidying up in the morning," Mark commented as they walked through Margaret's room.

Bessie sighed as she saw that writing utensils were scattered all across the floor again. "What are people doing in here?" she demanded.

"I think we need more staff helping Margaret," Mark said. "She seems to be a little bit overwhelmed."

"I'd be happy to help her," Bessie said. "But you'll have to find someone else to cover for Michael, then."

"I think Carolyn should do that," Mark said. "She is on the board for the charity, after all."

"Good luck," was all that Bessie could say to that.

Mark laughed. "I think I'll need it," he said. "I'll pick you up at ten tomorrow," he told her. "There's nothing that needs doing any earlier than that."

Bessie was happy to agree. She just hoped she might get a little extra sleep out of the later start.

"I'm parked on the next street," John told Bessie, taking her arm.

Bessie hated being coddled, but she was just tired enough to appreciate the extra support. John helped her into the car and shut the door for her before climbing into the driver's seat.

"You look tired," Bessie said sympathetically.

"I am," John admitted. "Inspector Lambert is on leave and I suppose I didn't realise how much she was actually doing around the office. I can't seem to get caught up with all the paperwork at the moment."

"When will she be back?"

"I don't know," John told her. "There are some issues that need working through, and that's all I have to say on the subject."

Bessie knew that the chief constable hadn't been happy with the way Anna Lambert had handled questioning a vulnerable suspect during a recent investigation, but this was the first she'd heard about the woman being away.

"How are you?" Bessie asked. "Besides tired," she added.

"I'm doing well," John told her. "I'm meant to be flying across on Christmas morning to spend a few days with the kids. I'm really hoping we can have this case solved by then so I don't have to cancel."

John and his wife had only recently separated. She'd moved back to the UK with their two children and Bessie knew John was finding it difficult being away from them. "You'll have to go anyway," she said firmly.

"Unfortunately, my job is more important than my personal life," John told her. "I knew that when I joined the police."

"Can't Inspector Lambert come back and take over the investigation?" Bessie demanded.

"I don't think anyone would like that idea," John replied. "For a number of reasons."

Bessie pressed her lips together to prevent herself from blurting out all of the questions that sprang to her mind.

"Anyway, I want you to tell me what you think was going on with Carolyn and Richard yesterday," John said.

Bessie shrugged. "I wish I knew," she said. "Or maybe I don't," she amended. "It seemed very much like they were both looking to start affairs and that they were flaunting it in front of one another. I hope I totally misread the situation, though."

"Do either of them have regular affairs?" John asked.

"I didn't think so," Bessie replied. "Richard had an affair with Carolyn, of course. That's how their relationship started. That much is common knowledge. I don't see them often, but I don't recall hearing any skeet about either of them over the years. As I said before, Carolyn sits on all the right boards and committees that make her look good, but beyond that I don't really know anything about her."

"Do you like her?"

Bessie frowned. "I don't dislike her," she said thoughtfully. "She's exactly what a committee like ours needs, as she's friends with all of the wealthiest families on the island. Her friends are going to be ninety per cent of the audience at the auction on Christmas Eve, and they should spend a lot of money bidding against one another on the various prizes. Just having her name on the invitations will have made MNH and the other charities quite a lot more money."

"So she's useful; but do you like her?"

"Not much," Bessie admitted. "She's polite and friendly enough while we're working together, but I can't help but feel that she wouldn't bother to speak with me if we ran into each other elsewhere."

"Who are her friends? I mean her real friends."

"I don't know that she has any," Bessie said after giving it some thought. "She's in the same position as a lot of wealthy men's wives. They get thrown together at events and things, but I don't think many of them like one another. I don't think I've ever seen her out having lunch with a friend or anything like that. Mary might be better able to answer that question, though, as she's in the same social circle. I'm not, obviously."

John laughed. "What about Richard? Do you know if he has friends?"

"Years ago he used to go across almost every weekend to spend time with his children," Bessie told John. "His first wife took the children and moved to London as soon as the divorce was mentioned. She used a London solicitor and he worked it somehow so that if Richard wanted to see the children, he had to travel to them. The children never visited the island."

"She must have had a good solicitor," John remarked.

"She did," Bessie agreed. "And it helped that Richard was head over heels in love with Carolyn. According to my sources, Richard would have agreed to just about anything to get the divorce pushed through."

"But the children are all grown up now?"

"Oh, yes, in fact, one or two of them have visited the island in the last couple of years. Richard and Carolyn had a huge party when his daughter came over to see him about five years ago."

"Did you go?"

"Oh, goodness, I wasn't invited," Bessie laughed. "But it was the talk of the island. They flew in some boy band that was popular at the time for entertainment and probably spent more on that one weekend than an average house is worth."

"So what does Richard do with his weekends now that his children are adults?"

Bessie shrugged. "Again, you should probably talk to Mary. She'll have a better idea of what goes on in that circle than I do. If it were me, I'd spend my weekends in my enormous library, trying to read every book I could get my hands on."

John grinned. "Somehow I don't think Richard is doing that," he said.

"No, I don't suppose he is," Bessie agreed.

At Bessie's cottage, John insisted on going inside to check that everything was okay.

"Mark doesn't do this," she said grumpily as she stood in the kitchen waiting for John to finish his quick inspection.

"Well, he should," John said as he rejoined Bessie. "This cottage is far too isolated, especially in the winter months when the holiday rentals are empty."

"There was a whole row of cottages on the beach when I bought this one," Bessie told him. "And we all lived here all year, too. When the island became a tourist destination, my neighbours soon discovered that they could rent out their homes during the summer for far more money than they'd ever imagined, and that was the end of this stretch of beach being properly residential."

"Now you're the only one left," John said.

"I do hope George and Mary get settled into Thie yn Traie quickly," Bessie said. "It will be nice to have neighbours again, even if they aren't all that close by."

135

"I'll feel better when they're moved in," John told her. "But that doesn't mean I won't stop checking your cottage when I bring you home at night."

Bessie shook her head. "I hate being treated like a small child," she grumbled.

"But you'll put up with it because you know I only do it because I care about you," John said.

Bessie nodded. "Now you'd better get home and get some sleep. Tomorrow is going to be a busy day."

"It is," John agreed.

In the doorway, he paused and looked back at Bessie. "You don't happen to have anything with Michael's handwriting on it, do you?"

Bessie thought for a moment. "I don't, but Mark will have his application for a place at 'Christmas at the Castle.' It wasn't long or complicated, but he will have written at least a few sentences on it."

"I'll have to ask Mark about that tomorrow," John said, making a quick note in his notebook.

Bessie shut and locked the door behind him, her mind churning. Michael must have left a note, she thought. So it was suicide? She shook her head. Thank goodness it was John's problem and not hers.

It was late and she was tired, but once she got into bed, she found she couldn't sleep. Nero and Archie were waiting on the nightstand and it took six chapters before she finally began to feel tired enough to rest. Sleep late, she told herself firmly as she drifted off to sleep.

At six, she found herself suddenly wide awake. She sighed and rolled over, trying to coax herself into another hour of rest, but it was no good. She was tired, but her brain was already hard at work, replaying memories of Michael over and over again.

She had her shower and got dressed. Feeling too tired to appreciate food, she poured herself some cereal and nibbled on it while she waited for the coffee maker to finish. The first cup of coffee helped to disperse the fog in her brain and a second left her feeling almost too awake. With several hours to fill before Mark was due, Bessie headed out for a long walk.

It was cold, windy, and foggy on the beach, but Bessie was determined to walk anyway. She made it as far as Thie yn Traie before stopping for a rest. Leaning on the cliff face, she stood and watched the waves as they pounded the beach.

While Bessie had planned to walk for longer, she was soaked through in spite of her heavy coat. She turned for home with a sigh. The walk back was straight into the wind, and when Bessie finally let herself into her cottage, she felt as if she'd had a real workout. After dripping in the kitchen for a moment, she squelched her way up to her bedroom and changed clothes. A few minutes with a mop cleared up the mess she'd left and the rest of the pot of coffee managed to warm her all the way through. She was just settling in with her book when someone knocked on her door.

"Maggie Shimmin, what brings you here?" Bessie asked as she let her guest in.

"I was just coming to check in on you, after all the trouble down south," Maggie said.

Bessie smiled. Maggie and her husband, Thomas, owned the holiday cottages that ran along the beach beyond Bessie's home. Maggie spent her summers keeping their guests supplied with groceries and baked goods and her winters keeping the rest of Laxey up-to-date on the latest gossip. If anyone was going to drop by unannounced, it was Maggie.

"I'm fine," Bessie said now.

"I didn't pay much attention when that designer was killed. I assumed someone from across came over and did him in, that's all. But then I heard someone was vandalising all of the decorations at 'Christmas at the Castle.' That's when I started worrying about you, you see."

"It wasn't all of the decorations," Bessie replied. "Someone smashed a few baubles in one room, that's all. 'Christmas at the Castle' is going ahead as planned anyway.'"

"Really? Even with Michael Beach's sudden death?" Maggie asked.

"As far as I know," Bessie told her.

"Well, that is good news," Maggie said, looking uncertain.

"There's something else on your mind," Bessie said. "What's wrong?"

"Oh, nothing," Maggie said, staring at the floor.

"Would you like some tea or coffee?" Bessie asked.

"Oh, no, I can't stay. I have to get back and help Thomas. We're going Christmas shopping today. We send little things to some of our best customers, you know, the sort of people who come every summer. Thomas is making a list and then we're going to try to find appropriate gifts for each of them."

"That sounds like a big job."

"It is, but it's a fun one. I love to shop, even if Thomas does moan the whole time."

Bessie nodded. Knowing Thomas, that's exactly what he'd do.

"I'd better go, then," Maggie said. She turned towards the door and then looked back at Bessie. "Could you put in a good word for me with your inspector friend? I mean, for my cousin Bethany?" she asked.

"With John?"

"That's the one," Maggie said. "Bethany's in a spot of bother, you see, and I know John will listen to you. She isn't a bad girl, really, she just made a little mistake."

"I haven't seen Bethany in years," Bessie said, thinking back. "The last I knew, she was working for an advocate in Douglas."

"Yeah, that didn't work out, really. She's been working for an estate agent for the last six months or so."

"And now she's in trouble with the police?" Bessie asked.

"The thing is, she thought Michael was serious about her. He swept her off her feet, you see, and she thought he was going to marry her."

"Bethany was involved with Michael Beach?" Bessie asked, feeling confused.

"Yeah, and that's why she gave him the keys."

Bessie felt as if the penny dropped. "Bethany gave Michael the keys to the house that was for sale. The one where they found his body."

"Yeah," Maggie said grimly.

"But what did Michael tell Bethany he wanted the keys for?" Bessie asked.

Maggie flushed. "I gather they were going to meet up there and, um, well, have some private time together. Bethany still lives with her parents and Michael's flat was tiny. From what Bethany said, they used to meet at different houses that she knew were empty, instead of going out."

"I see," Bessie said.

Maggie shook her head. "Bethany isn't the brightest child," she said. "She's going to get fired if word gets out, we know that, but we're hoping that she won't be in any trouble with the police on top of everything else."

"Was she supposed to meet him there on Friday night?" Bessie asked.

"No, in fact, they broke up about a week ago. He told her he had bigger fish to fry and left her heartbroken. She was so upset that she forgot that he still had a spare set of keys to that house in Lonan. When she remembered, she tried ringing him, but he never answered her calls."

Bessie shook her head. "She needs to talk to John," she said.

"She's going to do that today," Maggie told her. "As soon as her boss finds out that she gave Michael the keys, she's sure to get fired. I was hoping you could persuade John Rockwell to keep that a secret."

Bessie stared at Maggie for a moment. "I don't know if that's possible," she said slowly.

"But you'll try?" Maggie asked hopefully.

"I'll talk to John," Bessie said, deliberately not mentioning what she was going to say to the man.

"That's wonderful," Maggie exclaimed. "Thank you."

"I can't promise anything," Bessie cautioned her.

"But at least you'll try," Maggie said. "It's better than nothing."

"I think Bethany would be smart to go and tell her supervisor the whole story herself before she goes to the police," Bessie said. "It's the right thing to do."

Maggie made a face. "I'm not sure about that," she said. "But I'll pass it along to Bethany."

Bessie locked the door behind the woman and sighed deeply. She rang John at home and was pleased to find him in.

"It's good to have that particular mystery solved," he said when she'd finished telling him the whole story. "I'll talk to Bethany myself and urge her to tell all to her supervisor. She deserves to lose her job, if you ask me."

"Will you be down at the castle today?" Bessie asked.

"I don't know," John replied. "I find it next to impossible to plan my days when I'm in the middle of an investigation. What hours is 'Christmas at the Castle' open today?"

"From one until five," Bessie told him.

"I may just see you later, then," John replied.

CHAPTER 10

*B*essie filled the rest of her restless morning with more Nero Wolfe.

"I'm quite jealous of his genius," she told Mark on their drive to Castletown. "He can just sit in one place and work everything out. John seems to be running all over the island, talking to everyone and looking for clues all the time."

"But Mr. Wolfe has Archie to do all of those little jobs," Mark pointed out. "And Inspector Cramer and his men to take fingerprints and chase down leads."

"Yes, I suppose it isn't much different, really," Bessie said. "He just makes it look easier than what John has to do."

"It helps that he's fictional," Mark pointed out. "Rex Stout knows who the killer is from page one, so all he has to do is get Mr. Wolfe and Archie to spot him or her."

Bessie laughed. "I wish John knew who the killer was in the very beginning of every case," she said. "It would make his job much easier."

"I got the impression that the police don't think Michael was murdered," Mark said.

"John asked me if I had any samples of his handwriting," Bessie replied. "That suggests that they found a note of some kind."

"It does, doesn't it?" Mark replied.

When they arrived at the castle, Bessie went from room to room, helping the charity volunteers tidy up and prepare for the afternoon. It was midday when she reached the banquet room and found the rest of the committee was already there, along with most of the volunteers.

"I've ordered pizza," Mary told her. "If that doesn't sound good, you don't have to stay, but I've ordered more than enough for everyone."

"Pizza is fine," Bessie replied. "It saves me having to go out and then rush back."

"I think we all feel that way," Mark told Bessie.

"I'd rather go and have something nice, but I don't think I have time," Carolyn said, frowning.

"I was hoping you might be persuaded to stand in for Michael today," Mark told the woman. "You're on the board for the Alzheimer's Research Fund, after all. I'm sure you'd be best at answering questions about their work."

"Oh, goodness, I've no idea what they do," Carolyn laughed. "Richard writes them rather large cheques every year, that's why I'm on the board. I've only been to two or three meetings in the last ten years."

Bessie bit her lip. If the charity wanted to give out board positions to wealthy donors' wives, that was up to them, but it was a shame they hadn't been able to find someone who would genuinely care about what they did.

"Does anyone else want to volunteer to cover that room?" Mark asked, glancing around the room.

The pizza delivery interrupted any replies that might have been made. While Bessie filled her plate with pizza and garlic bread, she told herself that she didn't really mind covering for Michael again. She'd volunteered to be on the committee and she didn't regret it, even if some jobs she had to do were less fun than others. The subject didn't come up again until everyone was clearing up plates and cups and getting the room ready for the guests who were due to start arriving in only a few minutes.

"Bessie, I suppose I'll have to ask you to cover for Michael," Mark said.

"Or Bessie can cover for me and I'll cover for Michael," Margaret suggested. "I'm still recovering from all the children yesterday who wanted to write to Father Christmas. I'll happily let Bessie deal with today's crowds and cover Michael's room instead. I did a lot of volunteer work with the Alzheimer's Research Fund a few years back. My father suffered from Alzheimer's, you see."

Bessie wasn't sure that dealing with lots of overexcited children was a better option, but she could tell Margaret really wanted to switch rooms. "That's fine with me, if it's okay with Mark," she told Margaret.

"As long as the rooms are covered, I'm happy," Mark replied.

"I'm not far away if it all gets to be too much for you," Liz whispered to Bessie as the group began to disperse to their assigned locations. "I can change places with you for a while if you need a break."

"Thanks," Bessie said. "I hope I don't have to take you up on that."

In the end, Bessie made it through the afternoon. Most of the children were very well behaved, and when one or two began to cause trouble, a gentle reminder from a parent that Father Christmas was watching seemed to take care of everything. Bessie was relieved when five o'clock finally rolled around and the castle doors were shut. The room wasn't too untidy, and as they weren't open again until the final evening on Christmas Eve, there was no rush to straighten and clear up anyway.

"Oh, thank you, Bessie," Margaret said when the group reassembled in the banquet room just after five. "I hope it wasn't too much trouble."

"It was fine," Bessie assured her. "Some of the children were really lovely."

"I almost missed them," Margaret said with a laugh. "I'll be glad to have my own room back on Thursday night."

"I've spoken to the chair of the board at the Alzheimer's Research

Fund, and they're going to send someone to staff their room for Christmas Eve," Mark told them all.

Bessie smiled. She hadn't really minded working the rooms, but she would much rather be out and about, wandering around the castle and chatting to her friends on Christmas Eve.

"It's been a crazy weekend," Mark said. "But we're through it now. Only the big Christmas Eve auction to get through and the first 'Christmas at the Castle' is finished. Initial figures suggest that it has been somewhat more successful than we'd originally hoped, so at this point it seems likely that we'll do it again next year."

A few people clapped politely. Mark grinned. "I hope you'll all plan on being involved again next year. But that's for another day. For today, I'll just thank you all for your very hard work and send you home. No one has to be back until Thursday afternoon around two. That should give us plenty of time to tidy rooms and double-check that everything is ready. I'm having dinner catered in again, and then the doors will open at seven for three hours of fun, food and fundraising."

Having been told that they could leave, most people didn't stay long after Mark finished speaking. Only a short time later, he and Bessie were locking up doors and making their way out of the building themselves. Henry followed them, double-checking every door along the way. Bessie frowned as she noticed how tired he looked.

"Henry, are you okay?" she asked as they reached the street.

"I'm fine," he answered automatically.

"No, really, how are you?" Bessie asked.

"I just have to pop over the road and check on the catering for Thursday," Mark said before disappearing into the restaurant across from the castle.

"Henry, you look really tired," Bessie tried again, resting a hand on his arm as she spoke.

"I am a little tired," Henry admitted. He glanced around as if making sure they were alone, and then leaned in towards Bessie.

"Laura's been acting strangely," he whispered. "Like something is wrong, but she won't tell me what."

"I didn't see her here today," Bessie said.

"No, she asked to be moved to Rushen Abbey for a while."

"Oh, dear," Bessie frowned. She liked Laura and she thought that Laura and Henry made a lovely couple. "Did she say why she wanted to move?"

Henry shook his head. "She just said she wanted a change of scenery," he told Bessie. "She said that all the bad things happening here were giving her nightmares."

"The poor girl," Bessie exclaimed. "Perhaps I should ring her and see how she is."

"I think she'd like that. She's said nice things about you since your Thanksgiving party."

"I'm sure I have her number somewhere," Bessie said. "But give it to me again, just in case."

Henry recited the number from memory. Bessie jotted it down on a scrap of paper and tucked the paper in her bag.

"I'll ring her in the next few days and see how she is," Bessie promised. "Maybe she's just feeling a bit homesick with the holidays coming up."

"I doubt that. I asked her if there was anything she missed from across and she said something about being happy that she'd managed to get away. I'm not sure what she meant, actually."

"I'll try to talk to her and I'll tell you how it went on Thursday," Bessie said. "Here's Mark," she nodded towards the man who was now crossing the road back towards them.

"We're all set," he said. "Let me get you home," he said to Bessie.

Bessie gave Henry a quick hug and then followed Mark to his car. The drive back to Laxey was a quiet one as Bessie wondered and worried about Laura and Henry. She was surprised when Mark stopped at her cottage; she'd been so lost in thought she hadn't noticed where they were.

"See you on Thursday around half one," Mark told Bessie as she climbed out of the car.

"Lovely," Bessie muttered distractedly.

Inside her cottage, she made herself a light evening meal. She tried to divert herself with her book, but her mind wouldn't focus. As soon as she was finished eating, she found the scrap of paper and rang Laura.

"Hello, dear, it's Bessie Cubbon. How are you?"

"Oh, Miss Cubbon, I wasn't expecting, that is, I didn't, oh, I mean, I'm fine, really," the other woman stammered.

"I know you were quite upset by Mr. Hart's sudden death and the vandalism at the castle. When I didn't see you there today, I thought I would ring and make sure you were okay," Bessie explained.

"That's very kind of you. I'm fine, really. I just asked if I could be moved to a different site. You're right, the goings-on at Castle Rushen have upset me. I thought maybe a different site would make a nice change."

"Where are you now, then?" Bessie asked, pretending she didn't already know the answer.

"I'm at Rushen Abbey," Laura replied. "It's shut for the winter, so we're doing a lot of cleaning and polishing and rearranging a few exhibits before the spring."

"That does sound like more fun than dealing with the hordes of overexcited children at 'Christmas at the Castle,'" Bessie said with a laugh.

Laura chuckled. "I enjoyed that too, but the castle was, well, unsettling, I suppose."

"Do you have a day off this week?" Bessie asked impulsively. "I'd love to buy you lunch and get to know you better."

"Oh, why, that's very kind, but I don't, that is, I suppose I could, but you don't have to pay."

"I'll pay this time, and if we enjoy each other's company as much as I think we might, you can pay next time. Would that work?"

"I'd like that," Laura said. "I don't know many people on the island yet, aside from the people at work. I could do with making some more friends."

"Excellent, what day works for you?"

"I'm off on Wednesday," Laura told her.

"Is there anywhere you'd especially like to try?"

"Oh, I don't know. I don't really know my way around the island yet or anything. I don't even know where you live or what's convenient for you. I assume you live somewhere near Ramsey, as that's where you had your Thanksgiving feast, but that day was the only time I've been to Ramsey aside from when I've visited the Grove Museum."

"I live in Laxey," Bessie told her.

"I've been to the Laxey Wheel," Laura replied. "But I'm not sure I could find it again if I had to."

"Let's keep things simple," Bessie suggested. "You're in Douglas, right?"

"Yes, I have a flat near the museum," Laura replied.

Bessie named her favourite Italian restaurant. "It's right on the promenade and the food is wonderful. Shall we say midday on Wednesday?"

"That sounds wonderful," Laura told her. "I'm really looking forward to it now."

Bessie put the phone down with a smile on her face. Laura seemed like a nice woman, but moving to a new home later in life could make finding friends difficult. Bessie could only hope that she could help, by being a friend and also by introducing Laura to others. She was still making a mental list of people she wanted to introduce to Laura when someone knocked on her door.

"Doona and John? This is a pleasant surprise," she exclaimed when she'd opened the door. "Do come in."

"Hugh's on his way," Doona told Bessie after she'd given her a hug. "We thought it was time for a long conversation about what's happening at Castle Rushen."

"You should have rung first," Bessie replied. "I would have baked something."

"Hugh's taking care of that," John assured her, after his own welcoming hug.

Before Bessie could press for more details, Hugh was knocking on

147

the door. Bessie let him in, and once he'd set the bakery boxes on the counter, it was his turn for a squeeze.

"What did you bring?" Doona asked.

"Fairy cakes, fruit tarts and a selection of biscuits," Hugh replied. He flushed as everyone looked at him. "I was hungry," he said defensively.

"You're always hungry," Doona said with a laugh.

Bessie switched on the kettle and started a pot of coffee brewing as well. The conversation was mostly about Hugh and his girlfriend, Grace, as Bessie made the drinks.

"You are going to propose on Christmas, aren't you?" Bessie demanded. "The poor girl has waited long enough."

"I hope so," Hugh replied. "I've saved up just about enough for a nice ring, anyway. I'm taking one of Grace's friends with me ring shopping so she can help me get something that Grace will like. Then I just have to work up the nerve to actually ask."

"You should ask her father first," Bessie said. "I know it's an old-fashioned notion, but I think Grace would appreciate it."

"I asked her father a long time ago," Hugh said, blushing. "One night, when we were across on our summer holiday. I'd had a bit too much to drink, you see, just a few beers, really, but more than I usually drink. Everyone went to bed except Mr. Christian and me, and he asked me what my plans were for the future. I just blurted out that I wanted to marry Grace."

"And what did he say?" Doona asked when Hugh stopped for a moment.

"Oh, he said he was happy to give me his blessing," Hugh said. "I'm really glad it happened like that, actually, because I don't think I could work up the nerve to ask him now."

"Just see to it that you ask her," Bessie said.

"Yes, I will," Hugh said, looking down at the table.

Bessie sighed. The poor man was so smitten that he wasn't thinking straight. Well, if he didn't ask her at Christmas, Bessie decided she'd have to give him a gentle push.

"Right, are we all ready to talk about the case, or rather cases?"

John asked as they all sat down with hot drinks and plates full of treats.

"I'd rather not," Bessie replied. "I'd rather none of it had ever happened."

John patted her arm. "I am sorry that you're mixed up in another murder investigation," he said. "Maybe the new year will be better for you."

"I certainly hope so," Bessie said emphatically.

"But for now, I have two dead bodies and an act of vandalism to investigate and I can use all the help I can get," John added.

"I was hoping Pete would have the first case all wrapped up by now, at least," Bessie said.

"He's working on it," John said. "But it isn't as straightforward as we might have hoped."

"What does that mean?" Bessie demanded.

"We were hoping to find fingerprints or fibers or something left behind by the killer, but in a hotel room like that there is just too much of everything. Besides, a number of key suspects have excuses for having been in the room, which explains away their prints." He shook his head. "We weren't able to get anything off the body that even hints at who killed him."

"But it was definitely murder?" Bessie checked.

"It was definitely murder," John confirmed.

"So, motive, means and opportunity?" Hugh asked.

"It seems like a lot of people had motives," John said.

"But not good ones," Bessie argued. "I mean, the charity volunteers at the castle didn't like him, but I can't imagine any of them killing the man just because he didn't like their decorations."

"Michael Beach had more reason to dislike him than that," Doona pointed out.

"Because he could make a fuss over the punch," Bessie said. "But that still doesn't seem like much of a motive."

"What about Richard or Carolyn Teare?" Hugh asked.

"I don't know," Bessie said thoughtfully. "He and Carolyn had a fight about something, but she won't say what. It's hard to imagine that it could have been that serious, though."

"Is Richard the jealous type?" Doona asked.

"He's never seemed to be in the past, but I don't really know them well enough to be sure," Bessie said. "I think I'd suspect him over her, though, if I had to choose one of them as the murderer."

"Who else does that leave?" Hugh asked.

"The other committee members," John said.

"Oh, none of us had any reason to kill him, surely?" Bessie replied.

"He upset everyone at the castle, didn't he?" John asked.

"Well, yes, but Marjorie and Mary and I didn't really mind," Bessie said. "We just kept working on getting things ready and left Carolyn and Mark to fight it out with Mr. Hart."

"What if one of them decided they didn't like the direction Mr. Hart wanted to take the event?" Hugh asked.

"We weren't going to let Mr. Hart and Carolyn ruin anything," Bessie said firmly. "We told the volunteers they didn't have to change anything if they didn't want to. It would have all worked out in the end."

"So you don't suspect any of the committee members?" Doona asked.

"Not at all," Bessie said stoutly.

"What about Natasha Harper?" Doona suggested.

"I don't really know much about her," Bessie replied. "She didn't get along with Mr. Hart, but no one did, aside from Carolyn. He accused her of stealing his clients, but she didn't seem upset by it. If she had a motive, I don't know what it was."

"She replaced Mr. Hart at the event, didn't she? Was it worth killing for the job and the publicity?" Hugh asked.

"I can't imagine so," Bessie said. "She was already redoing Thie yn Traie for Mary. She just helped out at 'Christmas at the Castle' because she was already here. I suppose she might have received a bit of local publicity, but she works across mostly. She's only here because Mary is paying for her to be here."

"Maybe she fell in love with the island and wanted to stay forever," Doona said. "That does happen to people."

"But Mr. Hart wasn't her competition over here," Bessie pointed out. "He was only on the island because Carolyn brought him over, and he was just meant to be here for two days. He needed to get back to start filming a new television show, apparently."

"I wonder who'll be replacing him in that," John mused.

"I suppose, if it's Natasha, that could be a motive," Bessie said. "But I can't see how she'd be sure she'd get the job if something happened to him."

John made a note in his notebook. "I'll see what I can find out about that," he said. "What about the staff at the castle? Any of them have any reason to kill the visiting designer?"

Bessie shook her head. "He was horrid to Laura and upset her, which made Henry angry, but it's a long way from upset or angry to murder. Neither Henry nor Laura would hurt a fly."

"In your opinion," Hugh said.

"Laura has only been on the island for a few months," John said. "I'm not sure you can totally discount her. We're looking into her background to see if she knew Mr. Hart before she moved across."

"I hadn't thought of that," Bessie said. "But I still don't think she's a killer."

"What about the vandalism?" John changed the subject.

"I can see just about anyone doing that," Bessie said. "We all hated that room. It was pretty horrible."

"But actually destroying the room took some effort," John told her. "Do you really think Mary or Marjorie did it?"

"No," Bessie shook her head. "Actually, it's hard to imagine why anyone did it. It seems like pointless destruction. I can't see that anyone gained anything from it."

"Except the room isn't open to the public," Hugh pointed out. "Maybe this Natasha person didn't want anyone to think she'd worked on such an ugly room?"

"Actually, she did a great job with the room's centerpiece," Bessie said. "If anything, she should have been proud of what she'd accomplished."

"How does the vandalism tie in with the murder?" Doona asked.

"If we knew that, we'd be closer to solving both," John told her. "We aren't sure if they're connected or not, although we have to believe that they are."

"I thought Pete was pretty sure that Michael was responsible for the vandalism," Bessie said.

"He is," John said. "I'd feel better if we had some idea of a motive, though."

"He hated Mr. Hart and hated to see a tribute to him," Doona suggested.

"Possibly," John said.

"If he hated Mr. Hart that much, it suggests he could have killed him as well," Bessie said.

"And now we can't question him about it," Hugh said.

"What about his death? Was that murder?" Bessie asked.

"We're waiting for the autopsy results," John told her. "At this point, I'm not ruling anything out."

"I can't see any reason for anyone killing him," Bessie said after a moment's thought. "He was just an ordinary person."

"I understand he was flirting with Carolyn Teare quite heavily," John said.

"He was flirting with her and with Natasha," Bessie said. "But he was quite drunk as well."

"We're trying to retrace his steps from when he disappeared the first time," John said. "And we're talking to his friends and acquaintances on the island and across. It's possible that his death has nothing to do with the other incidents."

"But it doesn't seem likely," Bessie said.

John shrugged. "We're also talking to Carolyn and Richard Teare, and everyone at the Alzheimer's Research Fund. We're looking for motives for murder as well as any hint as to why he might have wanted to kill himself."

Bessie sighed. "We didn't talk about means or opportunity for any of this."

"It seems that just about everyone involved with 'Christmas at the Castle' knew that Mr. Hart had moved to the Seaside Hotel," John said. "No one appears to have an unimpeachable alibi for that evening."

"Michael told me that Mr. Hart was trying to blackmail him," Bessie said. "Maybe he was doing the same with others?"

"We're looking into Mr. Hart's finances," John told her. "I'm not sure if that will tell us anything or not, but it needs doing. No one else has come forward with a story like Michael's, at least not yet. We're also considering the possibility that someone came over just to kill the man, but that raises the question of how they knew where to look for him."

"Maybe he rang them when he got to the hotel," Doona suggested.

"Aside from his call to Michael, there were no outgoing calls from his mobile or his room. He might have rung someone from the Teares' home before he left there, but Carolyn says he didn't."

"We're jumping all over the place and I'm getting confused," Bessie said. She finished her tea and poured herself more. "So where are we?" she asked them all.

"For Mr. Hart's murder, it seems that everyone involved with 'Christmas at the Castle' had the means and the opportunity to kill him," John said. "Nearly everyone also had some sort of motive, although some are much stronger than others, of course. If you had to name a murderer from that list, who would it be?" he asked Bessie.

Bessie nibbled a biscuit while she thought. "I suppose, if I had to, I'd go for Richard Teare," she said eventually. "I think he had the strongest motive, even though I'm not really clear on what it was. If not him, then Michael. If Mr. Hart was trying to blackmail him, then he had a pretty strong motive."

"Anyone else want to throw a guess in?" John asked.

"I'd vote for Richard Teare as well," Doona said. "I don't want to blame poor Michael, as he has ended up dead, too."

"It would be neater if it was Michael," Hugh said. "He killed Mr.

Hart, destroyed the tribute room, and then killed himself. That makes perfect sense."

"Michael's death is complicated," John said. "The man kept disappearing, so it's impossible to say who knew where he was and who didn't. His phone had several cryptic texts on it that we can't trace. It seems someone was in contact with him when he was missing, but we don't know who."

"You can't work out where the calls came from?" Bessie asked.

"We're working on it," was all that John could tell her.

"I think we're just going around in circles," Bessie said after another biscuit.

"I don't think we've solved anything, that's for certain," Doona said.

"Sometimes it helps to just talk things through with a different audience," John said.

"But not this time," Bessie added with a rueful smile.

John shrugged. "I think it's helped me shuffle up the suspects a bit," he said. "I'll be taking a closer look at Richard and Carolyn Teare tomorrow."

"If Richard did kill Mr. Hart because he was jealous, then maybe he killed Michael for the same reason," Doona said.

"It's a possibility that needs looking into," John replied.

"I'm having lunch with Laura Meyers on Wednesday," Bessie told the others. "Maybe she saw or overheard something relevant, but she doesn't realise it."

"She has been questioned rather extensively," John said.

"But maybe no one asked her the right questions," Bessie countered with a smile. "I'm sure you didn't ask her who she thought the murderer was, but she might have her own ideas and they might be interesting."

"You know I don't like you spending time with suspects," John said.

"She isn't a serious suspect, surely," Bessie countered.

"We're still investigating her background," John reminded her. "Make sure you meet somewhere public."

"We're having lunch at that little Italian place on the promenade. It's very public," Bessie told him.

"Very good. Are you meeting with anyone else in the next few days?" John asked.

"I've nothing else planned, but it is a very small island," Bessie retorted.

"Please let me know if you hear anything that might be relevant," he instructed her. "Mr. Hart's killer was smart, and if Michael was murdered, it was very cleverly done."

"Did Michael leave a note?" Bessie asked.

John shook his head. "I can't answer that," he said. "But I will tell you that we're actively looking for handwriting samples from the man. I wish the autopsy results would hurry up, though."

"It's getting late," Doona said. "I have to work at eight and I know John will want to be in his office by eight at the latest."

"I'm not working until the afternoon tomorrow," Hugh said. "But I promised Grace that I'd take her to breakfast before she has to go to work."

"Did she find a teaching position, then?" Bessie asked.

"She's still working as a supply teacher, but she's covering someone's maternity leave at the moment, so she's going to be working for the rest of the school year," Hugh replied.

"How nice for her," Bessie said.

"She's teaching Reception, and she loves the little ones," Hugh said. "Most of them still listen pretty well. The big problem is keeping their attention for more than five minutes."

"Now you all must take some of these treats home with you," Bessie said as the party began to break up. "I can't possibly eat all of these on my own."

Bessie packed biscuits and tarts into small bags and handed them around. She took a few things for herself and then gave the bulk of the leftovers to Hugh. "I know you'll manage to eat them all," she said with a laugh.

She locked up the door behind them all and then checked that both doors were locked up tight. Switching off lights as she went,

Bessie headed for bed, her book in her hand. Once she was ready for bed, though, she decided it was too late to read. She slid under the covers and sighed deeply. Usually, after a session with John and the others, she felt as if they'd moved the investigation forward. Often she ended up with ideas for things she could do to help John learn what he needed to know. Tonight she felt as if they'd simply wasted their time. At least Hugh had brought biscuits and fairy cakes. The evening wasn't a total loss.

CHAPTER 11

*B*essie was in the shower on Monday morning when she started thinking about Christmas shopping.

"Christmas is Friday," she told her mirror image as she stepped out of the shower.

She stuck her tongue out at herself and then dressed quickly. She'd been so busy at Castle Rushen that she'd let the whole month of December slip away from her. While she preferred to do her shopping early in the month, before the shops became too crowded, she had no choice now but to head into Ramsey immediately.

Or almost immediately. She rang and asked for a taxi to Ramsey at half eight. Most of the shops wouldn't open much before nine, even if it was the week of Christmas. With some time on her hands, Bessie headed out for her morning walk. It was chilly and raining lightly, but she took deep breaths of sea air and didn't mind the weather one bit. The idea of Christmas shopping made her feel like a small child again and she found herself humming a Christmas carol as she walked. Shaking her head at her foolishness, Bessie returned home and made herself a mug of hot chocolate as a special treat.

When Dave, her favourite driver, arrived right on time, Bessie felt even more cheerful.

"Good morning, Dave," she called as she locked up her cottage. "And Happy Christmas."

"A very Happy Christmas to you too, Aunt Bessie," he replied. "But don't be so quick to lock your door. I have a little something for you."

He opened his boot and pulled out a small wrapped box. As Bessie reopened her door, he crossed to her.

"You shouldn't have," she exclaimed.

"It's just a little something," he said. "I told the wife that I've been driving you around for such a long time that it feels as if I should give you a present, and she found this and thought you might like it. If you don't like it, please pretend you do the next time you see her."

Bessie laughed. "I'm sure it will be perfect," she replied. "But I'll save it for Christmas if you don't mind."

"Oh, no, that's fine," Dave told her. "And please don't feel as if you have to reciprocate."

"But of course I have to get you something," Bessie protested. "The giving part of Christmas has always been my favourite part anyway."

Dave continued to protest as he drove Bessie to Ramsey. He let her out in front of the large bookshop that was one of her favourite places in the world.

"Please don't buy me a present," he said baldly.

Bessie just laughed. "I'll see you outside of ShopFast in three hours," she replied.

Inside the bookshop, Bessie couldn't resist spending a little bit of time looking at books for herself. She forced herself to stop after she'd found the fifth title she wanted. "Nothing like buying Christmas presents for oneself," she muttered as she made herself turn away from the mystery section.

In the self-help section, she found a book on basic home repairs that she thought would be helpful for Doona. Next she found a gorgeous cookbook full of quick and easy recipes that she hoped might be useful for Hugh. John was trickier to shop for, and Bessie found herself wandering around the shop a second time, happily browsing and thinking. Having no idea what the man liked to read in his free time, but knowing that that time was limited, she finally settled on a book of the best science fiction short stories of the past year.

Now she walked around again, this time looking for the one perfect present that could be given to just about everyone she knew. Every year she bought a simple little something that was appropriate for just about anyone and gave that same item out to her various friends around the island. One year it had been a simple but elegant candle holder, another year she'd found a small enamel box with the Laxey Wheel on it, and just last year she'd given everyone a photo frame with a Celtic design along the border. If she had more time, she'd have travelled into Douglas to look at the museum shop for something just right, but she was really hoping to get her shopping finished in this one trip.

After a while, she decided that she'd have to give up and move on. She paid for her purchases and headed out into the busy streets of the town. It only took a few minutes for Bessie to begin to feel fed up with the crowds. Everyone seemed to be pushing and shoving and trying to get ahead of everyone else. Babies were crying, cars were honking, and Bessie thought seriously about heading for a café to sip a drink until it was time for Dave to take her home.

Instead, she squared her shoulders and stood as tall as she could. At five feet, three inches she wasn't exactly intimidating, but she did her best to march through the crowd directly to where she wanted to go. The little specialty gift shop had a huge window display of very expensive cut crystal. Bessie pushed her way inside and sighed with relief. There were only a handful of other shoppers in this particular shop and several shop assistants were bustling around.

"Ah, Bessie, I'm so glad you stopped in," one of the women called. "I was going to ring you later today. We just received a shipment of something I think you'll quite like."

Bessie smiled at her. "Thank you for thinking of me, Carol," she replied, smiling at the woman who was co-owner of the shop. "I'd love to see what you're talking about when you've finished there."

Carol was just ringing up a customer, and of course the man in question had trouble getting his credit card to work and then changed his mind about half of his items. Finally, he wanted everything gift-wrapped. By the time he left, Bessie felt as if she'd thoroughly explored the entire small shop at least twice. While she found some lovely things, she couldn't find anything that she thought might be the special something Carol was talking about.

"Come with me," Carol said as she stepped out from behind the counter.

Bessie followed the woman through the shop and then through a door marked "Staff Only."

"They were meant to be here by the first of December," Carol told her. "But there was a problem with the production or something. Anyway, we finally received the shipment this morning and I haven't even put them out yet. We commissioned them ourselves and we're hoping to do one a year."

She opened a large box on the table in front of them and then pulled a much smaller box from inside it. Handing the small box to Bessie, she grinned.

"Go on, open it yourself," she suggested.

Bessie looked at the pretty red and green box. The top of it had the shop's name printed on it in silver letters. "The box is pretty," she remarked as she lifted the lid. She gasped with pleasure and surprise as she looked at the contents.

"It's pewter," Carol told her. "We commissioned a local artist to draw Castle Rushen in pencil and then had the drawing made into pewter ornaments."

Bessie pulled the round disc from its box. It was heavier than she'd expected it to be. It was the dull-silver colour of polished pewter, with Castle Rushen depicted on the front. The back of the disc had the name of both the shop and the artist as well as the year.

"How much are they?" Bessie asked, holding her breath.

When Carol named a price that Bessie felt was more than reasonable, she smiled. "I'll take, oh, lots of them," she told the other woman.

Carol laughed. "You might need to be a bit more specific than that," she said. "Or you can just buy the whole box and be done with it."

As there were a hundred ornaments in the box, Bessie decided not to buy them all. She quickly counted up how many she needed for friends, adding in all of the "Christmas at the Castle" committee members and charity volunteers to the list. When she was finished, she wasn't all that far off of buying at least half of the box.

"I'm going to give you a discount for buying so many," Carol told her at the till. "Come back and visit us in the new year. I'd love your thoughts on what other landmarks you'd like to see in future years."

"I will," Bessie promised. The charge on her credit card was large, but Bessie didn't mind. She loved the gorgeous ornaments and couldn't wait to start giving them out to her friends.

"Oh, can you wrap just one of them?" she asked before she left the shop. She enjoyed wrapping gifts herself, but she wanted to give Dave his present when he took her home, in case she didn't see him again before Christmas.

Feeling as if she'd accomplished a great deal, Bessie headed towards ShopFast. Along the way, she passed a shop that did custom gift baskets and found she couldn't resist stopping in.

"I need a basket for a friend who is in her early forties and needs to be spoiled," she told the woman behind the counter. It only took a few minutes for them to put together a basket of treats for Doona.

"Anything else today?" the woman asked.

While Bessie was very tempted to make up a basket for herself, the bag of books she'd bought herself weighed heavily on her arm and her conscience. "Not today," she said eventually.

"It will take me a few hours to make up the basket," the woman said once Bessie had paid for everything. "Do you want to stop back or should we deliver it somewhere?"

As Bessie's large shopping bag was full of books and Christmas ornaments and she still had grocery shopping to do, she opted to have the basket delivered. "Deliver it to me," she told the woman. "I'd like to give it to my friend myself."

ShopFast was nearly out of shopping trolleys because of the crowds. Bessie put her shopping bag into her trolley and shook her head. It took up far too much of the space she needed to put groceries in.

"Bessie, why don't I put that bag in my boot for you?" a voice at Bessie's elbow asked.

"Dave, what are you doing here?" Bessie asked, surprised to see her taxi driver standing beside her.

"I came in to get some things for my lunch," he explained. "I have about half an hour now before I'm meant to pick you up, so I thought it would be a good time to eat."

Bessie insisted on carrying the bag out to the taxi herself, even while Dave tutted at her.

"I'll see you in half an hour," she told him. "If I can get through the crowds by then."

"There's no rush," he assured her. "I don't mind a long lunch break."

Bessie rushed around the shop as much as she could, trying to focus on what she needed for meals for the rest of the week, excluding Christmas. She'd do another shop on Thursday morning for Christmas itself, she decided. For some reason the shops were usually nearly deserted on Christmas Eve, at least the ones that bothered to open, and the turkeys would be discounted as well. It was closer to a full hour when she finally paid for her shopping and headed out to find Dave.

"It's the time of year," he said over her apologies. "I sometimes think the island population doubles or something. Where are all these people the rest of the year?"

Bessie laughed, but Dave was right in a way. She could understand the crowds in the retail shops, but surely the grocery shops shouldn't be that much busier. People had to eat all year around, didn't they?

Dave helped Bessie take all of her shopping into the cottage when they arrived back.

"And this is for you and your lovely wife," she told him as she handed him the wrapped box.

"I told you you shouldn't," he protested.

"I'll take it back if you take yours back," she offered.

Dave chuckled. "Oh, no. The wife is quite pleased with herself for finding that. You'd better keep it."

"Then you'll have to keep yours," Bessie said with a grin.

"Fair enough," the man said. He gave Bessie a quick hug. "Happy Christmas, if I don't see you again before Friday," he said.

"Happy Christmas," Bessie echoed.

Bessie made a light lunch, promising herself something more substantial in the evening. She'd spent so much time in Castletown lately that she felt as if she hadn't taken a proper walk in months. With lunch tidied away, she headed out to walk until she was too tired to continue.

It didn't seem to take any time at all to get to Thie yn Traie, and from there Bessie pushed onwards, determined to give her legs a proper workout. An hour later she'd walked much further than she usually did and her legs were starting to complain. Turning back towards home, she slowed her steps and focussed on breathing deeply. She was convinced that sea air had a great deal to do with her continued good health and she was determined to take in as much as possible.

As she approached Thie yn Traie, she spotted someone standing near the bottom of the steps that went up the steep cliff.

"Bessie, there you are," Mary exclaimed as Bessie drew closer. "I was just thinking about sending a search party."

"I didn't realise I was missing," Bessie told her.

"I saw you walk past the other way," Mary explained. "We were working in the room the Pierce family called the 'great room,' the one with all the windows that look over the beach. Anyway, I saw you walk by and I thought I'd just pop down and catch you on your way back. But you didn't come back for ages. I'm just about frozen."

"I'm so sorry," Bessie told her. "Obviously, I had no idea, or I would have turned around sooner. I was just enjoying my first proper walk in a long time."

Mary flushed. "I don't mean to suggest that you should do anything to accommodate me," she said quickly. "And please don't think that I'm going to be spying on you every time you walk by, either. I just happened to notice you and I thought you might like to come up for a cuppa, that's all."

"I'd love one," Bessie said. Now that she was standing still, the cold air seemed to be going right through her.

"Come on up, then," Mary invited. "Natasha's here. We can show you our plans for the house."

Bessie followed Mary up the steps, holding on tightly. At the top she was reminded again of the vast size of the mansion that had been built as a summer home. From the beach, only the great room with its entire wall of windows could really be seen, but up close, the mansion seemed to spread out in every direction with several separate wings, a garage block and a small security booth.

"It is rather ugly, isn't it?" Mary asked brightly.

Bessie laughed. "And you still want to buy it?"

"We are buying it," Mary told her. "The Pierces are willing to take such a low price for it that George can't pass it up, even if he doesn't want to live here. Once the sale is complete and the renovations are done, then I can start trying to persuade George to actually sell the Douglas house and move out here."

"I hope you can persuade him quickly," Bessie told her. "I'd love to see the house occupied."

"Oh, Elizabeth, our daughter, will be moving in soon, even if George and I don't," Mary told her as she led Bessie to the side door. "She can't wait to get a little further away from us. Her wing is the first thing we're redecorating, in fact."

Bessie knew that Mary had been spending a lot of time at the house, but it still felt cold and empty when they went inside. She followed her friend down a long corridor, past the huge great room and into a large and modern kitchen. The cabinets were dark wood; the countertops were white, as were the tile floors. Stainless steel appliances shone all around the space, which Bessie thought was probably the same size as her entire cottage.

"Sit down, I'll put the kettle on," Mary told her.

Bessie perched on a stool that was in front of the long island that almost dominated the room. "Marble?" she asked as she touched the cold white surface in front of her.

"Yes, it wouldn't be my first choice, but George won't hear of replacing it. He thinks it's gorgeous."

"It is lovely," Bessie said. "But very cold."

"The entire house is cold," Mary replied "I'm hoping we can warm things up a little bit, but it isn't going to be easy or inexpensive. George doesn't care about kitchens, as he expects that we'll have staff to work in them, but I'd love to get rid of most of the staff and do at least some of the cooking myself. That means I really want to redo this kitchen to make it warm and inviting."

Bessie glanced around. "I'm not sure where you'd even start," she confessed.

"I think I'd start by cutting it in half," Mary told her. "It's far too large to feel cosy, but I suppose it works well if you have half a dozen people working in it."

"We don't want to add any walls," a voice said sternly from one of the doorways. "We can make the room feel much warmer with small changes," Natasha added as she walked in.

"Natasha and I haven't quite reached an agreement on what we want to do with this room," Mary told Bessie, smiling.

"Walls disrupt flow," Natasha said. "We need to change the floors; that will make a huge difference. And if we cover the windows with curtains in place of the cold metal blinds, that will help, as well."

She stopped and shook her head. "You didn't come to listen to us argue," she said to Bessie. "It's so nice to see you somewhere other than Castle Rushen."

Bessie laughed. "I only live a short distance down the beach from here. It's funny that we only ever see each other when we're both in the south of the island."

"We should see more of each other after the holidays," Natasha told her. "Assuming that Mary and George approve my plans, I'll be moving in to oversee the remodel. No doubt we'll see each other on the beach. I like to jog a few miles every morning."

"You know I love your plans," Mary said. "Except the ones for the kitchen, but we can talk about those after Elizabeth's wing and the master bedroom are finished. It's George you have to convince."

"And he isn't even going to listen to me until after the first of January," Natasha said with a sigh.

"George is quite excited about Christmas this year," Mary explained to Bessie. "He's decided to make up for all the years when he was too busy with work to pay any attention to the holiday. He has the entire house in Douglas covered in a thin layer of decorations, and he's bought presents for everyone from the children and grandchildren to the entire staff and dozens of people he's only met once or twice." She shook her head. "When the children were small, I used to ask him every year to get involved, but he was always busy. Now I'm sorry, because he's taken over every job and left me with nothing to do but work on the remodelling here."

"You've been busy with 'Christmas at the Castle,'" Bessie pointed out.

"Yes, and I am grateful that he's done as much as he has, really. But it's hard to feel in the Christmas spirit when you've not done any shopping or decorating," Mary said.

"I finally did my shopping today," Bessie told her. "And it has put me more in the spirit of things, although I do find 'Christmas at the Castle' makes me feel quite festive."

"It's lovely," Mary agreed.

"I've enjoyed being a part of it," Natasha told them both. "And it should look good on my CV as well."

"I was just talking to some friends about the television programme that Christopher Hart was meant to be making," Bessie said, hoping she wasn't changing the subject too obviously. "We were wondering what the people in charge will do now that he's no longer available."

"I've heard a rumour that they've asked Jason King to take over," Natasha told her. "It's only a rumour, but my source is pretty reliable."

"Should I know who Jason King is?" Bessie asked.

Mary laughed. "You don't watch television, do you? He was on a home improvement show for a few years, but then he had a fight with the producer about something or other and he left. Every time a new show like this is mentioned, his name comes up, but I don't know if he's ever been seriously considered for anything. He behaved quite badly, if the stories are to be believed."

"Oh, they should be," Natasha said. "I was a production assistant on that show, and the man was terrible to work with. He was late nearly every day and he always tried to blame other people when he didn't turn up on time. He was never happy with his dressing room, the food, the rooms he had to decorate, the quality of the materials he had to work with." She waved a hand. "I could go on, but I won't. I just hope he's learned something in his years away from the spotlight."

"I couldn't possibly ever be on telly. But you seem like you'd be a natural," Bessie told Natasha. "Is that a goal of yours?"

Natasha shrugged. "I just want to keep working," she said. "I'm passionate about designing. If someone offered me a show like the one Christopher was going to do, I'd do it, but for the publicity, not just to be on telly. What I really want is to be in demand so much that I can set my own prices and work only when I want to work. I want a flat in London and one in Paris and I want..." she trailed off. After a moment, she laughed. "Listen to me, babbling the dreams of my over-active imagination at you. Now you must share your crazy dreams with me, so I don't feel so bad."

Bessie smiled. "You mustn't feel bad," she said firmly. "You're still young, and it's only natural that you're ambitious. You're also very talented, so I hope you manage to achieve something like the success you're hoping for."

"I'll tell you what I dream of," Mary said. "I dream of owning a little cottage on the beach where I can live all by myself. The children can visit, of course, and George, too. I love him dearly, but sometimes living with him is hard work."

"I dream of living inside an enormous library," Bessie joined in. "I could have a little bed in one corner and I suppose I'd have to have someone bring me food three times a day, but all I would have to do is read all day long."

"You could have a spa tub in one corner, with some sort of shelf above the water level to hold your book while you soaked," Natasha suggested.

She opened the sketchpad she was carrying and began to draw. Before Bessie's eyes, her dream library began to take shape.

"This would be the sleeping corner," Natasha said. "We could put a small bed, maybe with a canopy and curtains so you could shut out the world if you wanted to." Natasha sketched a bed, piled high with enormous pillows.

"That looks wonderful," Bessie gasped.

"Then, in the opposite corner, a sumptuous bathtub." The woman drew the huge tub and then added water and bubbles to it. Bessie could almost feel herself sinking into it.

"Of course, we'd curtain off the tub area and probably add a small water closet in its own room as well," Natasha said, almost to herself. "A sink in with the water closet would be good. In another corner, you'd want a refrigerator and some cupboards for snacks and drinks in between those meals that will be magically delivered."

Bessie laughed. "You're far too good at this," she said as she looked at the sketch. "I'll just take this drawing to the planning board and see what they think of it as an extension to my cottage."

Natasha carefully pulled the sheet out of the book. "I know you're only teasing," she said. "But you may as well keep this. Maybe you will find a use for it some day."

"I should think you'd want to keep it," Bessie protested. "Surely you might be able to use it for someone?"

Natasha shook her head. "I don't think many of my clients want to live in libraries," she laughed.

"Now you must design my cottage," Mary said.

The trio talked about various floor plans for the imaginary cottage while Mary poured the tea and passed around biscuits and mince pies. Natasha sketched several different ideas while they debated.

"I think having everything on one level would be perfect," Mary said.

"But I'd worry about security," Natasha argued. "Maybe it's the

Londoner in me, but I like to be at least one flight of stairs away from intruders."

"I don't think you'd have to worry about that on the island," Bessie said. "It's very safe here."

"I'm not sure about that," Natasha muttered.

Bessie flushed. "I know Mr. Hart was murdered here, but I suspect his killer was someone from across who came over specifically to kill him. And we don't know what happened to Michael."

"I think Michael killed himself," Natasha said sadly.

"Why?" Bessie asked.

"He was very, well, depressed, just before he died," she replied. "He wouldn't really talk to me about anything. I thought we were becoming friends, but then he started drinking so much and hanging all over Carolyn Teare." She shook her head. "I don't know what happened, but he certainly changed just in the short time I knew him."

"You don't think he killed Mr. Hart, do you?" Bessie asked.

"I can't imagine why he would have," Natasha answered. "Unless Christopher was serious about the blackmail."

"What blackmail?" Mary asked, looking confused.

"Michael told me that Christopher threatened to press assault charges against him unless Michael paid him some money," Natasha explained. "Michael was worried that if Christopher did press charges, he'd lose his job and find it impossible to find another one."

"I didn't know that," Mary exclaimed. "Poor Michael."

"Murdering the man seems a bit extreme, though," Bessie said.

"Maybe it was an accident?" Natasha asked. "The police haven't said anything about what they found in Christopher's hotel room. Maybe Michael and Christopher had another fight and Michael hit him too hard or something like that. I can't see Michael killing Christopher in cold blood, but I really didn't know him all that well, either."

"I barely knew him at all," Mary said. "I thought he seemed like a nice young man, and if he had lost his job because of the altercation with Mr. Hart, I'd have found him a position somewhere else."

"Too bad he didn't know that," Natasha said sadly.

"He did," Mary replied. "We had a little chat right after the fight. I told him to come to me if he found himself in any trouble and I'd make sure it all worked out."

Natasha frowned. "He never told me that," she said. She stood up abruptly. "I really should get back to work. I'm drawing up the final plans for Elizabeth's bedroom."

"Can you leave the plans for the rest of the house with us so I can show them to Bessie?" Mary asked.

"As long as she promises not to talk about them with anyone. I've worked too hard on them to have them stolen at this point," Natasha answered.

"I won't say a word," Bessie promised.

Natasha nodded and then strode out of the room, leaving her sketchpad behind. For another half hour, Bessie admired the beautiful drawings that Natasha had made of the various spaces within Thie yn Traie.

"It all looks wonderful," Bessie said. "Before today, the only room I'd been in previously was the great room. Did I miss the sketch for that one?"

"There isn't a sketch for that one yet," Mary said. "It's just such a huge, cold and unwelcoming space, even Natasha hasn't been able to come with any ideas for redoing it."

"Maybe you should divide it up," Bessie suggested.

"George doesn't want to do that, and I understand his point. It's a wonderful room with fabulous sea views and adding walls anywhere would make it feel chopped up somehow. We're leaving it as it is for now, but I have high hopes that inspiration will strike at least one of us before the rest of the house is completed."

"How long will that take?"

"Oh, a year or more," Mary replied.

"That's a long time for Natasha to be over here," Bessie remarked.

"Oh, she's not going to stay here for the entire project," Mary replied. "She's spending Christmas here, and much of January, and then she'll go back to London and start work on something else. The plan is that she'll fly over once a month after that to make sure things stay on track, but we'll hire a local project manager to work on-site as well. Between them, things should go smoothly enough, and when everything else is just about finished, then we'll worry about the great room space."

Bessie nodded. She'd had her cottage updated and extended a couple of times since she'd bought it, but she'd never done anything on the sort of scale Mary was undertaking. "Well, I wish you good luck," she said.

"Thank you. I think we're going to need it," Mary laughed.

Bessie turned the pages of Natasha's sketchbook, admiring the beautiful drawings a second time. Towards the back of the book there were a few pages of notes, written in beautiful handwriting.

"What exquisite writing," Bessie exclaimed.

"Natasha does calligraphy," Mary told her. "Sometimes she writes out quotes and the like and then frames them as decoration in some of the rooms she designs."

"I've always wished I'd spent more time on my handwriting," Bessie said. "I'm just not patient enough. I want to write everything down as quickly as I can, but what I end up with is often illegible, even to me."

Mary laughed. "I know what you mean. I write lists for George of little chores that need doing, but he can't ever read them."

"Or maybe that's just what he tells you," Bessie suggested.

Mary laughed again and then insisted on taking care of the tidying up herself. "That's what I love about being out here," she told Bessie. "There isn't any staff, aside from Natasha, so I can do a bit of my own housework. I'm sure I'll soon grow tired of it, but for now it's quite the novelty."

Bessie walked the short distance home thinking about Mary's words. Housework certainly wasn't Bessie's favourite thing to do, but she did love taking care of her little cottage. Having staff would feel uncomfortable to her, she realised as she let herself into her home. She glanced around, noticing that the floors needed a good vacuuming. I suppose it's just as well I don't want staff, she thought to herself as she pulled out the vacuum.

CHAPTER 12

*B*essie woke up on Tuesday morning feeling like Christmas was suddenly much too close for comfort. After her shower, she dressed and had a quick breakfast of cereal and fruit and then headed out for her walk. It was raining heavily, so she kept the walk short, turning around as soon as she'd reached the holiday cottages.

It's a good thing I have lots to do today, she told herself as she stood dripping in her kitchen. She hung up her wet things and dried herself off as best she could. She then stood in the middle of the kitchen lost in thought for a moment.

Somewhere, in one of the bedrooms upstairs, she had a box of Christmas decorations. Most years she didn't bother with them, but this year she felt as if she should make an effort. Perhaps all the beautifully decorated trees at Castle Rushen had inspired her.

As she sorted through several boxes, most of which were filled with books, she thought about the Christmases she'd celebrated over the years. Christmas had been a much quieter affair when she'd been a child growing up in America than it was today. It had been mostly a religious celebration with less emphasis on shopping and presents and more on celebrating Christ's birth. When she'd first moved back to the island, she'd usually spent Christmas with one or another of her friends and their families. As those friends grew older and married and had families of their own, Bessie began to celebrate the holiday on her own, which she didn't mind in the slightest.

Bessie firmly believed that Christmas was for families and that those families could best enjoy their holiday if they didn't have to entertain guests. She had no shortage of places she could go if she'd wanted to; her advocate and his family invited her over every year, as did a number of other friends around the island, but she was quite content at home with a few good books. For the last two years, she'd had Doona over for Christmas dinner. Doona had grown up on the island, but didn't have any family still living on it. The two women enjoyed a traditional Christmas dinner together and exchanged small gifts in the afternoon, leaving Bessie to enjoy her alone time in the morning and evening. Nothing had been said yet, but Bessie assumed that Doona was planning on joining her again this year.

"Won't she be surprised when she sees the tree," Bessie chuckled to herself when she found the right box. It was right at the back, as it had been at least five or six years since she'd opened it.

Bessie carried the awkward box down into the kitchen and set it on the counter. After she cut through the tape she'd used to seal it, she opened it. Inside everything was neatly packed, just as she'd remembered.

The small artificial tree came out first. It was very old, one of the first artificial trees that she'd seen on the island many years earlier. She'd bought it on impulse that year, excited by the idea of having a tree that would last for years to come. It had definitely seen better days, even though it had been only used occasionally. After sliding it into the stand, Bessie did her best to straighten out the branches. With some effort, it began to look a little bit better.

Decorations will hide the worst bits, she thought eventually. She'd been working on the tree with it on the kitchen table, but it was just a little bit too big to remain there. Lifting it down to the floor, she looked around the small space. There didn't seem to be any good place to put it. Carrying it carefully, she headed into the sitting room, eventually standing it in one corner, partially blocking a bookshelf.

"It's only for a few days," she muttered to herself, suddenly seized with an irrational desire to rescue the hidden books. "You'll be fine back there," she told the books. "I haven't forgotten you, I promise."

Shaking her head at her foolishness, she went back into the kitchen to find the tree's decorations. An hour later the little tree was sparkling and festive. Bessie stood back and gave it a critical look.

It could do with Natasha's magic touch, but it didn't look too bad, she decided. Back in the kitchen, she pulled out a few other decorations, which she scattered around the house. At the very bottom of the box she found her childhood Christmas stocking. It was tattered and threadbare, and she was almost afraid to pick it up in case it simply fell to bits, but apparently it was sturdier than it looked and it held together while she inspected it.

It was plain red with a strip of white at the very top, exactly like Christmas stockings ought to be. Bessie was sure that her mother had sewn it herself. Her name, "Elizabeth," was stitched across the top in tipsy letters that Bessie remembered her older sister stitching for her when Bessie had been about five. Not wanting to put the stocking back into the now empty box and leave it as the only decoration not being used, Bessie wondered what she should do with it. Eventually she set it on top of another bookcase in the sitting room before she carried the empty box up to the spare bedroom and then headed back down to see how it all looked.

Deciding it was just about perfect, Bessie went back upstairs and pulled out rolls of wrapping paper. Feeling a bit overwhelmed by the sheer number of ornaments she'd purchased, she measured the first box and then cut several sheets of paper to size. Some considerable time later she sat back and surveyed the huge pile of brightly wrapped gifts. It had taken far too long, but the job was done and she was relieved. She carefully packed all of the ones for the people at Castle Rushen into a box and then piled everything else under her Christmas tree.

"Now it truly looks like Christmas in here," she said aloud. While she ate her soup and sandwich, she wondered what she wanted to do with her afternoon. The rain was still pouring down, which limited her options. She'd just finished the washing-up when an idea popped into her head.

I'll make Christmas cookies, she thought to herself. I haven't done that since I can't remember when. While not an English or Manx tradition, Bessie's mother had added Christmas cookies, which were becoming an American custom at the time, to their family holiday when Bessie had been small. Over the years, Bessie's sister had often sent her different recipes that they had enjoyed at their home in the US. Now Bessie pulled down her recipe box and began to look through it.

An hour later, with sugar cookie dough in the refrigerator and butter softening on the counter for chocolate chip cookies, Bessie decided to take a short walk. She walked as far as Thie yn Traie and then turned back for home. She'd only gone a few steps when she heard something behind her. Turning around, she saw someone climbing down the steps from the house above.

"Miss Cubbon? I was wondering if I could have a word with you," Natasha called.

Bessie stopped and waited for the girl to join her. "How are you?" she asked when Natasha had crossed to her.

"I'm okay, but I sort of wanted a bit of advice," she replied.

"It's too cold to stand still," Bessie said, shivering. "Why don't you walk back to my cottage with me? We can talk there."

"I suppose Mary won't miss me if I'm only gone for a short while," Natasha said. "She's gone into Douglas for something, anyway."

Back at the cottage, Natasha paused in the doorway. "Treoghe Bwaane," she read from the small sign at the door. "Is that Manx, like Thie yn Traie?"

"It is," Bessie told her. "It means Widow's Cottage."

"Oh, I didn't realise you were a widow. I thought Mary said to call you Miss Cubbon."

"I'm not a widow," Bessie explained. "I've never married. The cottage had the name when I bought it."

"Oh, I see."

"But you didn't come over to talk about my cottage," Bessie said. "What can I help you with?"

"It's Richard Teare," Natasha said. "I suppose I was flirting with him a little bit at Castle Rushen the other night, but he seems to have taken me rather more seriously than I'd intended. He keeps ringing me and I can't seem to find a polite way to discourage him."

"Why be polite?" Bessie asked as she put the kettle on.

Natasha laughed. "I'm tempted not to be, of course, but he's a very wealthy man with wealthy friends and my business relies heavily on word of mouth. I can't afford to anger him, but I don't intend to have an affair with him, either."

Bessie busied herself with teacups and saucers while she thought. "I assume you aren't answering his calls," she said eventually.

"I answered the first time he rang. He was talking about having me do some design work in his offices and I could really use the job."

"But that wasn't why he rang?"

"Oh, he started off talking about that, but then he asked me to have dinner with him and it became clear that he was hoping to, well, have more than just a professional relationship."

"And what did you say to that?"

"I told him I don't get involved with married men," Natasha replied. "He gave me some line about his marriage being a mess and how Carolyn had been cheating on him, but I said that didn't matter."

"Carolyn was cheating on him?" Bessie asked.

"Apparently," Natasha replied. "He said he'd been all wrong about that, though. He told me that he thought she was having an affair with Christopher Hart, but then he found out it was really Michael Beach that she was seeing behind his back."

"Really?" Bessie gasped.

"I don't know how true any of it is, though," Natasha added. "The man was trying to persuade me to start an affair with him. He might have just been making accusations to try to win my sympathy."

"I suppose so," Bessie said thoughtfully.

"Anyway, I don't suppose you have any advice for dealing with him?"

"I don't, really," Bessie told her. "The best thing you can do is avoid him, but if you really want that job with him, that won't be easy."

"I do really want that job," Natasha said fiercely. "It could open a lot of doors for me if he tells people he hired me to redo something that Christopher did for him."

"Did Mr. Hart leave behind a lot of unhappy customers?"

"Christopher did elaborate designs that told a story or painted a picture or some such thing," Natasha explained. "But a lot of what he did was totally impractical for day-to-day use. He charged ridiculously high prices, though, so no one was about to start making changes after he'd finished, at least not right away."

"I can only suggest that you try to limit any meetings you have with the man to very public places," Bessie said. The kettle boiled and Bessie poured them both tea.

Natasha sipped hers before she answered. "I can certainly try," she said. "I've told him I'm really busy at Thie yn Traie for now, which is true. We're meant to be meeting in the new year. Maybe he'll have found someone else by then."

"Maybe you need to hire an assistant and make sure he or she goes to any appointments with you," Bessie suggested.

"That's not a bad idea," Natasha said. "Richard suggested that we meet in London in January, which worries me. I think he's more likely to cheat on his wife when he's in London."

"I'd have to agree with that. I've never heard any rumours about him cheating on Carolyn, but if he was doing so when he was off the island, I probably wouldn't hear."

Natasha nodded. "He seems smart enough to keep his extramarital affairs away from such a small island where everyone knows everyone else's business."

The pair sipped their drinks and talked about the weather and Natasha's plans for Christmas.

"I was going to go home, but Mary invited me to stay at Thie yn Traie and keep working. It was too good of an offer to pass up. I'm hoping to get ahead on my plans there so I can start work on my next job as soon as possible."

"What's next?"

"I have a small office redesign to do for a company in Birmingham that just moved to a new building. It isn't going to win any awards or garner any excitement, but it's the sort of little job that keeps me going between the big assignments that I love."

"It isn't a career I ever considered, but it seems like it would be really enjoyable," Bessie told her.

"It's cutthroat at the top," Natasha said. "You have to be single-minded and focussed if you want to get to the sort of position that Christopher Hart held."

"And are you hoping to get there?"

"Oh, yes. I'm planning on it. I want to be doing television in the next twenty-four months and securing really big, high-profile clients in between. I'm hoping this job in Birmingham is my last little job ever."

"Well, good luck to you," Bessie told her. "You did wonderful things at 'Christmas at the Castle,' and your plans for Thie yn Traie are lovely. If I could afford it, I'd have you make over my cottage before you get too famous."

Natasha laughed and looked around the snug kitchen. "It could do with a total makeover, of course, but it really does suit you just the way it is."

When the girl had gone and Bessie was rolling out sugar cookies, she wondered what Natasha had really wanted. Bessie couldn't imagine why the girl would have come to her for advice on dealing with Richard Teare. The information she'd shared was interesting, and Bessie thought she ought to pass it along to John, but she wasn't sure she trusted that any of it was true. She frowned as she slid star and Christmas tree cutouts into the oven. After setting the timer, she grabbed her telephone.

"John, it's Bessie. I had a strange conversation today that I think I should share with you," she said when her call was connected.

"I'll come over after work," John offered. "I have a few things I want to talk with you about as well."

"I'll have Christmas cookies for you," she replied.

"I'll bring Chinese food, then, shall I?"

"That sounds good," Bessie agreed.

Bessie mixed up and baked chocolate chip cookies and then made some icing for the sugar cookies. She couldn't remember now what she'd even bought the small bottles of food colouring for, but she was glad that she had them. A thin layer of green icing covered her trees and she used yellow for the stars. She debated spending a bit more time on them, maybe doing something more elaborate on the trees, but then thought she might try one first. As she wiped away the crumbs from around her mouth, Bessie decided that the cookies were perfect just the way they were.

She was still tidying the kitchen when John knocked on her door a short time later.

"It smells like butter and vanilla in here," John remarked as he set the box of food down on the counter.

"Or it did," Bessie laughed. "Now it shall smell like sweet and sour chicken instead."

"You must tell me about Christmas cookies," John said as they sat down with full plates and fizzy drinks. "Is it an American tradition?"

"Yes, indeed. I'm sure it originally comes from some European tradition or another, but the Americans have really taken it to heart. When I was a child, my mother would bake both cookies and mince pies and Christmas cake, but my sister stopped doing anything other than cookies when her children were small."

"Cookie is just the American word for biscuit, isn't it?"

"Yes, although American cookies tend to be sweeter and more indulgent than a typical biscuit," Bessie replied. "You don't usually get chocolate chip biscuits or iced sugar biscuits, do you?"

John shook his head. "Chocolate-covered digestives are nice."

"But the digestive itself isn't very sweet," Bessie said. "American cookies are meant to be a real treat."

179

"I must make sure I don't eat too much dinner, then," John said. "I want to save room for a few cookies."

After the meal was cleared away, Bessie piled cookies on a plate and put it in the centre of the table. She handed John a small plate and then sat down with one of her own.

"This is delicious," John said after his first bite of a star.

Bessie managed to eat a Christmas tree of her own before the kettle boiled. While she made the tea, John seemed to be eating steadily. She passed him his drink and sat down with her own, smiling when she noticed that the large plate was now over half empty.

"You must take these away," John said, pushing the plate towards Bessie. "They are really good and I mustn't eat any more."

Bessie laughed and slid the plate as far from John as the table would allow. "It's Christmas," she pointed out.

"Yes, but that's the excuse I use at work when I eat mince pies and at Christmas dinner when I eat Christmas pudding. I can't keep indulging myself or I'll have to buy all new clothes before January."

"You'll be fine," Bessie assured him. "You've lost some weight. It would be good for you to put a few pounds back on."

"Anyway, you said you wanted to talk to me," John changed the subject.

"Yes," Bessie agreed. "Natasha visited me today. She said she wanted some advice."

John listened and took notes while Bessie recounted the visit. When she was finished, he looked at her thoughtfully. "What do you think she wanted?" he asked after a moment.

"I'm not sure, but I can't imagine it was advice on how to deal with Richard Teare," Bessie replied. "I'm hardly the person to give advice on dealing with extramarital affairs."

"Perhaps she just needed a sounding board," John said. "Everyone knows you're a good listener."

"I suppose," Bessie said.

"Anyway, it's interesting that she told you that Richard said his wife had had an affair with Michael Beach. That ties in with some of the other evidence we've gathered."

"Does it?" Bessie asked, surprised. "I didn't really believe that."

"No? Who did you think was lying, Richard or Natasha?"

Bessie sighed. "I can see Richard saying just about anything if he really was trying to get Natasha to start an affair with him," she said. "But I don't trust Natasha, either."

"Maybe you can talk to Carolyn," John suggested. "See if you can find out if it's true."

Bessie frowned. "I'd rather not," she said. "I hate prying into people's private lives, and I'm not terribly fond of Carolyn, either."

"It would be really helpful to know," John said seriously.

"I can try. But I won't see her until Thursday and we'll be busy with the Christmas Eve auction."

"Maybe you could ring her," John suggested.

Bessie shook her head. "I'm just about prepared to try to ask her about her romantic life when I see her, but I can't possibly ring her up and ask her who she was sleeping with. I simply can't."

John nodded. "No, I suppose you're right," he mused.

"I'm in Douglas tomorrow for lunch," Bessie said. "Maybe I'll see her in town. As I understand it, she spends a lot of time shopping in certain pricey boutiques. I can try stopping in a few."

"I'd appreciate it," John replied.

"Can you tell me why you need to know?" Bessie asked.

"It's all part of building up the bigger picture," John said. "We have two unexplained deaths and an act of vandalism. We're trying to tie them together or prove they aren't connected, one or the other."

"So who Michael was involved with at the time of his death could be relevant," Bessie said.

"Especially if it was the woman who was responsible for bringing Mr. Hart to the island," John said.

"You aren't suggesting that Michael killed Christopher because he thought the man was involved with Carolyn?"

"We're looking at every possibility," John replied. "If Carolyn was seeing Michael, it might explain why he was so quick to argue with Mr. Hart. There may have been some personal jealousy at work there."

"I'll see what Carolyn has to say. Did you talk to the girl at the estate agency who was involved with Michael?"

"I did, but I can't tell you anything she said," he replied.

Bessie laughed. "I'll just have to assume that they were no longer involved at the time of Michael's death."

"They weren't," John confirmed. "And she has an unbreakable alibi for the night he died, as well."

Bessie nodded. "I don't suppose you were able to get any fingerprints from the house where he was found," she said.

"We only fingerprinted the items we're pretty sure Michael, or someone who was with him, brought into the house. Only Michael's prints were found on everything at the scene."

"So you think he killed himself?"

"That's one possibility," John said. "We aren't ruling out any others, though."

A knock on the door interrupted their conversation. Bessie opened the door to Doona.

"I hope I'm not bothering you," she said. "But I just baked some mince pies and I wanted to share some with you before I ate them all myself."

Bessie laughed and let her friend in. "John and I were just talking about the case again," she told Doona. "Let me make you some tea and you can try some of my Christmas cookies."

Doona groaned. "I can't," she exclaimed. "I must have eaten half a dozen mince pies already today."

"The stars are really good," John told her as he pulled the plate back across the table. "And so are the chocolate chip ones."

"What's wrong with the Christmas trees?" Bessie teased as she poured Doona some tea.

"I haven't tried one of them," John replied. "In the interest of fairness, I suppose I must, though."

Bessie unwrapped the plate of mince pies that Doona had brought and put them on the table next to the cookies. She quickly refilled the cookie plate and then sat back down.

"I hope I'm not interrupting," Doona said after she washed a cookie down with her tea. "I won't stay if you need privacy."

"Oh, no, we were just talking in circles anyway," John said. "We need a breakthrough of some kind, I just wish I knew what."

"Maybe my talk with Carolyn will help," Bessie said.

"Every little bit of information helps," John told her.

"These are wonderful," Bessie said to Doona after she'd eaten her first bite of a mince pie. "Maybe I won't bother making any this year and just enjoy yours."

"I can't believe how nice these cookies are," Doona countered. "Why don't the British do cookies?"

"I have no idea," Bessie told her. "Of course this is just a small sampling. My sister used to make dozens of different varieties every year."

"I didn't know there were that many types of cookies," John said.

"Oh, you'd be surprised," Bessie replied. "She used to send me her two or three favourite new recipes every Christmas. I must have fifty or more cards from her from over the years."

"What could be better than these?" Doona asked, taking another chocolate chip cookie.

"Gingerbread, spritz, snowballs, thumbprints, double chocolate chip, oatmeal, peanut butter," Bessie laughed. "I went through the recipes today and those are just the ones I remember. There are so many more."

"Maybe once the holidays are over, I'll borrow a few recipes," John said. "I'd like to do more baking and cooking with the kids when they're here. Cookies seem like they might be fun."

"They are fun," Bessie agreed. "But they take time. You can only bake a dozen at a time on a tray, and most recipes make four or five dozen. They also need a lot of watching. Most of them are quite thin and can burn very quickly. I'll lend you a few of the easiest recipes to start with and you can work your way up to the more complicated things."

"Or maybe I'll just stick to the easy ones," John said.

"I'd love to borrow the chocolate chip recipe," Doona said. "But I don't think I can. I don't think I could be trusted to have them in the house. I'd just eat them all."

"Or you could bring them to me, like you did the mince pies," Bessie suggested.

"I live closer to you than Bessie does," John pointed out with a smile.

Doona laughed. "I actually stopped at your house first," she told him. "But you weren't home. I have a plate of mince pies in the car for you as well."

"I should stop eating all of Bessie's then," John said.

"I'll be making more," Bessie told him. "I have to do the mince pies tomorrow, actually. I told Mark that I'd bring some to the castle on Thursday for all of us hard workers to enjoy as we get everything ready."

When both plates were empty, John sat back from the table and sighed. "This has been wonderful," he said. "But I have to get home."

"I do, too," Doona said.

John stood up and began to stack dirty dishes by Bessie's sink.

"I'll just do the washing-up before I go," Doona said.

"Don't be silly," Bessie replied. "I can manage a few plates and cups. You both need to get home and get some sleep."

John insisted on helping Doona, though, and the pair quickly had Bessie's kitchen back in order.

"Before you go, you must see my tree," Bessie exclaimed as the pair finished.

"Oh, Bessie, it's lovely," Doona said, clearly delighted. "I'm so glad you decorated this year."

"I think 'Christmas at the Castle' has been a good influence," Bessie replied. "I felt like I had to do my part."

"It's really nice," John said. "Since I won't be here for Christmas, really, I didn't do any decorating at my house. Maybe I should have put up a small tree, though. It makes such a difference."

"This stocking looks very old," Doona remarked, holding up Bessie's stocking.

"It's from my childhood," Bessie told her. "I thought it made a nice extra decoration."

"It does," Doona agreed. "And so do all those presents."

Bessie looked down at the pile of gifts under the tree. "Somewhere under there are one or two things with your names on them," she told the pair. "But you shall have to wait for Christmas Day to have them."

Doona made a token protest, but Bessie could tell she was just pretending to be upset. Waiting for Christmas made the season much more special, especially for adults.

Bessie showed her friends to the door and let them out. She watched, smiling to herself, as Doona handed a plate of mince pies to John. John waited until Doona was safely in her car and driving away before following.

"That might just still work out," Bessie said aloud as she locked her door.

Upstairs, she got ready for bed and then read for a short while. She'd found a few mysteries set at Christmas from her collection, so now she lost herself in someone else's Christmas case. It was nice to forget about Christopher Hart and Michael Beach for a short while, anyway.

CHAPTER 13

*A*fter her usual morning routine, Bessie got busy making her mince pies. In the past, she'd often made her own mincemeat, but this year she simply hadn't had the time. When the pies were in the oven, they filled the house with the smell of spices and pastry. Bessie smiled to herself. The ones Doona had brought had been very good, but her own would taste better, just because she'd done them herself.

While they were cooling, Bessie took another short walk, as she was unlikely to find time to do so later in the day. She walked to the last of the holiday cottages and then returned home, feeling as if she didn't want to go as far as Thie yn Traie and find herself with company yet again. By the time her taxi arrived to take her into Douglas, the mince pies were all carefully put away and the kitchen was tidy.

Bessie's least favourite driver, Mark, was behind the wheel, and he didn't move up in her estimation as he honked from the parking area next to the cottage. Bessie had packed a couple of mince pies into a bag to give to her driver, but she was so rushed that she forgot to grab them. Once she was settled into the passenger seat, she was almost glad she had.

"And how are you today?" Mark asked.

"I'm well. How are you?"

"Oh, just dandy," Mark said grumpily. "I've to take you into Douglas and then pick up a box at one of the shops and run it up to Ramsey for a customer who's too lazy to go down to Douglas herself. Nothing like transporting inanimate objects, is there?"

"At least the box won't complain about your driving," Bessie pointed out, biting her tongue when she was very tempted to do just that as Mark swerved around a parked car.

"No one complains about my driving," Mark told her. "I'm a good driver. I've never had a ticket, well, except for parking tickets, and that's when I'm not driving." He laughed at his own joke and Bessie forced herself to smile.

"So are you ready for Christmas or is this a big shopping expedition to buy all your presents?" Mark asked.

"I'm done shopping. I'm just meeting a friend for lunch," Bessie replied. "Have you finished your shopping?"

"Oh, I don't do any of that. That's the wife's job."

"What about a present for her?"

"She'll buy something she wants and that'll be from me. I pay for it, so that's fair enough."

Bessie pressed her lips together. The woman had married Mark; she must have known what she was getting into.

"I hear you've been caught up in another murder or two," Mark said. "What is it with you lately? I've been driving you around for years, and now all of a sudden, everyone you know is getting murdered."

Bessie shook her head. "None of the cases have had anything to do with me," she said firmly. "I suppose I've just been in the wrong place at the wrong time lately."

"All the time, lately," Mark said.

"Yes, well, it isn't as if I enjoy it," Bessie snapped.

"No, I'm sure you wouldn't," Mark replied. He pulled up on the Douglas Promenade and stopped. "This close enough to where you're going?" he asked.

Bessie sighed. She loved to walk, but she didn't have a great deal of time before she was meant to be at lunch. If she got out here, she'd need to hurry to make it on time. She opened her mouth to protest and then shook her head. "This is fine," she muttered as she reached for the taxi's door.

"Happy Christmas to you," Mark said loudly as she climbed out. "Don't forget when you get your bill that we all appreciate a little Christmas bonus this time of year," he added.

Bessie kept her eyes straight ahead, not wanting to give the man the angry look she felt he deserved. He thought he warranted a Christmas bonus, did he? At least that explained why he'd been so chatty on the drive. That was his version of being friendly, apparently.

By the time Bessie reached her destination, she had calmed down. Mark was never going to change and she didn't have a choice but to put up with him as long as the taxi firm continued to employ him. The service was always in demand and she simply couldn't request her favourite driver all the time. Dave wasn't always available.

"I'm meeting a friend," Bessie told the host, who led her to a table for two in a quiet corner. Bessie had only just hung her coat on her chair when Laura rushed in.

"Oh, I knew I was late. I'm so sorry," Laura exclaimed when she reached the table. "I didn't know exactly how much time to allow for the walk over here and it turns out I didn't allow quite enough. I'm terribly sorry."

Bessie held up her hand to stop the flow of words. "I just arrived," she told the other woman. "You aren't late anyway; I was a minute or two early."

"I hate making people wait," Laura said, blushing bright red as she sat down across from Bessie.

"I'm nearly always early," Bessie told her. "But I'm quite content to sit on my own for a bit, as well."

"Not me," Laura said. "I always feel so conspicuous when I'm sitting on my own in a restaurant. I feel as if everyone is looking at me and thinking that I haven't any friends."

Bessie laughed. "I suppose people might think that about me," she said. "But I know it isn't true. I treat myself to lunch or dinner out once in a while and I never mind being alone. I always bring a book and enjoy myself."

"Maybe I should try that," Laura mused.

"I'm not sure Henry would understand why you'd want to be on your own, would he?" Bessie asked.

"No, he's such a dear man, though. I'd never do anything to upset him."

Bessie swallowed a dozen questions about Laura's relationship with Henry. It really wasn't any of her business. Bessie did feel quite protective of Henry, though, and she worried that Laura might break his heart one day.

"I hope you two are happy together," she said after a moment.

"We are," Laura told her. "He's just what I needed after, well, for my new beginning."

"How are you finding the island?" Bessie asked.

"I love it here," Laura told her. "It already feels like home and I can't imagine moving back across now."

"Do you still have family across?"

"An aunt that I was never close to and a few cousins I barely know. I'm sure they haven't even noticed I'm gone." Laura laughed, but Bessie thought she saw a flash of pain in the other woman's eyes.

"Well, we're certainly glad you're here," she told the woman. "Henry most of all."

The waiter arrived to take their order, and they requested drinks while Laura looked over the menu.

"What's especially good?" she asked Bessie after a short time.

"I haven't had anything here that wasn't good," Bessie told her. "If you like pizza, they make theirs with a very thin crust. The pasta is excellent and I love their Bolognese sauce. Whatever else we get, we have to get some garlic bread."

When the waiter returned with their soft drinks, both women ordered the spaghetti Bolognese. Bessie also asked for a plate of garlic bread.

"You'll love it," she told Laura. "I've never met anyone who didn't."

"Is everything at the castle ready for tomorrow night, then?" Laura asked as they sipped their drinks.

"I think so. We're all going to spend the afternoon there tomorrow making sure of it, anyway, though."

Laura laughed. "You are such a dedicated group of volunteers," she said. "Most of the volunteers I've worked with in the past were more interested in being seen to be helping than actually doing anything."

"I enjoy a bit of hard work," Bessie told her. "Especially when the outcome is so gratifying."

"I understand the event has already exceeded expectations in terms of money raised," Laura said. "And the auction should bring in quite a bit more, shouldn't it?"

"I certainly hope so. We've a lot of really wonderful prizes available."

"Including the contents of each room, right?"

"That's right. Did you want to bid on any of them?"

"I do like the rainbow room," Laura told her. "But I can't imagine what I'd do with all of those trees and their decorations. I have a one bedroom flat with just barely enough room for the small tree I put up last week."

"Yes, I think the room contents will all have to go to very wealthy people with huge houses to decorate. I know I don't have the space for any more decorations than what I already have," Bessie said. " Anyway, did you do something similar in the UK for work?" Bessie changed the subject.

"Yes, I worked for one of the stately homes in Derbyshire. I did all of their fundraising and special event planning."

"I'm always curious what makes people consider moving to the island," Bessie said. "It seems like a rather large lifestyle change."

"It has been," Laura agreed. "But I needed a change."

Bessie nodded. She was grateful that the garlic bread was delivered then, as Laura seemed to be somewhat upset with the way the conversation was going.

"So what do you like to do, aside from work?" Bessie asked after they'd both eaten their first slice of hot bread dripping in melted butter and garlic. "I'm not being nosy, I'm trying to think who you might enjoy meeting that might have similar interests," she added.

"I don't do much, outside of work," Laura said apologetically. "I like to read when I have the time and sometimes I do a bit of cross-stitch, but mostly I work and then sit and watch telly, aside from when I'm spending time with Henry, of course."

Bessie kept the conversation light and general as they finished off the bread and then ate their spaghetti. While she found herself liking the other woman, she felt as if Laura was deliberately keeping the conversation superficial. Bessie didn't want to push her, as they barely knew one another, but she also wanted to help the woman if she could.

"I'm sorry you were upset by the situation at Castle Rushen," she said after she'd insisted that they order pudding.

"I'm fine, really. I just felt like I needed a change of scenery," Laura said, staring into space.

"I hope it hasn't ruined the castle for you. It's a really beautiful place."

"It's one of the finest medieval castles I've ever seen," Laura replied. "It's beautiful, but I don't think I'll go back until after 'Christmas at the Castle' is all cleared away."

Bessie reached across the table and patted the other woman's hand. "I'm sorry that you were upset," she said softly.

Laura looked at her and then blinked back tears. "Thank you," she whispered.

Two decadent slices of chocolate cake, Laura's with ice cream and Bessie's with cream, arrived.

"Oh, this is too much," Laura exclaimed as the plate was placed in front of her. "I've been eating mince pies and all manner of lovely treats lately. I should have said no to this."

"Chocolate is good for the soul," Bessie told her firmly.

Laura took a bite. After she swallowed, she smiled at Bessie. "It's so good," she said. "And just what I needed."

Bessie nodded. "If you ever want to talk about whatever's upsetting you, I'm happy to listen, but only if you need a sympathetic ear."

Laura flushed and then bent her head over her plate. Bessie ate her own cake slowly, watching the other diners and leaving Laura alone with her thoughts. As the waiter cleared the plates, Bessie ordered coffee for them both.

"I don't have to rush away anywhere," she explained to Laura. "If you have somewhere else you need to be, though, don't feel that you need to stay."

"No, I'm fine for a bit longer," Laura said. "Coffee sounds perfect to wash down that rich cake."

"Are you spending Christmas with Henry?" Bessie asked.

"Yes, and all of his family," Laura told her. "He has an astonishing number of nieces and nephews, at least that's how it seems to me. I was an only child."

"Henry comes from a large family," Bessie recalled. "I hope they don't overwhelm you."

Laura nodded. "I've warned Henry that I'm used to very quiet Christmas celebrations. I've told him I might have to leave early if it all gets to be too much."

"They're all wonderful people," Bessie told her. "I'm sure they'll try to make you feel welcome, which might actually be worse than if they ignored you."

Laura laughed. "You could be right about that," she said. "The thing is, well, you see, my ex-husband, he didn't like crowds or family so we always spent Christmas just the two of us."

"Sometimes that's nice, too," Bessie said. "Just some quiet time together."

"But it wasn't nice," Laura blurted out. "He was, he, that is, he wasn't a very nice man."

Bessie patted Laura's hand. "I'm sorry," she murmured.

Laura blinked hard several times. "When Mr. Hart started yelling and screaming, it just reminded me so much of him," she said softly. "It took me ten years to finally walk away from being treated so badly and then I only managed it because he hit me so hard that I ended up in hospital. After they patched me up, they made me talk to someone about what was happening at home and I finally realised that I needed to leave."

"Good for you," Bessie said.

"It wasn't easy, but the divorce was final a few months ago."

"And you decided that you needed a change," Bessie said.

"I did," Laura agreed. "He'd moved a few miles away from the flat we'd shared, but I used to run into him once in a while, and everywhere I went I saw people who knew us as a couple. It was really difficult. Many of them thought I was making things up. He was the perfect gentleman in public, you see."

"Well, I'm glad you got away and I'm glad you ended up here," Bessie told her. "The island is lucky to have you."

Laura flushed. "Thank you," she said. "I hope you're right."

While they sipped their coffee, they talked more about Christmas and other neutral topics.

"I suppose I must get home and do something useful like laundry," Laura said eventually, after glancing at her watch.

"Yes, I have lots of little chores to get through today, as tomorrow is going to be busy and the next day is Christmas," Bessie replied. "But I've thoroughly enjoyed our lunch and I'd like to do it again sometime soon."

"I'd really like that," Laura told her. "You're the only person I've talked with about my ex-husband, well, aside from Natasha."

"Natasha?" Bessie said in surprise.

Laura flushed. "We had a chat one day at Castle Rushen," she said. "I was upset about everything that was happening and Natasha found me crying in one of the back rooms. She was so sympathetic that I ended up telling her all about my ex."

"It's good that you had someone you could talk to."

"Yes, and she really understood as well," Laura told her. "She and Michael had just had a fight and, well, she told me that he'd swung at her."

"She must have been very upset," Bessie said.

"Yes, she was," Laura agreed. "It was that day when she'd gone for a walk with him, before he disappeared for the afternoon."

"Can you remember what she said happened?" Bessie asked.

"I probably shouldn't be repeating it," Laura replied anxiously.

"I'm just surprised, that's all. Michael seemed like a nice man."

"But he punched Mr. Hart. He had a bad temper. Natasha said that he tried to kiss her and she told him to stop and that's when, well, he lost his temper. Luckily he missed when he swung at her."

Bessie nodded. "I hope she's told the police about the incident," she said.

Laura shrugged. "I'm not sure why she would. It isn't like she's going to press charges against Michael now."

"No, but the more they know about the man, the more quickly they can work out exactly what happened to him," Bessie explained. "It sounds as if his temper was getting the best of him just before he died."

"I think he killed Mr. Hart," Laura confided in Bessie. "He was really angry when he punched him, and then after Mr. Hart was killed, Michael started drinking all the time. I think he was trying to forget about the murder. It wouldn't surprise me if he committed suicide in remorse."

"It's all very sad," Bessie said neutrally. "I just hope the police can work it all out soon."

"I know I'll sleep better once they've closed the case," Laura said emphatically. "Even though I'm not still working at the castle, I still find the whole matter very upsetting."

"I'd better get home and finish up my pre-Christmas chores," Bessie said reluctantly. "I'll ring you in the new year and we'll do this again."

"Next time is my treat," Laura replied.

"Oh, and Happy Christmas," Bessie said, handing the woman the small wrapped box from her handbag. "I have something for Henry as well, but I'll give it to him at the castle tomorrow night."

"Oh, you shouldn't have," Laura exclaimed. "I didn't get you anything, and you bought lunch as well."

"It's only a little something," Bessie told her. "I bought the same little thing for everyone who worked on 'Christmas at the Castle.' I just hope it won't bring up bad memories when you see what it is."

"I'm sure I'll love it. Thank you so very much."

Bessie gave the woman a small hug and then they both headed out of the restaurant. Outside a cold wind was blowing and Bessie quickly buttoned her coat while she walked to the nearest taxi rank. Laura walked that far with her.

"Thank you again," she told Bessie.

"You're welcome. I'm so glad everything has worked out for you and that life brought you to the island."

"I am, as well."

With that, Laura continued on her way. Bessie was about to climb into a taxi when she remembered that she was meant to try to speak to Carolyn. With a sigh, she turned and headed for the nearest boutique. Half an hour later, she'd visited nearly all of Carolyn's favourite shops without any luck. As she pushed open the door to the last possibility, she heard a familiar voice.

"I'd like it better in green," Carolyn was saying to a harassed-looking shop assistant. "Or maybe blue would be better."

Carolyn turned slowly in front of the large mirror. She was wearing a red sequined dress that tightly hugged her slender figure. "No, the red is just all wrong."

"It's very festive," Bessie commented.

"Ah, Bessie Cubbon, how delightful to see you," Carolyn said. "But what brings you here? I can't imagine this is your sort of shop."

Bessie glanced around at the designer dresses and shoes that were elegantly displayed around her. "No, it really isn't," she agreed. "But I was walking past and I saw you and thought I'd stop and see how you are."

She hadn't seen Carolyn from outside the shop, but she hadn't tried looking in the window either. It didn't really matter, as Carolyn didn't question her words. "I'm fine, I suppose," Carolyn replied. "Just trying to find something suitable for tomorrow night."

"I'm really looking forward to tomorrow," Bessie told her. "And, dare I say it, I'm really looking forward to 'Christmas at the Castle' being over."

"Yes, I know what you mean," Carolyn replied. "It's been such hard work, and so upsetting at times. Losing dear Christo was so difficult."

"I know you two were good friends," Bessie said, hoping her emphasis on the word friend would spark a reaction.

"We were twin souls," Carolyn said, taking a tissue from the counter behind her and touching it to her eyes. "We understood each other perfectly. If I'd been a few years younger, we might have been lovers as well, but it's better that we weren't, I suppose. Taking our relationship further might have spoiled things between us."

"It's a shame you had that falling out just before he died," Bessie said, feeling mean as she did so.

"We didn't have a falling out," Carolyn snapped. "Richard and Christo had a disagreement, that's all. I had to pretend to take Richard's side, of course, but Christo knew I didn't mean it."

"The vandalism of the room you were decorating in his honour must have been a huge shock," Bessie suggested.

The shop assistant had been hovering around Carolyn with a bored look on her face, but now she looked interested. Carolyn noticed and waved her away. "I'm talking to my friend," she said. "Go and see if you have anything else that might suit me while I do that." She turned back to Bessie. "The vandalism was heartbreaking," she said. "And it's even worse thinking that Michael might have been responsible for it."

"You and Michael were friends, too," Bessie commented in her most innocent tone.

Carolyn frowned. "We were friends," she agreed. "I'm on the board of the charity where he works, so we knew each other before 'Christmas at the Castle.' I was on the committee that hired him, actually. Then, working at Castle Rushen together naturally brought us even closer."

"Did you think he had a violent temper?" Bessie asked.

"Because he punched Christo?" Carolyn laughed. "Christo was being difficult," she explained. "And, dare I say it, I do think that

Michael was just the teeniest bit jealous of my friendship with the man. Michael seemed to think that he and I could, well, be more than friends, if he played his cards right."

"I see," Bessie said.

"Of course I'd never cheat on Richard like that," Carolyn added. "But it is such fun to flirt, just a little bit. I didn't mean to give Michael the wrong idea." She glanced around the tiny shop and then leaned in close to Bessie.

"I do worry that I drove him to it," she whispered.

"Drove him to what?" Bessie asked.

"Drove him to kill Christo and then himself," Carolyn answered.

"I thought you thought Richard killed Christo," Bessie replied.

"Oh, that was just a passing fancy," Carolyn said with a wave of her hand. "Richard wouldn't hurt a fly, really."

The shop assistant returned from the back of the shop with a huge pile of gowns in her arms. "This is all we have in your size," she told Carolyn.

Carolyn yawned. "This is taking too long. Send them all to my house and I'll pick one and send the rest back," she said. The girl frowned but nodded.

"I must get changed and get back to the house," Carolyn told Bessie. "Natasha is coming over to help me redesign a few rooms."

"Really? I thought Mr. Hart did your whole house last year."

"He did, but some of the rooms are ready for a change," Carolyn said. "See you tomorrow."

She disappeared behind a curtain, leaving Bessie with the frazzled assistant.

"Did you need something?" the girl asked Bessie, her look clearly suggesting that she doubted they would have anything that might suit Bessie.

"No, thank you," Bessie said politely. She headed out into the cold and made her way back to the taxi rank. There she climbed into the first cab in the queue. It wasn't from her usual service and Bessie didn't know the driver. She found herself giving the man directions, first to Laxey and then to her cottage.

"This sure is pretty," he said when he pulled up in front of her home. "I didn't even know this was here. Maybe I'll bring the wife and kids over to play on the beach in the summer."

"It's a small beach and it can get quite crowded," Bessie cautioned him. "But I think it's the nicest beach on the island."

"We've only just moved here from Cumbria. The kids are looking forward to splashing in the sea when it gets warmer."

Bessie paid him, including a generous tip, and then headed into the cottage. Even though she was still quite full from lunch, she found herself nibbling on the mince pies that she'd intended to give to her morning taxi driver. She was just finishing off her ironing pile when someone knocked on her door.

"Hugh? This is a lovely surprise," she said. "And Grace? What brings you two here?"

"We were driving by and we thought we'd stop and see how you are," Hugh told her.

Bessie stood back and let the pair into the house. She smiled as Hugh stepped back to let Grace enter in front of him. His manners were certainly improving now that he was seeing the pretty blonde teacher.

"Happy Christmas," Grace said happily. She handed Bessie a small bag.

Bessie looked inside, expecting to see cakes or biscuits, but instead she found several small wrapped parcels. "But what is all this?" she asked.

"Just a few little things to help make your Christmas," Grace told her.

"You shouldn't have," Bessie replied.

"But we had such fun shopping for you," Grace exclaimed. "Didn't we?" she asked, turning her big blue eyes on Hugh.

"Oh, um, yes, er, that is, it was really fun," Hugh said unconvincingly.

Bessie laughed. "I have a few little things for you two as well," she said. She led the pair into her sitting room and gestured towards the tree. "They're under there with a lot of things for other people. I was hoping you two might stop in on Christmas itself, so I'm afraid I put your things towards the bottom of the piles."

"We can stop back on Christmas," Grace said quickly. "We weren't sure what your plans were, but we'd be happy to come over if you're sure we won't be intruding on your celebration."

"Oh, goodness, not at all," Bessie told her. "Doona is coming for lunch, but I'll be up at six. You're welcome any time from seven until, I don't know, nine or ten o'clock that night."

Grace laughed. "I think we'll probably drop in on our way back from Douglas. My family is having us for our traditional Christmas breakfast and then we're having Christmas dinner with Hugh's family. We'll try to stop here between the two."

"That would be lovely," Bessie said. "I won't worry about your gifts for now, then."

Bessie insisted that the pair sit down in the sitting room where they could all enjoy the tree and the decorations. "I'll make some tea and bring through some Christmas cookies," she told them. When she returned with a tray, Grace was holding her Christmas stocking.

"This is beautiful," she said. "It looks as if you've had it for many years."

"It was mine when I was a child," Bessie replied. "I won't tell you how many years ago that was, though."

Grace chuckled. "Too bad you don't have anywhere to hang it."

"I had the fireplace in here removed when I had central heating put in," Bessie told her. "At the time, it seemed sensible to simply get rid of it, but I do rather miss it sometimes."

The trio sipped their tea and ate their way through a plate of cookies, although Hugh managed to eat most of those.

"This is another American tradition I'm firmly in favour of, like Thanksgiving," he said after his fourth cookie.

"I'm happy to share the recipes with you if you want to make your own next year," Bessie told him.

"I'd love to have them, but I'm not sure I want to wait for next Christmas. It seems like I probably want to practice making them between now and then," he replied.

Bessie and Grace both laughed. "Why don't you weigh twenty stone?" Grace demanded.

"I don't know, I'm just lucky, I suppose," Hugh said, grabbing another cookie.

"You'll probably have to be more careful when you get older," Bessie told him. "But enjoy it now while you can."

"I do," Hugh assured her.

Bessie laughed again. Anyone who knew Hugh knew that.

After the happy couple helped Bessie tidy up from their impromptu tea party and left, Bessie found herself staring at the pile of presents under her tree. She'd bought gifts for a great many people and she had no idea when she'd see most of them next. She needed to sort out how to deliver them all, and soon. It was nearly Christmas. In previous years she'd spent most of December visiting various friends around the island and sharing gifts with them. This year she'd been so busy that she hadn't had the chance.

She made a list of everyone she'd bought a gift for and then began to ring them all up, one after another. When she was finished, some time later, she'd spoken to nearly everyone or at least left messages on their answering machines. Feeling that such devices were an excellent invention, she sat back and sighed. Now that she'd invited everyone to stop and visit her at home over Christmas or Boxing Day, she needed to bake again.

She took a quick walk up the hill to the little shop at the top and bought the ingredients for more Christmas cookies. The girl behind the counter was one Bessie had never seen before, but she rarely visited the shop in the late afternoon or evening. The shop assistant was polite, at least, and Bessie left carrying several heavy bags.

"At least it's downhill home," she muttered to herself as she began the walk back to the cottage.

"Let me give you a ride," a voice called.

Bessie turned around and smiled at John Rockwell who had stopped his car on the road next to her. "That's very kind of you," she said. "But it's out of your way."

"Not far. You can thank me with a few more Christmas cookies if you feel you must," he told her with a grin.

Bessie laughed and piled her shopping into the backseat before climbing into the passenger seat.

"Should I ask what's in the bags?" John asked.

"I've invited nearly everyone I know to stop and visit me on Christmas or Boxing Day," Bessie explained. "Now I need to make lots more Christmas cookies so I have something to offer them all."

"And you need to do it tonight as you're at the castle all of tomorrow," John guessed.

"Exactly. I don't like to buy baking supplies at the corner shop. The prices are much higher than they are at ShopFast. But this was an emergency."

"And it's Christmas," John added.

He insisted on carrying the bags into the cottage for Bessie. She put several cookies on a plate for him before she started putting her shopping away.

"I don't want to overstay my welcome," John said after the first cookie was gone. "It looks as if you're going to have a busy evening."

"I'm glad you're here, actually," Bessie told him. "I was going to ring you, but I forgot. I had lunch with Laura today and she told me something I thought you should know, and I also had a chat with Carolyn."

"You'll have to start by reminding me who Laura is," John replied.

"Oh, sorry. I mean Laura Meyers. She works for Manx National Heritage and was working at Castle Rushen until recently."

John nodded. "Pete interviewed all of the staff members there," he told Bessie. "I've read through his notes, but I didn't remember the name."

Bessie repeated everything that Laura had said about the conversation she'd had with Natasha. After a few minutes, John started taking notes.

"Interesting," he said as he slid his notebook back in his pocket after Bessie had finished. "I'll follow up with Pete and then with Natasha."

"If you can avoid telling her that Laura repeated the story, I'd appreciate it," Bessie said. "I don't want Natasha angry at Laura."

"I'll see what I can do," he replied.

"I don't think anything Carolyn said is at all helpful, but I tried," she said before she recounted her chat with the woman.

"So now she's settled on Michael as the killer," John mused. "That's very convenient for her and Richard."

"It's also convenient for the killer, assuming Michael didn't do it," Bessie said.

"Yes, and it's a solution that the Chief Constable is leaning towards as well," John said. "It would be nice to think that it's that simple."

"But you don't," Bessie said.

"It's almost too neatly packaged," John replied. "But I'm going to get out of your way now. Good luck with your baking. I need to ring Pete."

Bessie spent her evening baking dozens of cookies in several different varieties. She finally went to bed much later than normal, feeling both exhausted and as if she'd accomplished a great deal.

CHAPTER 14

Thursday morning was Christmas Eve. Bessie woke up and felt a small thrill of excitement. Even at her age, perhaps especially at her age, Christmas was something special. She showered and lavished on her dusting powder, thinking about Matthew and also about a Christmas long ago when another man had asked her to be his wife. I wonder where I'd be now if I'd said yes, she thought. The most likely answer was Australia, as that was where the man was living when he'd visited the island and met Bessie. She shook her head to chase the memories away. Everything had worked out for the best. He'd eventually married someone else and she'd stayed on the island she loved, in the cottage that was home.

By the time she'd finished her walk, she was anxious to get to ShopFast and get her groceries. Although Christmas Eve was usually quiet, as most people preferring to get their shopping done early, this year might be different. She didn't want to waste time waiting in long queues if at all possible. She was so eager to get going that she didn't mind that her driver turned out to be Mark again. He always drove too fast, and for once she wasn't unhappy about that.

"I'll be back in an hour," he told Bessie when he dropped her off.

"I just hope I'm done by then," she replied.

"I can wait," Mark assured her.

Assuming his unexpected courtesy was due to his desire for a large Christmas bonus, Bessie nevertheless hurried around the shop. It wasn't nearly as busy as she'd feared and as she waited behind a harassed mum with two toddlers at the checkouts, Bessie remembered why she liked to shop on Christmas Eve. Her turkey had been marked down to half-price, the sprouts had been marked down even further than that and the bakery was practically giving away apple pies. The shop would be shutting early this evening and be closed on Christmas Day. They needed to get rid of anything that wouldn't keep or be wanted for Boxing Day.

Bessie had a house full of Christmas cookies and mince pies, but she bought several of the discounted apple pies to take to Castle Rushen. She was back outside the shop with two minutes to spare, her trolley full of very full grocery bags. Mark was waiting at the agreed-upon spot.

"Let me help," he said, climbing out of the taxi to help Bessie load her bags into the boot.

With the bags safely stowed away, Bessie climbed into the passenger seat and settled back with a sigh. It was only the very beginning of what was going to be a very long day.

"So, do you have big plans for the rest of the day?" Mark asked as he drove.

"Tonight is the last night of 'Christmas at the Castle,'" Bessie told him. "We're auctioning off all of the decorations in the rooms and several other prizes that have been donated to Manx National Heritage."

"I hope no one else gets themselves killed down there tonight," Mark said.

Bessie stopped herself from snapping back at the man. In a weird way, she felt like he was genuinely trying to be nice. "I'm sure we'll have a lovely evening," she said after a moment.

Back at her cottage, Mark insisted on parking and carrying Bessie's shopping inside for her. "This is really nice," he said, looking around Bessie's kitchen. "I don't think I've ever been inside before."

"No, I don't think you have," Bessie said, thinking of all the times he'd sat in the car and honked rather than come to her door. "Let me pack you up a few Christmas cookies to keep you going," she said. She quickly filled a small bag with cookies and handed it to the man. "Happy Christmas."

"Ah, thank you," he said. He gave her a crooked smile and then ducked his head. "Happy Christmas to you, too," he said.

Bessie watched him walk back to his car, surprised to find that she didn't dislike him quite as much as she usually did. She even decided to add a larger than normal tip to his fare when she received the bill from the company. She laughed at herself. Mark had clearly been hoping for just that, but for today, she didn't mind.

After she put her shopping away, she carefully packed up several boxes with the things she needed to take to Castle Rushen. By the time Mark Blake arrived to collect her, she was more than ready.

"It's been a long morning," he complained as he loaded Bessie's boxes into his boot. "I was starting to think it would never be time to head south."

"You'll be relieved when tonight is over," Bessie suggested as she settled into the passenger seat.

"I will," Mark agreed. "It's been much more successful than we'd hoped, but it's also been incredibly stressful."

"Two unexplained deaths and an act of vandalism didn't help," Bessie said dryly.

"That's certainly true. But in less than twelve hours it will all be over, bar the tidying up, at least, and I can get back to my other responsibilities. I can't tell you how much I'm looking forward to boring meetings."

"Our committee meetings were never boring," Bessie said with a laugh.

"Not with Carolyn on the committee," Mark agreed. "I do think she managed to disagree with someone about nearly everything."

"I think she's a very unhappy woman, really," Bessie said. "Volunteer work doesn't suit her."

At the castle, Mark insisted that Bessie head inside while he made multiple trips with her boxes. "We're all meeting in the banquet room, of course," he told Bessie.

Bessie wasn't surprised to find that she was the first to arrive. Mark had been a few minutes early and the drive hadn't taken as long as it sometimes did. The roads had been quieter than normal. It wasn't long before the others began to wander in, though.

"Hello, Bessie," Marjorie called as she walked in carrying a large box. "How are you this lovely Christmas Eve?"

"I'm well," Bessie replied. "How are you?"

Before Marjorie could reply, they were joined by Mary and Natasha. The charity volunteers trickled in as Bessie chatted with first one person and then another. Once Carolyn arrived, Mark called them all to order.

"I want all of our volunteers to spend some time making sure their rooms look their absolute best," he told them. "The committee is going to start by going through the auction room, making sure that's ready, and then we'll be coming around and helping with each room."

"I do hope I'm in the right place," a voice said from the doorway. "I'm Lawrence Wright. I'm a volunteer from the Alzheimer's Research Fund. Someone asked me to come down and help out tonight."

"You are absolutely in the right place," Mark assured him. "I'll show you your room when we're done here."

Bessie smiled at the new arrival, grateful that he would be dealing with Michael's room tonight. The man had grey hair that matched his beard and mustache, and Bessie thought that he could have passed himself off as Father Christmas with the right clothing. He certainly had the little round belly, she thought, trying not to giggle at the idea.

"If anyone has any questions or concerns, please ask. Henry is here from Manx National Heritage if anyone needs a ladder or any tools," Mark told them. "We'll meet back here at five for dinner. From the looks of all the different boxes, it seems that we have a great many Christmas treats as well."

A few people clapped and then the group began to disperse around the castle. Bessie joined the rest of the committee as they headed down to the room that was set up for the auction. It didn't take them long to iron out a few small issues. Carolyn was unusually quiet as they worked.

"Are you okay?" Bessie asked her as they crossed paths.

"I'm fine," she said with a tight smile. "I have a headache, that's all."

Bessie offered her some tablets, but Carolyn refused. "I have to be careful what I take," she said. "I might just go home."

Bessie knew that Mark was counting on Carolyn to cajole her wealthy friends into spending a lot at the auction. If Carolyn left now, it could have a serious impact on the evening's success.

"Maybe you'll feel better after we eat something," Bessie suggested.

Carolyn shrugged. "We'll see."

The committee spent some time checking the room that they'd decorated, and then they split up to help the others. Bessie found that most of the charity volunteers were simply sitting in their rooms, waiting.

"We really didn't need to come in this early," Agnes said. "That isn't a complaint, though. I didn't have anything better to do."

"I think Mark was afraid the rooms would suffer from the crowds more than they did," Bessie replied. "Everything looks good everywhere, though."

As Bessie headed back up to the banquet room to see if she could find Mark, her mobile rang.

"Bessie, it's Doona. I'm bored and I was wondering if you could use a hand down there."

"Oh, goodness, we don't have enough for us to do," Bessie said with a laugh. "But it's nearly time for dinner. Why don't you come down and join us? I'm sure there will be plenty, and I'd love to see you."

"Oh, I can't invite myself to your dinner," Doona protested. "But I will come down a little early. I'll plan to be there around six, if that's okay."

"Of course it is," Bessie said. "Ring me when you arrive and I'll come and get you. Henry will probably be at the entrance anyway."

"Great, I'll see you soon."

In the banquet room, the caterers were setting up for dinner.

Bessie lent them a hand as everyone else trickled in. Before anyone started eating, Bessie passed out the small wrapped gifts she had for everyone. She was happy when no one opened them immediately, which would have spoiled the surprise for everyone else.

For the next hour everyone enjoyed the delicious food, but Bessie felt as if there was something odd in the atmosphere. While everyone was superficially festive, there were tensions everywhere.

"Mary, what's wrong?" Bessie hissed to her friend. Bessie had noticed her frowning whenever she didn't think she was being watched.

"I've had a bit of a falling out with Natasha," Mary said. "It isn't anything serious, but I think I might need a new designer."

Bessie looked over at the woman, who was standing very close to Mark and talking. The pair looked very cosy all of the sudden.

"Do you want to talk about it?" Bessie asked.

"Not tonight," Mary replied. "It isn't anything, really, but I don't think we can keep working together."

"That sounds quite serious," Bessie said.

Mary shrugged. "She's very focussed on her career."

"Isn't that a good thing?"

"Not if it gets in the way of proper behaviour," Mary replied.

Bessie gave her a questioning look, but Mary ignored it. "I'll tell you about it another day," she said. "Now isn't the time."

"She's suddenly very friendly with Mark," Bessie said.

"Yes, maybe he wants a room or two in his house redesigned or something."

Bessie watched the couple for another minute. "It seems like she wants to do more than decorate for him," she muttered as Natasha leaned in closer to Mark and whispered in his ear.

"I didn't approve when she flirted with Michael and Richard Teare, but it wasn't really my business," Mary said. "But flirting with George is going too far."

"She was flirting with George?" Bessie gasped.

"We'll talk about it another time," Mary told her. "For now I'm just trying to work out a way to get rid of her without upsetting her."

"She deserves to be upset," Bessie said.

"But I'd rather not deal with a lawsuit for breach of contract," Mary replied.

"I can't believe there isn't champagne," a voice announced from the doorway.

Richard Teare was standing there, his arms full of champagne bottles.

"Oh, darling, what a wonderful idea," Carolyn called, crossing to him quickly.

"It was a good idea," Natasha purred. She turned away from Mark, quickly walked over to Richard, and grabbed a bottle. "Glasses?" she shouted.

A member of MNH staff quickly brought in some of the glasses that were meant to be for guests later in the evening. Within minutes, everyone was being handed a glass full of the bubbly drink.

Bessie thought about refusing, as she didn't really want to drink, but it would have seemed rude to not take it. Intending to dump it out as soon as she could find a safe place to do so, she took the glass and joined in a toast to Mark. As everyone chatted, she worked her way around to Natasha.

"Are you okay?" she asked the woman.

"I'm fine, why?" Natasha shot back.

"You just don't seem yourself," Bessie replied.

"Mary's been complaining about me, hasn't she?" Natasha demanded. "I didn't mean to upset her, though. It was all a misunderstanding, that's all."

"I'm sure it was," Bessie replied.

"You'll have to excuse me now, though," the woman added. "I'll see you later."

"Where are you going?" Bessie asked.

"Oh, I need to freshen up before the crowd gets here," she replied.

Bessie watched her leave and then shrugged. It seemed as if everyone was acting oddly tonight. She took another sip of her drink as her phone began to buzz.

"I'm here," Doona announced happily. "I'm in the courtyard and it's magical. I can't believe how beautiful it looks."

"We're up in the banquet room," Bessie told her. "Come on up and have some champagne."

She barely finished speaking when something somewhere in the castle made a horrible crashing noise. As everyone stopped talking, another bang was followed by a short silence. Before anyone spoke, a third booming noise came as the lights went out and everything went completely dark.

"Um, Bessie? Are you still there?" Doona's voice startled Bessie.

"I am," Bessie replied. "In total darkness, but here."

"It's only very dark in the courtyard," Doona told her. "It's pretty cloudy, so there isn't much natural light. What's going on?"

"I have no idea, but I'm sure Henry and Mark are working on it," Bessie replied.

"Well, what shall we talk about?" Doona asked with a laugh.

Before Bessie could reply, she heard a scream from Doona's end of the conversation. "What was that?" she demanded.

"I'm not sure," Doona replied. "I'm afraid someone might have just fallen down the stairs."

"You should stand still," Bessie told her. "Wait until someone with a torch arrives to find out what happened."

"I'm just going to walk towards the stairs," Doona told her. "Someone might be hurt. I'm putting you on speaker phone so you can hear what's going on."

Bessie pressed the phone to her ear, trying to hear what was happening in the courtyard.

"Hello?" she heard Doona shout. "Is there someone there? Are you hurt?"

"Too bloody right I'm hurt," a voice snapped.

"Who's there?" Doona asked.

"What difference does it make?" the voice shot back. "Do you have a torch?" Bessie recognised the other voice as Natasha's.

"No, I'm afraid not," Doona said.

"I might have broken my ankle," Natasha said. "And I really need to get out of here."

"I think we'll just have to wait for the lights to come back on," Doona said.

Bessie could hear Mark somewhere behind her on his mobile, issuing instructions to the various staff members who were on-site.

"I hit my head, too," Natasha said. "I'm feeling quite dizzy."

Bessie covered the bottom of her mobile with her hand and spoke loudly. "Someone needs to ring for an ambulance. It sounds as if Natasha is hurt."

"My mobile doesn't give off much light," Doona was saying in Bessie's ear. "I'm afraid I'm going to trip over something if I keep walking towards you."

"I'm due on a flight at seven," Natasha said angrily. "I have important business meetings to get back across for."

"If you're hurt, you might not be able to fly," Doona said. "Anyway, it's Christmas tomorrow. Surely you won't be having meetings on Christmas."

"This is all Christopher Hart's fault," Natasha raged. "Try to do a little long-range career planning and you end up with a broken ankle. My head hurts."

"Maybe you should keep talking," Doona suggested. "I don't know how hard you hit your head, but I know they say you shouldn't go to sleep with a concussion."

"It would be just my luck I'd end up with a concussion," Natasha replied. "All my careful planning was wasted, wasn't it? Did you ever play with dolls when you were little?"

"Um, yes," Doona replied, sounding puzzled.

"I didn't," Natasha said. "I played with doll houses. All I ever wanted to do was be a designer. Do you know how hard it is to make it big in this business?"

"Very hard?" Doona guessed.

"I don't mean finding jobs. It's easy enough to find people who want a few rooms doing over, especially now when half the shows on telly are about redecorating. I'm talking about making it big, being on one of those telly shows and designing rooms for the rich and famous."

"That must be very difficult," Doona replied.

"It's nearly impossible," Natasha told her. "You can't blame a girl for eliminating a bit of the competition now and then, can you?"

Bessie wasn't sure she'd heard that correctly. She tapped the nearest person on the shoulder. "We need the police, too," she whispered. "Ask them to send John Rockwell and Pete Corkill."

Bessie recognised Liz's whispered "okay," before she went back to listening to the conversation that was happening in the courtyard.

"...difficult getting noticed is," Doona was saying.

"There's just too much competition," Natasha replied. "And men like Chris Hart get all the publicity because they do outlandish things that everyone secretly hates, but no one wants to admit that they hate it because it's meant to be artsy and conceptual and whatever other stupid description the designer can come up with."

"So what happened to Christopher Hart?" Doona asked.

Bessie pressed the phone to her ear and held her breath.

"Oh, I killed him," Natasha said with a laugh. "We were staying in the same hotel, so it was easy enough to find him. Mary sent me an email to ask if I would be prepared to help out down here if Carolyn and Christopher didn't make up in time, so I heard about their disagreement."

"You killed him because he was a competitor?" Doona asked.

"Well, yeah. I'll do anything to get ahead in this business. Sometimes you have to do things you don't want to do in order to further your career, you know? Like sleeping with old men or combining colours that don't go together because that's what the client wants. Or maybe even making sure that the star of the show you work on keeps being told the wrong start time every day."

"Or killing someone," Doona added.

"That was really unpleasant," Natasha said. "I didn't realise how hard it would be, and it was messy, too. I planned better for the next one."

"You killed Michael, too," Doona said sadly.

"I just put a bunch of tablets in his wine. He just fell asleep and didn't wake up. That was much better. That's what I'll do next time, too."

"You're planning to kill more people?"

"I've made a list. I'll just keep taking them out, one at a time, until I start getting the recognition I deserve," Natasha said.

"What about the vandalism here?" Doona asked.

"Oh, that was Michael," Natasha told her. "I suggested it. I was hoping it would make him look as if he hated Christopher, you see, and make his motive look stronger. Besides, it was an awful and ugly room."

"So you got Michael to smash everything in it."

"I told Michael that I hated Christopher and I hated the idea of a tribute to him. He was already drinking a lot. He was an alcoholic, you know. He quit drinking a few years ago, but when Christopher threatened to sue him, he went back to it."

"It sounds like he confided in you," Doona remarked.

"Oh, yes, he thought we were friends, and was hoping for more," Natasha replied. "He wasn't a bad guy, really, but I needed someone to take the blame for Christopher's murder, you see. I got him to smash up that horrid room and then I arranged to meet him at the empty house."

"And the suicide note?"

"Oh, I can fake just about anyone's handwriting if I try. I spent years mastering calligraphy. I had him write down the address and directions to the house where we met, so I would have something to work with."

"The poor man," Doona muttered.

"I'm sure he would be happy to know that his death wasn't in vain," Natasha said. "His suicide note explained how he killed Christopher, so the police can close the investigation and I get away with it. Michael did say once that he'd do anything for me."

Bessie thought she'd seen a lot in her many years on the planet, but what she was hearing now shocked her deeply. Natasha seemed to be completely without a conscience.

"How are you feeling?" Doona asked Natasha.

"Sleepy," Natasha replied. "My head and my ankle hurt too much to let me sleep, though."

"I'm sure help is on the way," Doona assured her.

"Just not the police," Natasha giggled. "You won't repeat what I told you, will you? I mean, I'll just deny it all anyway, so you might as well not bother."

"There's someone with a torch coming," Doona said. "Maybe he can get the lights back on."

"It's me," a voice called in the darkness. Bessie struggled to hear who was speaking to Doona.

"It's Henry. If I can't repair the problem, I can switch on the emergency generator. One way or another, we'll have lights in a few minutes."

"Then I can get to the airport," Natasha said.

To Bessie it sounded as if she was slightly slurring her words.

"Or to hospital," Doona suggested.

"Hospitals are too white. I've always wanted to redesign a hospital. I'd put colour everywhere," Natasha said. "But not red. Blood is red and it goes all over the place when you stab someone. Did you know that? I didn't expect it to get all over me. I had to throw all the clothes I was wearing away, except for the shirt I left with Michael. It was a really big shirt, so it could have been his."

Henry was as good as his word. A moment later, lights began to flicker on around the castle. Bessie glanced around at everyone else and then shook her head. They had no idea what she'd been hearing through her mobile.

"Natasha fell down the stairs on the way to the courtyard," she told Mark. "She's just confessed to killing Mr. Hart and Michael."

Mark was on his mobile as Bessie hurried from the room. She was still listening on her mobile as Doona began to give instructions to the newly arrived ambulance team. By the time Bessie reached the bottom of the stairs, Natasha was on her way out of the castle, safely strapped down to a stretcher.

"Are you okay?" Bessie asked Doona as the pair hugged.

"That was horrible," Doona gasped. "She just kept talking and telling me things I didn't want to hear."

"I know," Bessie said soothingly.

"Yes, I suppose, of all people, you do understand," Doona said. "I never realised how awful it has been for you, though."

"How badly hurt is she?" Bessie asked.

Doona shrugged. "Her head had a nasty lump on it and they seemed to think the ankle was broken. They'll take her to Noble's. I rang John and suggested he meet them there."

"Where she'll deny everything," Bessie said with a sigh.

"At least the police know where to look now," Doona replied. "I'm sure John and Pete will be able to find plenty of evidence to support what Natasha told me."

"I hope so," Bessie said. "The thought of her getting away with it is terrifying."

"But what happened with the lights?" Doona asked.

"It looks as if the main switch was turned off," Henry, who was just passing by, said. "I can't imagine how that happened."

Bessie shivered.

"You don't think Mr. Hart's ghost…" Doona began.

Bessie shook her head. "No, I don't," she said firmly.

"Anyway, we're meant to open in ten minutes, and everyone is all upset," Henry said. "Do you think we should cancel the auction?"

"No, I don't," Bessie said firmly. "Let's go find Mark and make sure he isn't thinking of doing anything silly."

Back in the banquet room, Mark was pacing anxiously. "Is Natasha okay?" he asked.

"She's on her way to Noble's," Doona told him.

"Did you actually say that she confessed to killing Mr. Hart and Michael?" he asked Bessie.

"I did, and she did," Bessie replied.

"Maybe we should cancel the auction," Mark began.

"After all of our hard work?" Bessie demanded. "Natasha is in hospital with a police guard. They'll sort out that mess. It has nothing to do with 'Christmas at the Castle.'"

Mark looked uncertain. "Committee members, we need a quick decision," he announced. Everyone gathered around him. "Natasha has confessed to killing Mr. Hart and Michael and is on her way to hospital. The question is, do we still go ahead with the auction?"

For a moment no one spoke, and then a chorus of "yeses" filled the space. Carolyn sighed deeply and then gave Richard a hug.

"I didn't really think you'd killed anyone," she said loudly.

"Of course not," Richard muttered, patting her back.

CHAPTER 15

en minutes later the doors opened on the first annual 'Christmas at the Castle' charity auction. Bessie stuck close to Doona, who still looked upset. After an hour, and a few glasses of wine, both women were feeling better when Doona's mobile rang. It was a short conversation.

"John's tied up at Noble's, but he sends his apologies for not being here," she told Bessie. "Apparently, Natasha started out by denying everything and now she's demanding that they stop questioning her because of her head injury. They're going to search Thie yn Traie next. Apparently, Mary has already given them permission."

Carolyn's mood seemed to have improved dramatically after Natasha's confession, and Bessie watched happily as the other woman coaxed her wealthy friends into bidding outrageously on the various items up for auction. Mary had her own group of wealthy friends to bid against them. By the time the doors closed behind the last of the guests, the event had raised at least twice as much as they'd hoped for MNH and the various charities, and Bessie found herself the proud owner of the mystery box of books.

"That was a huge success, in spite of the power failure," Mark told everyone as they gathered for one last time in the banquet room.

"Did Natasha really confess to murdering Mr. Hart and Michael?" Liz asked.

"I think we'll have to wait and see what the police say about that," Doona told her. "She hit her head when she fell. It's possible she was just confused."

Bessie didn't speak, but there was no doubt in her mind that Natasha had been telling the truth when she'd told Doona what she'd done.

"Everyone should go home and have a very happy Christmas," Mark told them. "As for our lovely charity volunteers, your work here is done. The committee is responsible for packing up your rooms and delivering their contents to the winning bidders from tonight's auction. Please make sure that you haven't left any personal belongings in your room. MNH will be sending out cheques to each of you once the numbers are finalised."

"When can we apply for a space for next year?" Agnes asked. "I definitely want to do it again. It was a lot of work, but if we raised what you've suggested, it was worth it."

"I'll be talking to my supervisor about that in the next few weeks, once we've finished up here and finalised all of the numbers," Mark replied. "I'm sure if we do it again, we'll start planning much earlier in the year. I'll definitely be in touch with you all, one way or another."

The committee members agreed to meet in early January to start clearing out the castle. There was a flurry of hugs, and calls of "Happy Christmas" and "Happy New Year" filled the air as everyone gathered their things and headed for home. Doona offered to take Bessie home, to save Mark the trip, and he was happy to agree.

"I'm totally exhausted," he admitted to Bessie. "I think I might just sleep through Christmas."

"I'll come over around one tomorrow, if that's okay," Doona told Bessie on the drive back to Laxey. "I plan to have a very lazy start to the day."

"That's fine," Bessie agreed. "I'll plan our Christmas lunch for two."

"Perfect."

At Bessie's cottage, Doona insisted on coming inside to make sure everything was okay. "Don't argue," she told Bessie as she took the box of books from her boot.

Bessie bit her tongue and let her friend into the cottage. She hung up her coat and slipped out of her shoes while she waited for Doona to finish her inspection.

"I'll see you tomorrow," Doona said as she hugged Bessie in the doorway. "Happy Christmas."

"Happy Christmas," Bessie replied.

She locked the door and then checked that all the doors and windows were shut and secure. After tucking the box of books into a corner to inspect later, she headed up to bed.

Upstairs, she changed into the new nightgown that she'd bought herself earlier in the month. When she was a child, every Christmas Eve she'd been given a new nightgown by her grandmother, and that always made the night feel even more special. Bessie didn't buy one for herself every year, but this year she'd needed something new, and Christmas was the perfect time to get it. Now she snuggled down under her duvet feeling almost as if she were a small child again. When she woke up it would be Christmas, and she felt as if she were almost too excited to sleep.

It felt as if only minutes had passed when she next opened her eyes, but it was already just past six. Bessie got up and showered and dressed. After a short walk on the beach, she made herself an extra-special breakfast with pancakes dripping in the maple syrup that she had loved since childhood. For years she'd been unable to get maple syrup on the island, but increasingly exotic foodstuffs were being imported regularly now. After she put the turkey in the oven, she filled a large platter with Christmas cookies and filled the kettle with water. Now she just had to wait for friends to arrive. She didn't have long to wait. John Rockwell was the first to knock on her door.

"I hope I'm not too early," he said as he gave her a hug. "I have to get to Ronaldsway for my flight."

"You know I'm always up early," Bessie told him, switching on the kettle.

"You are," he agreed. "I'm afraid I woke Doona."

Bessie laughed. "She did say she was going to have a slow start today."

"I wish I'd known," John said. "I would have left her present on her doorstep and not knocked."

"I'm sure she was happy to see you anyway," Bessie said.

"I'm not," John laughed.

"I'm so glad you're getting to go across. I was worried that Natasha's confession might complicate your getting away."

"Actually, it's made things much easier," John replied. "Pete's taking care of wrapping everything up, but we found the clothes she was wearing when she killed Mr. Hart in plastic bags at Thie yn Traie. I suppose she didn't realise that Mary isn't having the rubbish collected at the moment."

Bessie sighed. "And she really just killed him to advance her career?" she asked. "It seems a strange motive."

"She was already on our short list, because we spent some time looking into her past. There were a few accidents that happened to rivals of hers over the years that made her one of our chief suspects. She wouldn't have been allowed to get on that plane. Anyway, I'll be taking a closer look at all of that once I'm back."

"Oh, goodness," Bessie exclaimed.

"No one else ever died," John told her. "But one man in particular had some very serious injuries that put him out of work for many years."

"How awful," Bessie said.

"Let's talk about happier things," John suggested. "What have you asked Father Christmas for this year?"

Bessie laughed as the kettle boiled. She made tea and offered John cookies. The pair chatted happily for a few minutes, until he glanced at his watch.

"I'm going to have to go," he said. "But I do have a small present for you." He handed Bessie a wrapped box.

"I'd like to save it for later, if I may," Bessie told him. "Doona is coming for lunch and I thought that I'd wait and open all of my presents once she's gone and I'm settled in for the night."

"You may do whatever you like with it," John assured her.

"Your gifts are under my tree," Bessie told him. The pair walked into the sitting room and Bessie found the small pile of things for John. "There are some book tokens there for the children," she told him as she handed everything to him.

"You shouldn't have done that," he protested.

"It's books. Everyone should get books for Christmas," Bessie said firmly.

John laughed. "If you insist."

A knock on the door sent Bessie back to the kitchen. She was greeting and hugging another friend when John walked back through.

"I'd better go," he said. He gave Bessie another hug before he left.

From there it felt to Bessie as if a steady stream of visitors flowed through her cottage. The stack of presents she'd purchased went down slowly as the pile of gifts for her grew. By the time Doona arrived, Bessie was feeling as if Christmas couldn't get much better.

Doona brought her own pile of gifts for Bessie. They settled in the sitting room with their gifts to one another at once. Bessie wanted to save everything else for after she was done having visitors for the day.

She was delighted to see that her friend had had the same idea she'd had. "What a beautiful gift basket," Bessie said, examining bottles of wine and bubble bath and expensive chocolate.

"Oh, snap," Doona laughed as she opened her own basket of treats. "I have something else for you," Doona told her. "And I don't want any objections from you about it."

Bessie frowned. "What have you done?" she asked nervously.

Doona laughed. "I've bought you something I know you want, but I also know you'll think it was too expensive."

"If it was expensive, I don't want it," Bessie said firmly.

"I used some of my inheritance," Doona explained. "I thought it would be nice to put it to good use. You've no idea how grateful I am for your friendship. Please let me give this to you."

"What is it?" Bessie asked suspiciously.

Doona laughed. "It would be easier to discuss it if you knew what I was on about," she said. She left the room and Bessie listened as her front door opened and closed and then opened and closed again. When Doona came back, she was carrying a huge parcel that looked familiar to Bessie.

"I can't accept that," Bessie said before she'd even opened it.

"You don't even know what it is," Doona argued.

"It's the painting that Grant Robertson tried to give me, isn't it?"

"Yes," Doona admitted. "I bought it at the auction."

"It sold for a lot of money," Bessie recalled.

"Not that much. I can afford it," Doona said. "All of the money raised went to repaying the people Grant stole from, so it's good that it sold for a lot."

"But you want to pay off your mortgage and remodel your bathroom," Bessie argued.

"I should have enough to do both those things once the estate is finally settled," Doona told her. "Please, let me give you this one thing to thank you for supporting me when my marriage fell apart and again when Charles died."

Bessie felt torn. She hated that her friend had spent so much money on her, but she loved the painting very much. While she was thinking, Doona spoke.

"At least unwrap it," she suggested.

Bessie pulled off the paper and sighed deeply. It was even more beautiful than she remembered. Somehow it seemed to capture the beach at her very favourite time of day. The sun was just rising and the beach was deserted except for a few seagulls that were flying in lazy circles over the gentle waves.

"It's gorgeous," she said softly.

"Where will you hang it?" Doona asked.

"Maybe in my bedroom," Bessie said. "As the view out the window here is much the same as the painting."

"Of course the view in here isn't always quite as nice as the painting," Doona said. She pointed out the window and Bessie laughed.

The painting showed the beach on a spring or summer morning with clear skies. At the moment, the skies were grey and a heavy rain was falling on a windswept and sodden beach. Doona was right; the beach in the painting looked much nicer than the one outside Bessie's window.

"Maybe it should go down here, then," Bessie said. "I'll decide after I take the Christmas decorations down."

"Let me know if you want any help with hanging it," Doona said. "It's rather heavy."

"I suppose I must keep it, then," Bessie said. "As it already feels as if it belongs here."

"Thank you," Doona said happily.

"No, thank you."

Lunch was delicious, and Doona insisted on doing all of the washing-up. Bessie refilled the cookie tray in anticipation of still more visitors in the afternoon, and she wasn't disappointed. Mary and George Quayle arrived on foot from Thie yn Traie as Bessie was letting Doona out.

"Bessie, Happy Christmas," Mary said, hugging Bessie tightly once the pair had removed their wet things. "I can't believe that woman was remodeling our new house," she added, shaking her head.

"I hope that doesn't put you off buying it," Bessie replied.

"Oh no, we've actually just arranged to sign the papers next week," Mary told her. "We had ever so much trouble getting everyone to agree to do it during the week between Christmas and New Year, but it's all arranged now. And to help clear out all the ghosts, we're having that New Year's Eve party I mentioned. You must come."

Bessie smiled. She didn't really like New Year's Eve parties, but of course she would go anyway, for Mary's sake.

They exchanged presents, but the Quayles couldn't stay long, as they still had their children and grandchildren, who were scattered around the island, to visit.

"Elizabeth is moving into Thie yn Traie over the next few days," Mary told Bessie. "So don't be surprised if you see lights on at all hours. She decided she doesn't want to wait for her rooms to be finished, so she'll be staying in the east wing while we finish the west wing for her."

The next few hours flew past as Bessie welcomed more of her

friends for short visits. When Hugh and Grace arrived, she tried to look at Grace's left hand without being obvious about it. Apparently she wasn't being as subtle as she'd hoped, because after a few minutes, Hugh caught her eye and shook his head. Questions rushed to Bessie's lips, but she swallowed them all and served tea and cookies to the pair. She was relieved when Grace excused herself for a short while.

"She said no?" Bessie asked, shocked.

"No, I haven't asked yet," Hugh told her. "I was going to ask this morning, before breakfast, but then I got nervous and couldn't talk properly. Now I can't seem to find the right time to ask."

"Take her for a walk on the beach and do it," Bessie suggested.

Hugh looked out the window and shook his head. "I want it to be romantic, not windy and rainy."

Bessie would have said a great deal more, but Grace returned then and a short time later the pair left. By eight o'clock Bessie was tired of talking and almost out of Christmas cookies. There were still a few friends who hadn't visited, but she assumed they'd come by on Boxing Day. If she did run out of cookies, she'd serve them mince pies.

She switched on the radio and found a station playing Christmas music, then she sat down with her pile of presents and began to unwrap them, taking careful note of exactly what she'd received so that she could write thank-you notes the next day.

An hour later, she was feeling overwhelmed by the generosity of her friends. She wouldn't need to shop for bath products or chocolate for some time to come. Even better, she'd received a small fortune in book tokens. She could hardly wait to start spending those. The last present she unwrapped was the pile of books she'd purchased for herself and impulsively wrapped and put under the tree. She looked through them and chose one to take up to bed with her. She still had the box of books from the auction to go through, but she decided to save that for another day. Today had been wonderful enough.

After walking through the cottage, turning off lights and checking the doors, she stopped in the sitting room and smiled at the tree. She was so glad she'd decided to decorate it this year. It had been a strange and often unhappy year, but today couldn't have been any better. She unplugged the tree and then walked to the stairs. Glancing back into the room, she frowned. What was the strangely shaped object on top of the bookshelf?

Switching on the nearest lamp, Bessie crossed the room and looked in surprise at her old Christmas stocking. Someone, and she wasn't sure she could guess who, had filled the small sack with tiny presents. Bessie poured them out and opened a bottle of bubble liquid, a bouncy ball, miscellaneous chocolates and a toy car. She smiled to herself as she headed up the stairs. She'd been wrong only a moment earlier. Christmas had managed to get just a little bit better.

GLOSSARY OF TERMS

MANX LANGUAGE TO ENGLISH

- **cloan** — children
- **fastyr mie** — good afternoon
- **kys t'ou** — How are you?
- **moghrey mie** — good morning
- **ta mee braew** — I'm fine.

HOUSE NAMES – MANX TO ENGLISH

- **Thie yn Traie** — Beach House
- **Treoghe Bwaane** — Widow's Cottage (Bessie's home)

ENGLISH/MANX TO AMERICAN TERMS

- **advocate** — Manx title for a lawyer (solicitor)
- **bin** — garbage can
- **biscuits** — cookies

- **boot** — trunk (of a car)
- **car park** — parking lot
- **crisps** — potato chips
- **cuddly toy** — stuffed animal
- **cuppa** — cup of tea (informal)
- **CV** — resume
- **duvet** — a comforter with a removable cover, usually filled with feathers and down
- **fairy cakes** — cupcakes
- **fairy lights** — Christmas lights (string lights)
- **fizzy drink** — soda (pop)
- **flat** — apartment
- **fortnight** — two weeks
- **holiday** — vacation
- **jelly** — gelatin dessert (most commonly Jell-O in the US)
- **jumper** — sweater
- **lie in** — sleep late
- **loo** — restroom
- **midday** — noon
- **notes** — paper money (bills)
- **pram** — stroller
- **pudding** — dessert
- **queue** — line
- **rubbish** — garbage
- **shopping trolley** — shopping cart
- **skeet** — gossip
- **supply teacher** — substitute teacher
- **sweets** — candy
- **telly** — television
- **till** — check-out (in a grocery store, for example)
- **trainers** — sneakers

OTHER NOTES

Book tokens are gift certificates that can be used in most bookshops throughout the United Kingdom, regardless of where they were purchased.

Bessie calls someone a "pot," which is a reference to the expression "the pot calling the kettle black." She is suggesting that the person who is complaining is sometimes guilty of the same behaviour as the person he or she is complaining about.

Boxing Day is traditionally December 26th (although it can be moved to the 27th if the 26th is a Sunday, as it is a public holiday). In the past it was the day when tradesmen were given their "Christmas boxes."

In the UK, people sometimes say "snap" to mean that two things are the same (from the card game where you say "snap" when someone lays down the same card as the previous one).

Noble's is Noble's Hospital, the main hospital on the Isle of Man. It is located in Douglas, the country's capital.

Reception is the first year of full-time education in UK (and Isle of Man) schools. It is similar to US Kindergarten, but students begin in the school year when they will turn five, which is generally about a year earlier than their US counterparts.

In the UK, people measure their weight in terms of stones and pounds, rather than just pounds. A stone is equal to fourteen pounds, so if someone weighs ten stone they weigh 140 pounds.

Ronaldsway is the area of the island where the airport is located. Although officially called the "Isle of Man Airport," nearly everyone on the island calls the airport "Ronaldsway" when talking about it.

CID is the Criminal Investigation Department of the Isle of Man Constabulary (Police Force).

When talking about time, the English say, for example, "half seven" to mean "seven-thirty."

The emergency number in the UK is 999, rather than 911, as used in the US.

A "full English breakfast" generally consists of bacon, sausage, eggs, grilled or fried tomatoes, fried potatoes, fried mushrooms and baked beans served with toast.

ACKNOWLEDGMENTS

Thanks to everyone on my team. I couldn't do this without
My editor, Denise.
My beta readers, Charlene, Janice, Ruth and Margaret.
My photographer for cover art, Kevin.
And, most importantly,
My readers, who mean the world to me! Thank you to everyone who has taken the time to get in touch and share their thoughts on Bessie and her friends. I love hearing from you!

Bessie's story continues in....

Aunt Bessie Knows

An Isle of Man Cozy Mystery

By Diana Xarissa

Aunt Bessie knows she's in for a long evening when she joins her friends to celebrate New Year's Eve.

In Elizabeth Cubbon's experience, New Year's Eve parties are never as fun as they ought to be. When she's invited to share the night with her new neighbours at Thie yn Traie, she reluctantly agrees, in spite of her misgivings.

Aunt Bessie knows that gorgeous redhead, Gennifer Carter-Maxwell is drunk and slightly out of control.

But when Gennifer starts flirting with Hugh Watterson, the young police constable who is Bessie's friend, Gennifer manages to upset Hugh's girlfriend, Grace. By the time midnight arrives, Bessie is more than ready to head for home, but first she agrees to join in the search for the now missing Gennifer.

Aunt Bessie knows that Hugh Watterson didn't kill anyone.

And she's certain that his supervisor, John Rockwell, knows it too. Unfortunately, it's Inspector Anna Lambert heading up this particular investigation. As evidence against Hugh seems to be piling up fast, Bessie knows she's going to have to do some of her own detective work.

This is book eleven in the Isle of Man Cozy Mystery Series.

ALSO BY DIANA XARISSA

The Quinton Case

The Rhodes Case

The Isle of Man Romance Series

Island Escape

Island Inheritance

Island Heritage

Island Christmas

ABOUT THE AUTHOR

Diana Xarissa grew up in Erie, Pennsylvania, earned a BA in history from Allegheny College and eventually ended up in Silver Spring, Maryland. There she met her husband, who swept her off her feet and moved her to Derbyshire for a short while. Eventually, the couple relocated to the Isle of Man.

The Isle of Man was home for Diana and her family for over ten years. During their time there, Diana completed an MA in Manx Studies through the University of Liverpool. The family is now living near Buffalo, New York, where Diana enjoys writing about the island that she loves.

Diana also writes mystery/thrillers set in the not-too-distant future under the pen name "Diana X. Dunn" and fantasy/adventure books for middle grade readers under the pen name "D.X. Dunn."

She would be delighted to know what you think of her work and can be contacted through snail mail at:

Diana Xarissa Dunn
PO Box 72
Clarence, NY 14031.

Find Diana at:
www.dianaxarissa.com
diana@dianaxarissa.com

Made in United States
North Haven, CT
06 November 2023

43689073R00137